François II.

THE HOROSCOPE, *Frontispiece.*

THE HOROSCOPE ❧ A ROMANCE OF THE REIGN OF FRANÇOIS II.

❧ ❧ ❧ ❧ ❧

BY ALEXANDRE DUMAS

❧ ❧ ❧ ❧ ❧

Fredonia Books
Amsterdam, The Netherlands

The Horoscope:
A Romance of the Reing of François II

by
Alexandre Dumas

ISBN: 1-4101-0089-8

Reprinted from the 1897 edition

Fredonia Books
Amsterdam, The Netherlands
http://www.fredoniabooks.com

In order to make original editions of historical works available to scholars at an economical price, this facsimile of the original edition of 1897 is reproduced from the best available copy and has been digitally enhanced to improve legibility, but the text remains unaltered to retain historical authenticity.

INTRODUCTORY NOTE.

THE list of characters who play parts of more or less prominence in the romance of "The Horoscope," includes hardly a name with which we have not been made familiar in the earlier volumes of this series. François de Guise, the conqueror of Calais and protector of Gabriel de Lorges, Comte de Montgomery, at whose hands King Henri II. met his death in the lists, is a leading figure in the "Two Dianas," in which we also make the acquaintance of Louis de Condé, *ce petit prince tant joli,* from whom all the later Condés and Contis were descended, and of Coligny, the great general and noble-hearted man, whom, with his scarcely less great brother Dandelot, we meet again in the "Page of the Duke of Savoy," fighting valiantly under the banners of the despicable race, whose most formidable enemies they were destined later to become. Again, in "Marguerite de Valois," we have seen Coligny, on that terrible Saint Bartholomew's night in 1572, shot down like a dog in that same house on Rue de Béthisy, by the hired bravos of his deadly foes, the Guises.

In "Ascanio" we have our earliest glimpse of Catherine de Médici, then newly arrived at the French court, and newly wedded to him who was then only a younger son of France, but who came to be King Henri II. In the "Two Dianas" we meet her again, first as the despised and neglected consort of the king, compelled to submit to the humiliating ascendency of the beautiful Diane de Poitiers, but content, with her brood of possible kings about her, to bide her time; and later, after the king's sudden and extraordinary death, beginning to play the part which, under Dumas' auspices, in the matchless romances of the Valois series, we have watched her play throughout the reigns of Charles IX., whom she loved but little better than François II., and Henri III., who was the dearest to her heart, as he was almost the most despicable of all her sons. In the "Two Dianas" poor François is shown to us in a somewhat more favorable light than in the "Horoscope." Weak, spiritless creature that he was, the fervent, devoted love which he is commonly supposed to have felt for his queen, the ill-fated Mary Stuart, has seemed to be the only ray of sunshine and romance in his brief and gloomy reign.

The Baron de la Rénaudie will be remembered as a prominent actor in that part of the "Two Dianas" which deals with the earlier religious troubles and the conspiracy of Amboise.

The execution of Anne Dubourg, which is also referred to in the "Two Dianas," aroused intense excitement, and caused the most poignant regret and sorrow throughout France. It did more than anything else to hasten the outbreak of the first religious war.

"The Maréchal de Saint-André," says Larousse, "married Marguerite de Lustrac, — Dame de Fronsac, — by whom he had one daughter, *Catherine* d'Albon, maid of honor to Catherine de Médici. After his death, Catherine d'Albon, whose hand he had promised to one of the sons of the Duc de Guise, was confined in the monastery of Longchamp. She died there shortly after, poisoned, so it is said, by her own mother; according to some, at the instigation of the queen-mother, who dreaded to see the marshal's immense fortune in the hands of the Guises; according to others, from jealousy, she and her daughter both being in love with the Prince de Condé. The Prince de Condé having lost his wife, the Maréchale de Saint-André, being then widowed, entertained for a moment the hope of marrying him."

Of the group of poets introduced to us in the queen-mother's salon, Ronsard is the only one whose name is at all known to-day. Brantôme, however, has always been a favorite of lovers and students of French literature and history, and he has recently become even more widely known through the publication by the Société de l'Histoire de France of his complete works in eleven volumes, together with a very learned and interesting notice of the man by M. Ludovic Lalanne, the editor appointed by the society. His work was very miscellaneous in character, and he did not pretend to write history, but he was a prominent figure at court throughout the reigns of the later Valois, and many of the facts recorded by him in his unique and inimitable style have been universally accepted as authentic and worthy of a place in more serious chronicles.

Let us say a word concerning the horoscopes cast by the old witch, as related in the fourth chapter of the tale before us.

In April, 1561, the Maréchal de Saint-André, the Duc de Guise, and the Connétable de Montmorency formed a league known as the "triumvirate," ostensibly for the purpose of stamping out the Protestant heresy, but really from motives of self-aggrandizement. Catherine de Médici, then queen-regent, fearing that her own power might be diminished by the union of the three most powerful French subjects, ordered the marshal to return to his post as governor of Lyon. "Shortly after," says Larousse, "the war between Catholics and Protestants having broken out, Saint-André took Poitiers, . . . and on December 9, 1562, fought the battle of Dreux against the Prince de Condé. As he was pursuing the fugitives, he was surrounded and taken prisoner by certain Calvinists. One of them had taken him up behind him on his horse, and they were riding away, when a Catholic named *Aubigny* or *Bobigny*, whose property he had confiscated, shot him dead with a pistol."

The Prince de Condé, shortly after the date assigned to the events of this tale, was convicted of participation in the Conspiracy and so-called Tumult of Amboise, and sentenced to death; but the death of François II., and Catherine's consequent temporary leaning toward the Huguenots — through fear of the Guises — saved him, and for several years thereafter he was one of the recognized leaders of the Protestant armies. "He was wounded at the battle of Jarnac," — we quote again from Larousse, — "and having been made a prisoner, he was assassinated in a most cowardly way by Montesquiou, captain of the guards to the Duc d'Anjou, — afterwards Henri III., — who blew out his brains with a pistol shot while his wound was being dressed at the foot of a tree."

The Duc de Guise was the recognized chief of the Catholic party during the first religious wars, which he and his brother, the scarcely less famous Cardinal de Lorraine, did so much to foment. He was besieging Orléans in 1563, when he was killed by a pistol shot fired by a Protestant gentleman named Poltrot de Méré. As the Duc de Guise, whatever his merits, was more prominent in the history of the time than either of the others, historians have had more to say about his death and his assassin. Brantôme, who was an eye-witness of the assassination, gives many interesting details concerning the duke's last moments, and also concerning his assassin, whom he had frequently seen at the duke's table.

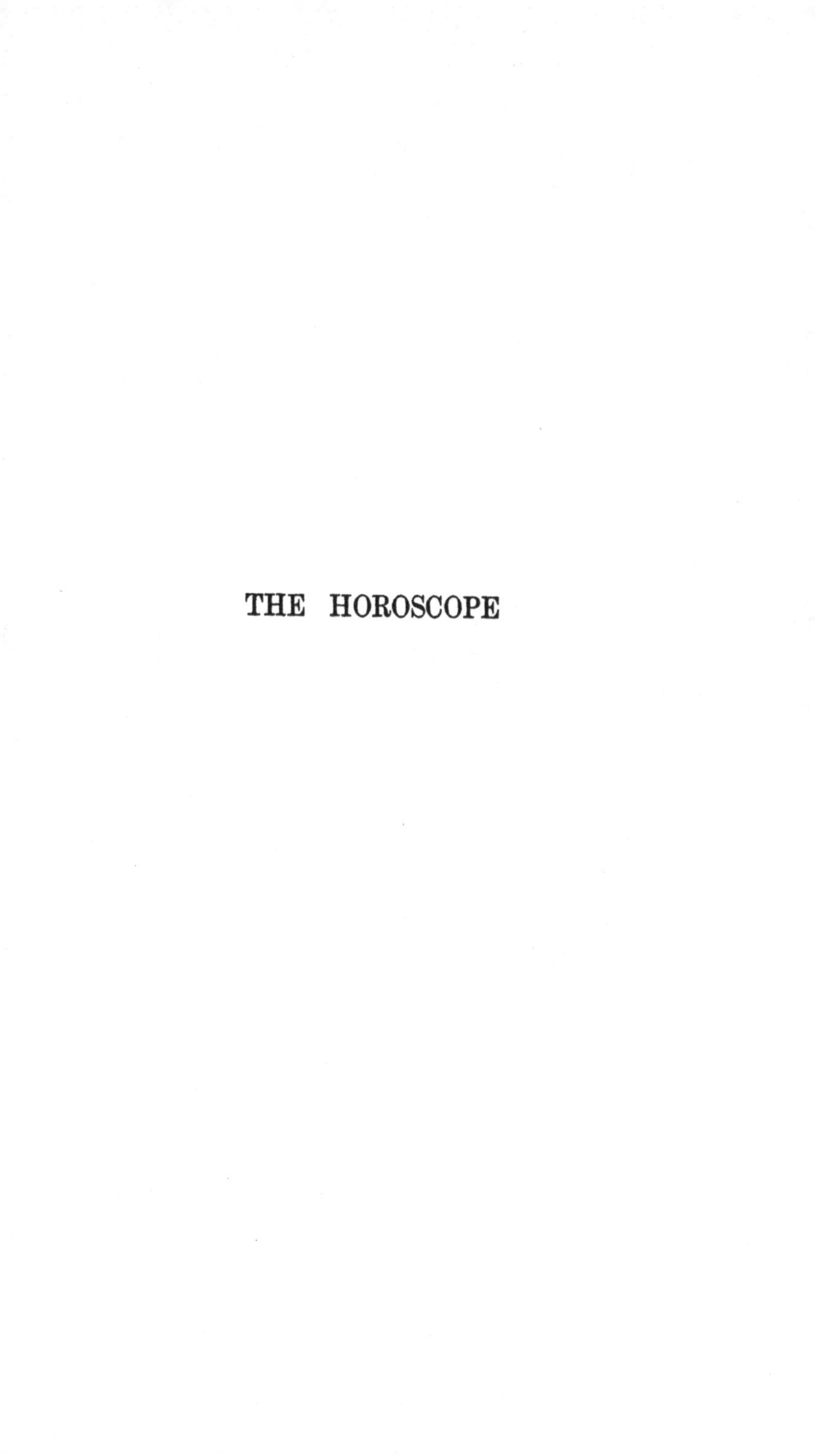

THE HOROSCOPE

LIST OF CHARACTERS.

Period, 1559.

FRANÇOIS II., King of France.
MARY STUART, his queen.
CATHERINE DE MÉDICIS, the queen-mother.
FRANÇOIS DE LORRAINE, DUC DE GUISE.
PRINCE DE JOINVILLE, his son.
CARDINAL DE LORRAINE.
LOUIS DE BOURBON, PRINCE DE CONDÉ.
PRINCE DE MONTPENSIER.
JACQUELINE OF HUNGARY, his wife.
DUC DE MONTPENSIER.
PRINCE DE LA ROCHE-SUR-YON.
M. DE MOUCHY, grand inquisitor of the law.
MARÉCHAL DE SAINT ANDRÉ.
CHARLOTTE DE SAINT ANDRÉ, his daughter, the king's mistress
JACQUES BAUBIGNY DE MÉZIÈRES, her page.
MAÎTRE ANTOINE MINARD, president of the parliamentary council
MADAME MINARD, his wife.
JULIEN FRESNE, clerk to President Minard.
POLTROT DE MÉRÉ, a Gascon adventurer.
M. DE CHAVIGNY, commander of the Archers of the Guard.
M. DE CARVOYSIN, first equerry to the King.
BRANTÔME, SEIGNEUR DE BOURDEILLES.
RONSARD,
BAIF,
REMI BELLEAU,
PONTUS DE THIARD,
JODILLE,
} poets at the French court.

LANOUE, maid to the queen mother.

ADMIRAL GASPARD DE COLIGNY,
MADAME DE COLIGNY, his wife,
DANDELOT DE COLIGNY, the admiral's brother,
GODEFROI DE BARRI, BARON DE PÉRIGORD, SEIGNEUR DE LA RENAUDIE,
M. MONTESQUIEU,
ANNE DUBOURG, councillor of parliament,
ROBERT STUART, his natural son.
} Huguenots

PATRICK, an archer of the Scotch Guards,
MÉDARD,
} friends of Robert Stuart.

LANDRY,
PERRETTE,
} bourgeois.

HOST OF THE RED HORSE INN.

A SOOTHSAYER.

CONTENTS.

THE HOROSCOPE.

I.

THE FÊTE DU LANDI.

One radiant spring morning about the middle of the month of June, in the year 1559, the Place Saint Geneviève was blocked by a crowd which might approximately have been estimated at thirty or forty thousand persons.

A man freshly arrived from the country and suddenly coming into the Rue Saint Jacques, where he could command a view of this crowd, would have been greatly perplexed to say for what purpose it had gathered in such numbers in this quarter of the capital.

The weather was superb: they were not, therefore, about to bring forth the relics of Saint Geneviève, as in 1551, to obtain a respite from the rains.

It had rained two days before: certainly, then, they were not looking to the relics of Saint Geneviève for rain, as in 1556.

They had not to deplore a disastrous battle, like that of Saint Quentin: hence they were not, as in 1557, marching in procession with the relics of Saint Geneviève in order to secure the protection of God.

It was clear, nevertheless, that this vast concourse of people, gathered on the site of the old abbey, had assembled to celebrate some great event.

But what event?

It was not of a religious nature, for although a few monks' robes might be seen here and there in the crowd, yet the consecrated robes were not sufficiently numerous to lend a religious character to the fête.

It was not a military gathering, for the soldiers in the crowd were few in number, and those few carried neither halberds nor muskets.

It was not an aristocratic assemblage, for one failed to see emblazoned pennons fluttering overhead, or plumed helmets of noble lords.

The predominant element of this motley throng, in which were intermingled gentlemen, thieves, monks, bourgeois, *filles de joie*, old men, jugglers, sorcerers, bohemians, artisans, beggars, and venders of cerevisia; some on horses, others on mules, some on asses, others in coaches (coaches had been invented that very year); the most of them, too, coming and going, pushing, swarming, and struggling to reach the middle of the square, — the predominant element of this multitude, we say, was made up of students, students of the four nations, Scotch, English, French, and Italian.

This, in fact, was the occasion: it was the first Monday after Saint Barnabas's Day, and all this crowd had assembled for the purpose of attending the Fête du Landi.

But perhaps these three words, smacking of the speech of the sixteenth century, mean nothing to our readers. Let us therefore explain what the Fête du Landi was.

Attention, dear readers! we are about to expound a point in etymology, not unlike a member of the Academy of Inscriptions and Belles-Lettres.

The Latin word *indictum* signifies a time and place appointed for an assembling of the people.

The *i* was changed at first to *e*, the *e* finally became *a*. People said successively, instead of *indictum*, *l'indict*, *l'endit*, then *l'andit*, and, at last, *landi*.

Hence this word signifies the time and place appointed for an assembly.

From the days of Charlemagne, the Teutonic king who made his capital at Aix-la-Chapelle, the holy relics within the chapel were shown to pilgrims once a year.

Charles the Bald transported these relics from Aix to Paris, and once a year they were exhibited to the people in the market-place near the Boulevard Saint Denis.

The Bishop of Paris, in view of the increasing piety of the faithful, and considering the market-square to be not at all in keeping with its guests, fixed upon the Plain of Saint Denis for the Fête du Landi.

Thither in procession the clergy of Paris conveyed the relics. The bishop went along to preach and to give his blessing to the people; but it was with the blessings as with another's goods or a neighbor's fruit, — not every one had the right to distribute them: the clerics of Saint Denis claimed that they alone had the right to bless upon their own territory, and they denounced the bishop to the parliament of Paris as a usurper.

The matter was obstinately argued and debated on both sides, with such eloquence that the parliament, not knowing in favor of which of the contestants to decide, decided unfavorably for both, and, in view of the trouble they were making, forbade the bishops on the one hand and the abbés on the other to set foot near the Fête du Landi.

The contested privileges fell to the rector of the University; to him was accorded the right to repair every year to the Fête du Landi, on the first Monday after Saint Barnabas's Day, and there select the necessary parchment for all the colleges: the merchants convening at this fair were even forbidden to sell a single leaf before Monsieur Le Recteur had made his entire purchase.

The rector's excursion, which lasted several days suggested to the students the idea of accompanying him; they begged permission. The permission was granted, and from that time forth the visit was made every year with due pomp and with all imaginable splendor.

Regents and students gathered on horseback in the Place Saint Geneviève, and from there marched in orderly array to the ground where the fair was held. The cavalcade arrived quietly enough at its destination; but, once arrived, its members found ready to join them all the bohemians and sorcerers of Paris (there were thirty thousand of them at the time); every girl and woman of doubtful character (no statistics have ever given their number); and, dressed in boys' clothes, all the demoiselles of the Val d'Amour, the Chaud-Gaillard, and the Rue Froid-Mantel, — a veritable army, something like one of the great migrations of the fourth century, with the difference that these women, instead of being barbarians or savages, were only too civilized.

Having reached the Plain of Saint Denis, every man halted, dismounted from his horse, ass, or mule, brushed the dust from his boots and hose, — from his shoes and spatterdashes, if he had come on foot, — and mingled with the honorable company whose pitch he endeavored to reach or to raise. They lounged around, ate puddings, sausages, and pastry; they drank to the continuance of the bloom on their ladies' cheeks in frightful numbers of pots of white wine from the neighboring hills, — Saint Denis, La Briche, Épinay-lez-Saint-Denis, and Argenteuil. Their brains reeled with love and drink: then,—"the flagons began to pass, the meats followed, the fragments flew. 'Stop your brawling! pour me Rousse without water; toss off this glass like a man, my friend; white wine! white! pour, everybody, pour, in the devil's name! a butler needs Briareus' hundred hands to pour without tiring. My tongue peels; again, comrade!'" They were acting the fifth chapter of "Gargantua."

That was a fine age,—a merry age, rather, you will agree,—in which Rabelais, curé of Meudon, wrote "Gargantua," and Brantôme, abbé of Bourdeille, wrote "Les Dames Galantes."

Once drunk, they sang, kissed, quarrelled, babbled nonsense, abused the passers-by,—what the devil! they must have sport!

With the first, then, who came to hand, they began a chaffing that ended in laughter, insults, or blows, according to the temperament of the victim.

It required twenty decrees of parliament to remedy these disorders; and in the end they were forced to the expedient of removing the fair from the plain into the town of Saint Denis itself.

In 1550 it was decreed that the students should attend the Fête du Landi only in deputations of twelve, including the regents from each of the four Collèges aux Nations, as they were then called.

But here is what then happened.

The students not included in this number discarded the university garb, and, arrayed in short mantles, colored caps, and slashed hose, the sword, which had been forbidden them, being added under cover of this species of Saturnalia to the dirk, which from time immemorial they had arrogated to themselves the right to carry, they repaired to Saint Denis by every possible route, in virtue of the saying, " All roads lead to Rome; " and as, in their masquerading, they eluded the vigilance of their masters, the rioting became infinitely greater than before the issue of the ordinance designed to restrain it.

Such was the state of affairs in 1559; and, witnessing the order with which the cortège set out, one would be a thousand leagues from imagining the irregularities to which they would abandon themselves when once they reached the fair.

On this occasion, as usual, the cavalcade began to move methodically enough, and entered the broad Rue Saint Jacques without producing any great commotion; while passing in front of the Châtelet it sent up one of those howls of malediction such as only Paris mobs know how to give; for half the members comprising this crowd certainly knew the subterranean prisons of this structure otherwise than by hearsay. After this manifestation, which was at least a slight relief, it entered the Rue Saint Denis.

Let us press on, dear reader, and engage a place in the abbatial town of Saint Denis, that we may be present at an episode of the fête which is connected with the story we have undertaken to relate to you.

The official fête was entirely within the town, in the high street of the town even; and it was within the town, and particularly in the high street, that the barbers, cerevisia-venders, upholsterers, haberdashers, linen-drapers, harness-makers, saddlers, rope-makers, spur-makers, leather-dealers, leather-dressers, tanners, shoemakers, wood-carvers, woollen-drapers, money-changers, goldsmiths, grocers, and publicans especially were established in the wooden booths which they had constructed two months in advance.

Those who attended the fair at Beaucaire, twenty years

ago, or even the Fête des Loges at Saint Germain, ten years ago, can, by magnifying to gigantic proportions the scenes they beheld in those two localities, have some idea of the Fête du Landi.

But those who are in the habit of attending regularly year after year this same Fête du Landi, which is still celebrated in our time in the sub-prefecture of the Seine, would by no means be able, from seeing what it is, to imagine what it was.

In reality, instead of the sombre black habiliments which, amidst all festivities, sadden in spite of themselves even those who are least inclined to melancholy, as a reminder of mourning, a sort of protestation of grief, the queen of this poor world, against gayety which seems only a usurper, this entire mass of people wore garments of dazzling hues, of gold and silver fabrics, embroideries, laces, bindings, feathers, braids, puffs, velvets, taffetas ribbed with gold and satins wrought with silver; the entire body glittered in the sun and seemed to flash back at him his most ardent rays. Never, in fact, had such splendor been displayed by all, from the highest ranks of society down to the lowest. Although, in the year 1543, King François I., and later King Henri IV., promulgated twenty sumptuary laws, these laws have never been obeyed.

The explanation of this unheard of splendor is very simple. The discovery of the new world by Columbus and Americus Vespucius, and the expeditions of Fernando Cortez and Pizarro to the famous realm of "Cathay," indicated by Marco Polo, had flooded all Europe with such a quantity of coin that a writer of that century complains of the invasion of luxury and of the rise in the price of food, which, he says, had more than quadrupled in eighty years.

But the picturesque side of the fête, however, was not to be found in Saint Denis itself. True, the decree of parliament had transported it into the town; but the decree of the populace, mightier in its way, had transported it to the bank of the river. The fair, then, was held in Saint Denis, but the fête was at the water-side. Having nothing to buy, we will betake ourselves to the water-side below the Isle of Saint Denis, and, once there, we will look about and listen to what is going on.

The cavalcade which we have seen start from the Place Saint Geneviève, proceed along the Rue Saint Jacques, greet the Châtelet with a howl, and file through the Rue Saint Denis, made its entry into the royal necropolis between eleven o'clock and half-past eleven; then, like sheep arrived at the pasture and turned loose, the students escaped from the regents and scattered abroad, some into the fields, others through the town, others along the bank of the Seine.

For care-free hearts, — rare hearts, but they exist, nevertheless, — it was a delightful spectacle to see stretched at length here and there in the sun, on the high grassy bank, for a league away, the fresh students of twenty years, lying at the feet of beautiful girls with red satin bodices, pink satin cheeks, and white satin necks.

The eyes of Boccaccio should have been able to pierce heaven's azure curtain and gaze delightedly upon this gigantic "Decameron."

The first part of the day passed well enough; they were warm, and they drank; they were hungry, and they ate; they sat down, and were rested. Then the conversations began to wax heated, the heads to grow hot. God knows the number of tankards, full, emptied, refilled, re-emptied, again refilled, and finally broken, whose fragments they hurled at one another.

About three o'clock, the river-bank, strewn with tankards and plates, some whole, others broken, brimming cups and empty bottles, with couples embracing and strolling over the turf, husbands taking strange women instead of their wives, wives taking their lovers instead of their husbands,—the river-bank, we repeat, but lately as green, fresh, and glistening as a village on the banks of the Arno, now resembled a Teniers landscape depicting a Flemish *kermis.*

Suddenly, a formidable cry arose:—

"Into the water! into the water!"

Every one sprang to his feet; the shouts were redoubled.

"Into the water with the heretic! Into the water with the Protestant! Into the water with the Huguenot! Into the water with the Baptist, the Colas cow! into the water! into the water! into the water!"

"What is the matter?" cried a score, a hundred, a thousand voices.

"He has blasphemed,—that is the matter! He has doubted Providence,—that is the matter! He says it will rain!"

It was, perhaps, the last accusation, on the face of it the least damaging, that produced the greatest effect on the multitude. The multitude was enjoying itself, and would have been furious at having its enjoyment interrupted by a storm; the multitude was wearing its Sunday clothes, and would have been maddened had its Sunday clothes been spoiled by rain. The explanation given, the vociferations began again louder than ever. The people pressed toward the place whence the cries came, and gradually the crowd became so dense at this point that the wind itself could with difficulty have penetrated it.

In the centre of the throng, and almost stifled by it,

stood a young man of twenty years, whom it was easy to recognize as a disguised student; with pallid cheeks, blanched lips but clinched fists, he appeared to be waiting until some of his assailants bolder than the rest, not content with shouting, should lay hands upon him, that he might beat down all who should encounter the two weapons of defence made by his doubled fists.

He was a tall, fair young man, rather spare and rather delicate, resembling in appearance one of the worthy demoiselles dressed in boy's clothes whom we have just mentioned; his drooping eyes bespoke the utmost candor, and could Humility have taken on a human countenance, she would have chosen no other type than the one presented by the face of this youth.

What crime then could he have committed that all this rabble should be at his heels, the whole pack in full cry, that all these arms should be outstretched ready to cast him into the flood?

II.

IN WHICH IS EXPLAINED WHY, WHEN IT RAINS ON SAINT MÉDARD'S DAY, IT RAINS FOR FORTY DAYS.

As accused in the preceding chapter, he was a Huguenot, and he had announced that it was about to rain.

This is the way the affair began; it was a very simple matter, as you will see.

The fair young man, who appeared to be expecting a friend, was walking along the river. From time to time he stopped, he looked at the water; then, when he had looked at the water long enough, he looked at the grass; when he had looked at the grass long enough, he raised his eyes and looked at the sky.

One would certainly pronounce it a monotonous pastime, but it must be admitted that it was inoffensive. However, certain people, who were celebrating the Fête du Landi in their own fashion, took it ill that this young man should celebrate it in his. In fact, during the last half hour, several bourgeois, with a sprinkling of students and artisans, had shown themselves visibly irritated by the young man's triple contemplation; and they were the more irritated that the youth seemed to take not the slightest notice of them.

"Ah!" said a woman's voice, "I am not curious, but I should like very much to know why that young man is so bent upon contemplating the water, the earth, and the sky, one after the other."

"Do you care to know, Perrette of my heart?" inquired a young bourgeois who was gallantly drinking wine from the lady's glass and love from her eyes.

"Yes, Landry, and I will give a smacking kiss to the one that tells me."

"Ah! Perrette, for so sweet a recompense, I wish you had set a harder task."

"I shall be content with that."

"Will you give me a pledge?"

"There is my hand."

The bourgeois kissed the girl's hand, and rising said,—

"You shall soon know."

Thereupon the one whom the girl called Landry turned away, and, approaching the silent and solitary observer, he said: —

"Hey, there! young man, may I ask, without seeming to presume, why you are looking at the grass like that? Have you lost anything?"

The young man, perceiving that he was the person addressed, turned around, politely removed his hat, and with great courtesy answered his interlocutor: —

"You mistake, monsieur, I was not looking at the grass; I was looking at the river."

And, having pronounced these few words, he turned away. Master Landry was somewhat disconcerted; he had not expected so civil a reply. Such civility impressed him. He returned to the company scratching his ear.

"Well?" demanded Perrette.

"Well, we were deceived," said Landry, pitifully enough: "he was not looking at the grass."

"What was he looking at, then?"

"At the river."

A shout of laughter rose in the face of the messenger, who felt the blush of shame rise to his cheek.

"And you did not ask why he was looking at the river?" inquired Perrette.

"No," returned Landry; "he was so civil I thought it would be indiscreet to put a second question to him."

"Two kisses to the one who will go and ask him why he is staring at the river," said Perrette.

Three or four lovers rose.

But Landry signified that, as he had undertaken the matter, he was the one to carry it out.

The justice of his claim was admitted.

He returned to the blonde youth, and for the second time he asked,—

"Hey, there! young man, why do you stare at the river like that?"

The same by-play was repeated. The young man turned, removed his hat, and, still civil, replied to his questioner,—

"Excuse me, monsieur, I am not staring at the river; I am watching the sky."

And with these words the young man bowed and turned away.

But Landry, for the moment as disconcerted by this reply as he had been by the former, believing his honor to be involved, and hearing in the distance his comrades' shouts of laughter, took courage, plucked the student by the cloak, and insisted,—

"Then, young man, will you be kind enough to tell me why you are watching the sky?"

"Monsieur," returned the young man, "will you do me the favor to say why you ask?"

"Well, I will be frank with you, young man."

"You will oblige me, monsieur."

"I ask you, monsieur, because my companions are so

annoyed at your standing here like a post for the last hour, and executing the same manœuvres."

"Monsieur," replied the student, "I remain here because I am waiting for a friend; I stand up because by standing I shall be able to see him coming in the distance. Then, because he does not come, and I am tired of waiting for him, and because the ennui that I suffer compels me to move about, I look at the ground so as not to cut my shoes on the broken tankards with which the grass is strewn; then I look out upon the river as a change from looking down at the ground; then, finally, I look up at the sky as a relief from looking at the river."

The bourgeois, instead of accepting this explanation for what it was,—that is, for the pure and simple truth,—believed that he was being hoaxed, and he turned as red as the poppies that were to be seen in the distance blossoming in the fields of clover and corn.

"And do you intend, young man," persisted the bourgeois, settling himself on his left hip with an exasperating air and squaring back his shoulders, "do you intend to devote yourself much longer to this unpleasant occupation?"

"I had intended to continue it until my friend came, monsieur; but—"

The youth glanced up at the sky.

"I do not think I shall be able to await his pleasure," he concluded.

"And why will you not wait?"

"Because there is going to be such a rain-storm, monsieur, that in a quarter of an hour from now, neither you, nor I, nor any one else will be able to remain out of doors."

"It is going to rain, do you say?" interrogated the

bourgeois, with the expression of a man who thinks he is laughed at.

"It will pour, monsieur!" tranquilly returned the youth.

"You are undoubtedly joking, young man."

"I assure you I have not the least idea of doing so, monsieur."

"Then you are making game of me," suggested the exasperated bourgeois.

"Monsieur, I give you my word that I have no such thought."

"Then why do you tell me that it is going to rain, when the weather is magnificent?" roared Landry, becoming more and more exasperated.

"I say it will rain, for three reasons."

"Will you give me your three reasons?"

"Certainly, if it will oblige you."

"It will oblige me."

The young man politely bowed, and with a manner that seemed to say, "You are so amiable, monsieur, that I can refuse you nothing."

"I am waiting for your three reasons," said Landry, clinching his fists and grinding his teeth.

"The first, monsieur," said the youth, "is that, as it did not rain yesterday, there is good reason for its raining to-day."

"You are quizzing me, monsieur."

"By no means."

"Then give me the second."

"The second is that the sky was overcast all the night, all the morning, and is still so at this moment."

"Because the weather is cloudy is no certainty of rain, you know."

"There is likelihood of it, at least."

"Let me have your third reason; but I warn you that if it is not better than the first two, I shall lose my temper."

"Should you lose your temper, monsieur, you would be displaying a petty disposition."

"Ah! do you tell me that I have a petty disposition?"

"Monsieur, I spoke of a possibility, not of a probability."

"The third reason, monsieur, — the third reason?"

The young man extended his hand.

"The third reason for its raining, monsieur, is that it is raining."

"Do you pretend that it is raining?"

"I do not pretend it, — I affirm the fact."

"This is intolerable!" declared the bourgeois, quite beside himself.

"It will presently be much more so," remarked the young man.

"And do you think I will stand it?" cried the bourgeois, scarlet with rage.

"I do not think you will stand it any longer than I," returned the student; "and if I were going to give you advice, it would be to do what I am about to do, — that is, look for shelter."

"Ah! this is too much!" roared the bourgeois, turning toward his associates.

Then, addressing himself to all within range of his voice, he shouted, —

"Come here, all of you! Come on, everybody!"

The bourgeois seemed so enraged, that every one came running at his call.

"What is the matter?" inquired the women, in a shrill key.

"What is the matter?" demanded the men's hoarse voices.

"What is the matter?" retorted Landry, sensible of support. "Incredible things."

"What?"

"Merely that monsieur would have us see the stars in broad daylight."

"I beg pardon, monsieur," rejoined the student, with great suavity; "on the contrary, I have informed you that the weather is extremely cloudy."

"A figure of speech, master student," answered Landry. "Do you understand?—a figure of speech!"

"In that case, your figure is bad."

"Do you say that I have a bad figure?" yelled Landry, who, deafened by the blood throbbing in his ears, misunderstood, or did not wish to understand. "Ah! this is too much, messieurs; you see for yourselves that this knave takes us for fools."

"Takes you for a fool," said a voice,—"that is quite possible."

"You and me and all of us; it is a poor jester that amuses himself with brewing mischief and wishing it may rain to spite us."

"Monsieur, I take my oath that I do not wish it to rain; for, if it rains, I shall get as wet as you, and even wetter, since I am three or four inches taller than you."

"Is that as much as to call me a runt?"

"I used no such term, monsieur."

"A dwarf?"

"That would be a gratuitous insult. You are nearly five feet high, monsieur."

"I don't know what keeps me from throwing you into the water!" shrieked Landry.

"Ah! yes, into the water with him!" cried several voices.

"Should you throw me into the water, monsieur," said the young man, with his usual politeness, "you would not get any the less wet."

As this response proved that he alone possessed more wit than the rest together, the rest turned against him. One tall fellow approached, and, half banteringly, half threateningly, said, —

"Tell us, rascal, why dost thou say it is now raining?"

"Because I felt the drops."

"Raining in drops," cried Landry, "is not a downpour, and he said it would pour."

"Art thou, then, in league with some astrologer?" said the tall fellow.

"I am in league with no one, monsieur," answered the young man, who was growing angry; "not even with you, who 'thee and thou' me."

"Into the water! into the water!" cried several voices.

And then it was that the student, conscious of the gathering storm, doubled his fists and prepared for the encounter. The circle began to close in upon him.

"Stop!" exclaimed a new-comer. "It is Médard!"

"Who is Médard?" demanded several voices.

"He is the saint whose fête falls on to-day," said a wag.

"Well," cried the one who had recognized the young man, "this one is no saint,—he is a heretic."

"A heretic!" shouted the crowd; "into the water with the heretic! into the water with the Baptist! into the water with the Reformer! into the water with the Huguenot!"

And all the voices joined in chorus, —

"Into the water! into the water! into the water!"

These were the cries that had disturbed the fête just as we were well under way to describe it.

But at that very moment, as if Providence had meant to send the youth the help of which he stood in such dire need, the friend whom he was expecting arrived,—a handsome cavalier of twenty-two or twenty-three years, whose high-bred air bespoke the gentleman, and whose appearance betrayed the foreigner; he came at a run, and, thrusting aside the crowd, he found himself within twenty paces of his friend just as the latter, seized before, behind, by the feet and by the head, was struggling with all his might.

"Defend yourself, Médard!" cried the new-comer. "Defend yourself!"

"It really is Médard, you see!" cried the one who had called him by this name.

And as if to bear the name were a crime, the whole mob shouted,—

"Yes, it is Médard! it is Médard! Into the water with Médard! into the water with the heretic! into the water with the Huguenot!"

"What audacity for a heretic to bear the name of so great a saint!" screamed Perrette.

"Into the water with the sacrilegious wretch!"

And those who had seized poor Médard dragged him toward the bank.

"Help, Robert!" cried the youth, feeling that he was no match for such numbers, and that death was to be the end of the joke.

"Into the water with the ruffian!" shrieked the women, as mad in hate as in love.

"Defend yourself, Médard!" again cried the stranger, drawing his sword. "Defend yourself; I am coming!"

And, striking out right and left with the flat of his sword, he swept down the slope like an avalanche. But he reached a point where the crowd was so dense that, whatever desire its individuals might have had to disperse, their efforts were unavailing; they took his blows and howled with pain, but they did not scatter. After howling with pain, they howled with rage.

The new-comer, who from his foreign accent could be recognized as a Scotchman, kept on raining blows, but without advancing; or he advanced so little that it was easy to see that his friend would be in the water before he could reach his side. About twenty peasants and five or six boatmen were in the fray. In vain poor Médard clutched with his hands, struck out with his feet, and bit with his teeth; every second brought him nearer to the brink.

The Scotchman no longer heard anything but his calls, and they were perceptibly nearing the water's edge. He himself ceased calling, — he roared; and with every roar the broad side of his blade or the butt of his sword fell upon some head. Suddenly the shouts redoubled; then followed silence; then was heard the splash of a heavy body striking the water.

"Ah! ruffians! murderers! assassins!" screamed the young man, as he strove to make headway toward the river, to save his friend or to die with him.

But it was impossible. As well might he have tried to overturn a wall of granite as this living wall. He recoiled, worn out, grinding his teeth, his lips foaming and his forehead streaming with perspiration. He retreated to the brow of the slope to see if, when above the crowd, he could not catch a glimpse of poor Médard's head reappearing on the surface of the water. And as he stood there, on the crest of the slope, leaning on his sword, and saw nothing reappear, he bent his gaze upon the furious mob, and regarded the human pack with loathing.

Thus, standing quite apart, pale and in black garments, he looked like the destroying angel, resting for a moment with folded wings. But, the moment past, the rage that was seething within his breast, like lava in a volcano, mounted hot to his lips.

"You are ruffians; you are assassins; you are infamous wretches all! Forty to one, you have drowned, murdered, a poor lad who had done you no harm. I challenge you all! There are forty of you; come on, and I will kill the whole forty, one after the other, — curs that you are!"

The peasants, bourgeois, and students to whom this invitation to meet Death was addressed, did not appear to care to risk the chances of a side-arm combat with a man that handled the sword so masterfully. Seeing this, the Scotchman disdainfully returned his sword to its sheath.

"You are as craven as you are vile, cowardly knaves!" continued he, with a sweeping gesture above their heads, "but I will avenge this death on others less despicable; as for you, you are not worthy a gentleman's sword. Away, then, clowns and poltroons! and may the rain and hail destroy your vineyards, and lodge your grain, and pour down upon your fields as many days as you have employed men to slay one!"

But, as if justice demanded that this murder should be avenged, he drew from his belt a great pistol, and, firing upon the crowd without taking aim, he cried, —

"God speed the ball!"

There was a report, the ball whistled, and one of the men who had just cast Médard into the water uttered a cry, clapped his hand to his breast, staggered, and fell mortally wounded.

"And now, adieu!" said he. "You shall hear from me again. My name is Robert Stuart."

As he finished speaking, the clouds, heaped in the sky since the day before, suddenly burst, and as the unfortunate Médard had predicted, there fell one of those torrent-like rains that never come in the season of rains.

The young man walked slowly away.

The peasants would certainly have fallen upon him, seeing his maledictions produce immediate effect, had not the roaring of thunder, which seemed to them to be trumpeting the last day, the water falling in torrents, and the blinding lightning, engaged their attention infinitely more than thoughts of revenge; and it became at once a case of each for himself.

In a short time the river-bank, recently thronged with from five thousand to six thousand people, was as deserted as the shores of one of the streams in the New World which had so lately been discovered by the Genoese navigator.

It rained forty days without ceasing.

And this is why,—so at least we think, dear reader,—when it rains on Saint Médard's Day, it rains for forty days.

III.

AT THE RED HORSE INN.

We will not undertake to tell our readers what became of the fifty or sixty thousand people who assisted at the Fête du Landi, and who, taken unawares by this modern deluge, sought shelter in alcoves, houses, taverns, and even in the royal sanctuary.

At this period there were barely five or six inns in the town of Saint Denis, which were almost instantly so overcrowded that some of the people began to leave them more hastily than they had entered, preferring to be drowned by the rain rather than suffocated by the heat.

The only inn that remained comparatively empty — and this distinction it owed to its isolation — was the Red Horse Inn, situated on the highway, within range of a gun-shot or so from the town of Saint Denis.

For the time being, three persons were occupying the great smoke-blackened room that was pretentiously called the guest hall, and which — save for the kitchen and a loft overhead serving as a sleeping-room for belated muleteers and cattle-dealers — comprised in itself alone the entire inn. It was something like an enormous cart-house, lighted by the door, which reached almost to the roof; the ceiling was made on the model of the ark, with visible timbers following the shape of the roof.

As in the ark, a goodly number of animals — dogs, cats, hens, and ducks — swarmed over the floor, and instead of the raven that came back with empty beak, and the dove that brought the olive branch, swallows were seen flitting in and out among the blackened joists by day, and bats by night. As for the furniture of this hall, it was limited to the articles indispensable to an inn, — that is, to rickety tables, crippled chairs, and wabbling stools.

The three persons occupying the room were the inn-keeper, his wife, and a wayfarer of thirty or thirty-five years of age.

Let us describe the grouping of these three people, and tell how they were engaged.

The inn-keeper, whom in his character of master of the house we mention first, was doing nothing; he sat before the door, astride upon a straw-bottomed chair, with his chin propped on its back, and grumbled at the foul weather.

The inn-keeper's wife, sitting a little behind her husband, in such a position, however, as to catch the light, was plying her spinning-wheel, moistening at her lips the thread she was twisting between her fingers and drawing from the hemp of her distaff.

The wayfarer of thirty or thirty-five years, instead of seeking the light, sat, on the contrary, in the remotest corner of the room, with his back turned to the door, and appeared to be a customer, judging from the tankard and cup before him.

Yet his thoughts did not seem to be fixed upon his drink; with his elbow on the table and his head in his hand, he was lost in revery.

"Beastly weather!" growled the host.

"Do you find fault with it?" said his wife. "You were the one that wanted it."

"So I did," admitted the inn-keeper; "but I was wrong."

"Then don't complain."

At this admonition, containing small comfort but full of logic, the inn-keeper, heaving a sigh, bowed his head and was silent.

The silence endured about ten minutes; then the inn-keeper raised his head and growled again, —

"Beastly weather!"

"You have already said that," remarked his wife.

"Well, I say it again, then."

"It will not mend the matter, if you keep on saying it till night, will it?"

"True; but it does me some little good to storm at the thunder, rain, and hail."

"Why do you not rail at Providence, and be done with it?"

"If I thought that Providence sent such weather — "

The inn-keeper hesitated.

"You would rail at Providence. Come, confess, now!"

"No; because — "

"Because what?"

"Because I am a good Christian, instead of a dog of a heretic."

At the words, "a dog of a heretic," the traveller, who had been caught in the Red Horse Inn like a cat in a trap, came out of his revery, raised his head, and struck such a blow on the table with his pewter cup that the tankard began to dance and the cup was dented.

"Here, here!" cried the inn-keeper, bouncing on his chair like the tankard on the table, supposing that his guest was summoning him; "coming, my young master!"

The young man swung his chair around on one of its hind legs, and, swinging with it, he came face to face with his host, who was standing before him; after scanning him from head to foot, without raising his voice, but with lowering brow, he said,—

"Was it you that just said, 'dog of a heretic'?"

"Yes, my young master," stammered the tavern-keeper, with reddening face.

"Well, if it was you, master knave," replied the guest, "you are but an ill-bred ass, and deserve to have your ears cropped."

"Pardon, your honor; I did not know that you were of the reformed religion," said the inn-keeper, trembling in every limb.

"Which should prove to you, scamp that you are," continued the Huguenot, without raising his voice so much as a half tone, "that an inn-keeper, who deals with everybody, ought to keep his tongue in his head; for it is quite possible that while he thinks he has to do with a dog of a Catholic he is dealing with a respectable follower of Luther and Calvin."

And, as he said the last words, the gentleman raised his felt hat. The inn-keeper did likewise. The gentleman shrugged his shoulders.

"Come," said he, "another measure of wine, and do not let me hear you utter the word 'heretic' again, or I will tap your old wine-cask of a stomach; do you hear, my friend?"

The inn-keeper backed away, and took himself off to the kitchen to get the wine.

The gentleman, meanwhile, described a half-turn to the right with his stool, and resumed his position with his back to the door, his face again being in the shadow when the landlord returned to set his small measure of wine before him.

Then the uncommunicative gentleman held out his

battered drinking-cup to be exchanged for a new one. The inn-keeper, without breathing a word, rolled his eyes and nodded his head, as much as to say: "The devil! From all appearances, when that fellow smites, he smites hard;" and he returned with a sound glass for the disciple of Calvin.

"Very good," said the latter; "this is the sort of inn-keeper I like."

The host bestowed his most agreeable smile upon the gentleman, and went away to resume his station in the foreground.

"Well," inquired his wife, who, on account of the restraint which the Protestant had placed on his voice, had not overheard a word of what was passing between her husband and his guest, "what did the young gentleman have to say to you?"

"What did he say?"

"Yes, that is what I asked."

"Very flattering things," answered the other: "that my wine was excellent, that my inn was marvellously neat, and that he was surprised that such a house should not have more custom."

"And what did you reply?"

"That this beastly weather was our ruin."

Just as our friend was indirectly reviling Providence for the third time, Providence, as if to give him the lie, caused two new guests to arrive at the same moment, although from opposite directions, — one on foot, the other on horseback. The pedestrian, who appeared to be a knight of fortune, was advancing from the left, — that is, from Paris; the rider, who wore a page's costume, was approaching from the right, — that is, by the Flanders road.

But, just as he was clearing the threshold of the inn,

a foot of the pedestrian was stepped on by the horse. The pedestrian discharged an oath and turned pale. The mere oath announced the speaker's part of the country.

"Ah! *cap de Diou!*" he cried.

The rider, like an accomplished horseman, executed a half-turn to the left with his horse, lifting him to his hind feet, and, springing to the ground before the animal's fore feet had struck the earth, he rushed toward the injured man, and in tones of earnest solicitude exclaimed, —

"Oh, captain, I offer you every apology!"

"Do you know, master page," said the Gascon, "that you have nearly crushed me?"

"Believe me, captain, I am excessively chagrined."

"Well, console yourself, young gentleman," returned the captain, as he made a wry face, showing that he had not entirely mastered his pain; "console yourself; without suspecting it, you have just done me an enormous service, and I really do not know how to thank you."

"A service?"

"An enormous one!" repeated the Gascon.

"*Mon Dieu!* in what way?" demanded the page, who could see from the nervous twitching of the speaker's face that he was exercising great self-control to refrain from swearing instead of smiling.

"It is very simple," returned the captain; "there are but two things in the world that vex me beyond endurance: they are old women and new boots; well, ever since morning I have been encumbered with a pair of new boots, in which I have had to walk from Paris. I was casting about for an expeditious means of breaking them in, and here have you, to your undying glory, wrought the miracle in a twinkling. I pray you, then, in return for the favor, on every occasion to command my person, which declares itself your humble servant."

"Monsieur," said the page, bowing, "you are a man of spirit, which does not surprise me, after hearing the oath with which you greeted me. You are courteous; nor does that surprise me, considering you are a gentleman: I accept all that you offer, placing myself, in turn, quite at your service."

"I presume you are intending to stop at this inn?"

"Yes, monsieur, for a short time," replied the youth, tying his horse to a ring fastened in the wall for that purpose, — a proceeding which the inn-keeper watched, his eyes beaming with joy.

"And I, also," said the captain. "Come, you lout of a landlord, set out some wine, and of the best!"

"Immediately, messeigneurs!" cried the inn-keeper, hastening to his kitchen, — "immediately!"

Five seconds later, he returned with two tankards and two glasses, which he placed on a table near the one at which the first gentleman sat.

"Monsieur host," demanded the youthful page, in accents as gentle as a woman's, "has your inn a room where a young gentlewoman can rest for an hour or two?"

"We have only this room," returned the inn-keeper.

"Ah, *diable!* that is a pity."

"You are expecting your wife, my galliard?" mysteriously inquired the captain, seizing the end of his mustache with his tongue, and beginning to nibble at it.

"She is not a wife for me, captain," gravely responded the youth; "she is the daughter of my noble master, Monsieur le Maréchal de Saint André."

"*Haü! grand double et triple Diou vivant!* Then

you are in the service of the illustrious Maréchal de Saint André?"

"I have that honor, monsieur."

"And do you think that the maréchal will descend here and creep into this kennel? Do you imagine that, my young page? Come, now!" protested the captain.

"He must do so; for the last fifteen days Monsieur le Maréchal has been ill at the Château de Villers-Cotterets, and, as it was impossible for him to return on horseback to Paris, — whither he goes to be present at the tournament that takes place on the twenty-ninth, on the occasion of the marriage of King Philip II. with the Princess Elizabeth, and that of the Princess Marguerite with the Duke Emmanuel Philibert of Savoy, — Monsieur de Guise, whose château is near the Château de Villers-Cotterets —"

"Monsieur de Guise has a château in the neighborhood of Villers-Cotterets?" interposed the captain, desirous of showing that he had knowledge of the court; "and where do you place this château, young man?"

"At Nanteuil-le-Haudouin, captain; it is a purchase which he has recently made that he might be on the king's route when the king goes to and from Villers-Cotterets."

"Ah! ah! well played, that, it seems to me!"

"Oh," smilingly remarked the page, "that player does not lack skill."

"Nor a game," said the captain.

"As I was saying," resumed the page, "Monsieur de Guise brought his own coach for the maréchal, and they are coming on at a walking gait; but, notwithstanding the coach is so easy and the horses are proceeding to Gonesse so slowly, Monsieur le Maréchal experiences great fatigue, and Mademoiselle Charlotte de Saint

André has sent me ahead to find an inn where her father can get a little rest."

Hearing these words spoken at the table next his own, the first gentleman, who had waxed so wroth when the Huguenots were insulted, pricked up his ears and appeared to take the keenest interest in the conversation.

"*Per la crux Diou!*" ejaculated the Gascon. "I swear, young man, that if I knew of any room within two leagues around fit to receive the two generals, I would yield to no one, not even to my own father, the honor of conducting them thither; but, unfortunately," he added, "I know of none."

The Huguenot gentleman made a gesture which might have been construed as a sign of contempt. This movement drew the captain's attention to him.

"Ah! ah!" he drawled.

And, rising, he bowed to the Huguenot with studied courtesy; this done, he turned his attention to the page. The Huguenot rose, as the Gascon had done, bowed politely but grimly, and turned his attention to the wall. The captain poured wine for the page, — who took up his glass before it was a third full, — then he resumed: —

"You say, young man, that you are in the service of the illustrious Maréchal de Saint André, the hero of Cérisoles and of Renty. I was at the siege of Boulogne, young man, and witnessed his efforts to enter the town. Ah! *per ma fé!* there was a man that did not steal the title of 'maréchal.'"

Then he suddenly paused, and seemed to reflect.

"*Cap de Diou!*" he exclaimed; "now I have it! I am from Gascony; I have abandoned the château of my ancestors to serve some prince of renown or illustrious leader. Young man, is there not a place in the household of the Maréchal de Saint André that a brave officer like me could with propriety fill? I will not stand upon trifles in the matter of salary, and, provided I am given no old women to amuse or new boots to break in, I will endeavor to perform to my master's satisfaction whatever duty it may please him to assign me."

"Ah! captain," said the page, "I am truly very sorry, but, unfortunately, Monsieur le Maréchal's household is complete, and I doubt whether, should he wish to do so, he could accept your obliging offer."

"*Morbleu!* so much the worse for him, for I can boast myself a treasure to my employers. Now, grant that I have said nothing, and let us drink."

The young page had already raised his glass for the captain's gratification, when, suddenly assuming a listening attitude, he set the glass down again upon the table.

"Your pardon, captain," said he, "but I hear the sound of a coach, and, as coaches are somewhat rare, I think I can safely assume that it belongs to the Duc de Guise; with your permission, I will leave you a few moments."

"Do so, my young friend; do so," said the captain heartily; "duty first of all."

The permission sought by the page was asked from simple courtesy, for, even before the captain responded, he had hastily rushed out of the inn, and disappeared at a bend of the road.

IV.

THE TRAVELLERS.

THE captain took advantage of this interval to reflect, and, while reflecting, to drink up the wine he had before him. The first tankard of wine emptied, he called for another. Then, as if he lacked food for reflection, or that brain-work could be accomplished only by painful effort by reason of his infrequent indulgence in the exercise, the captain turned again to the Huguenot, saluted him with the exaggerated politeness that he had already displayed, and said, —

"*Per ma fé*, monsieur, it seems to me that I recognize a compatriot."

"You are deceived, captain," answered the one appealed to; "for, if I mistake not, you are from Gascony; I am from Angoumois."

"Ah! you are from Angoumois!" cried the captain, with an expression of admiring surprise, — "from Angoumois! Well! well! well!"

"Yes, captain; does it please you?" inquired the Huguenot.

"I should think so! permit me to congratulate you You have a magnificent, a fertile country, coursed by beautiful rivers; your men are full of courage, — his late Majesty, François I., for instance; your women sparkle with wit, — Madame Marguerite de Navarre, for example. In short, I confess, monsieur, that were I not of Gascony, I would be of Angoumois."

"Really, you do my poor province too much honor, monsieur," returned the gentleman from Angoumois. "I know not how to thank you."

"Oh, nothing is easier, monsieur, — merely to show me the slight return of taking my brutal frankness in good part! Do me the honor to touch my glass to the glory and prosperity of your compatriots."

"With the greatest pleasure, captain," responded the Huguenot, as he transferred his tankard and glass to a corner of the table at which the Gascon was seated, and of which the page's departure had left him in sole possession.

After the health drunk to the glory of the sons of Angoumois, the Huguenot gentleman, not to be wanting in courtesy, proposed the same toast to the prosperity and glory of the sons of Gascony.

Then, the courtesy shown him by the other having been paid in kind, the gentleman from Angoumois picked up his tankard and glass, in readiness to return to his own place.

"Oh, monsieur," said the Gascon, "this would be interrupting our acquaintance too soon! Pray do me the favor to finish your pot of wine at this table."

"I was afraid of causing you inconvenience, monsieur," returned the Huguenot, politely but coldly.

"Causing me inconvenience? Never! Besides, monsieur, in my opinion the best and most perfect friendships begin at the table. A pot of wine rarely yields less than three glassfuls, does it?"

"Assuredly, monsieur, very rarely," replied the Huguenot, visibly at a loss to know what his interlocutor meant.

"Well, let us propose a toast for each glass. Do you agree to a health for each?"

"A health for each, monsieur."

"When two persons join heartily in drinking the health of three men, it is because they have similar dispositions, opinions, and principles."

"There is some truth in what you say, monsieur."

"Some truth! some truth in it, you say, — *par le sang-Diou!* monsieur, it is truth unalloyed."

Then, with his most pleasing smile, he continued, —

"To begin our acquaintance, monsieur, and to expose the similarity of our views, permit me, then, as the first toast, to propose the illustrious Constable de Montmorency."

The gentleman, who had already confidently raised his glass with brightening countenance, became grave, and replaced it on the table.

"You must pardon me, monsieur," said he; "but with respect to that man, it is impossible for me to oblige you. Monsieur de Montmorency is my personal enemy."

"Your personal enemy?"

"As much as a man in his position can be such to a man in mine; as much as the great can be the enemy of the lowly."

"Your personal enemy! In that case, from this hour he becomes mine, and all the more that I do not know him at all, and have no deep-seated affection for him. He has a bad reputation; he is miserly, overbearing, dissolute; gets beaten like a ninny and caught like a fool. How in the devil's name, then, did I come by the idea of offering you such a toast? Allow me, now, to make amends by proposing another, — To the illustrious Maréchal de Saint André!"

"Faith! you are farther astray than before, captain," answered the Huguenot, with the same pantomime at mention of the Maréchal de Saint André as at the name of the constable. "I cannot drink the health of a man whom I do not esteem, — a man capable of doing anything for advancement or money, a man who would sell his wife or his daughter as he has sold his conscience, if he were paid the same price."

"Oh, *cap de Diou!* what is that you say?" cried the Gascon. "What! was I about to drink the health of such a man? Where the devil are your wits, captain?" he continued, reprimanding himself. "Ah! my friend, if you wish to preserve the esteem of honest men, you must make no more such blunders."

Then, shifting his audience, and addressing himself to the Huguenot, he said, —

"Monsieur, henceforth I hold the Maréchal de Saint André in the same contempt that you yourself entertain for him. And now, not willing to leave the impression of my mistake on your mind, I will propose a third health, with which, I hope, you will have no fault to find."

"Whose, captain?"

"The health of the illustrious François de Lorraine, Duc de Guise! to the defender of Metz! to the conqueror of Calais! to the avenger of Saint Quentin and of Gravelines! to the repairer of the blunders of the Constable de Montmorency and the Maréchal de Saint André! — Ah!"

"Captain," said the young man, growing pale, "you are unlucky, for I have made a vow."

"What is it, monsieur? Be assured that, if I can be of assistance in its fulfilment —"

"I have sworn that the man whose health you propose shall die only by my hand."

"*Pécaire!*" exclaimed the Gascon.

The Huguenot moved as if to rise.

"Why!" cried the Gascon. "What are you about now, monsieur?"

"Monsieur," answered the Huguenot, "the trial is ended; the three toasts have been proposed, and, as we do not seem to entertain the same opinion of the men, it is to be feared that matters would be much worse were we to touch upon their principles."

"*Haü! grand double et triple Diou vivant!* it shall not be said that congenial souls have fallen out over men they did not know; for I know neither the Duc de Guise nor the Maréchal de Saint André, nor do I know the Constable de Montmorency; let us assume, then, that I have been so imprudent as to propose the healths of the three great devils, — Satan, Lucifer, and Ashtaroth; you cause me to see, at the third toast, that I am risking my soul, and I promptly withdraw them. Here I am, then, at the point whence I started, and, as our glasses are full, we will, if you please, drink them to our respective healths. God give you long and prosperous days, monsieur! I speak from the very depths of my heart."

"The desire is too courteous not to be reciprocated, captain."

And this time the Angoumois emptied his glass, following the example of the captain, who had already drained his own.

"Well, that matter is settled," declared the Gascon, smacking his lips, "and we are getting on famously; and so, henceforth, monsieur, you can dispose of me as of your most devoted friend."

"I place myself equally at your disposal, captain," responded the Huguenot, with his usual courtesy.

"As for me," continued the Gascon, "I will add,

monsieur, that I await but the opportunity to do you a service."

"And I, for you," responded the Angoumois.

"Sincerely, monsieur?"

"Sincerely, captain."

"Well, then, the occasion you seek for doing me a favor is, I think, at hand."

"Is it possible that I am to have this happiness?"

"Yes, *per la crux Diou!* either I very much mistake, or you hold it in your hand."

"Speak, then."

"This it is: I have come from Gascony; I have left the château of my ancestors, where I was visibly fattening to an alarming degree; my barber recommended exercise, and I have come to Paris for the purpose of devoting myself to some salutary exercise. It is unnecessary to say that I have chosen the military career. Do you not know in Angoumois of some good place which a Gascon captain could fill,—providing they give him no old women to amuse or new boots to break in? I venture to flatter myself, monsieur, that, in such a case, I shall properly fulfill the duties with which I am intrusted."

"I wish I knew of such a place, captain," replied the Angoumois; "unfortunately I left my country very young, and I know no one there."

"*Par les entrailles du saint-père!* monsieur, that is quite unfortunate; but, while I think of it, my dear monsieur, may you not know of some little place in another province,—I have not absolutely set my heart on Angoumois, which is, to be sure, a fever district,—or, indeed, of some virtuous lord of noble race to whom you could recommend me? Should he not be quite virtuous, I would still make shift with him, providing

God had endowed him with as much valor as he had denied him virtue."

"I regret exceedingly, captain, to be unable to serve in any way a man so easily suited; but I am a poor gentleman like you, and had I a brother, I could not keep him alive from my surplus of either purse or credit."

"By the holy thief!" cried the Gascon, "decidedly, it is very unfortunate; but, as your will is good, my dear monsieur," he continued, rising and fastening his sword-buckle, "I am, on my honor, under the same obligation to you."

And he saluted the Huguenot, who returned the salute, took up his glass and pot of wine, and went back to his former seat.

Now the arrival of the coach produced a different effect on each of the actors introduced in this scene.

As we have said, the gentleman from Angoumois resumed his former place, which permitted him to turn his back to the door. The Gascon captain remained standing, as befitted a younger son in the presence of the illustrious personages announced by the page; the innkeeper and his wife hastened to the door to place themselves at the disposal of the travellers whom good luck was bringing them.

The page, who, to keep his attire from contact with the mud, was standing erect on the footboard of the coachman's seat, leaped to the ground and opened the door. A man of about forty years, haughty of mien, descended first.

It was François de Lorraine, Duc de Guise. He wore the white scarf with fringe and fleurs-de-lis of gold, the insignia of his rank as lieutenant-general of the king's army. His hair was cut short and straight across. He wore a black velvet toque with white plumes, in the style of that period; a doublet of pearl-gray and silver, which were his favorite colors; hose and velvet mantle of scarlet; and long boots, which, as occasion demanded, could be drawn up to the thigh or turned down below the knee.

"Why, this is a veritable deluge," said he, as he gained a footing among the puddles of water that tesselated the space before the door of the inn.

Then, turning to the coach and leaning over into the interior, he continued, —

"Look here, dear Charlotte, you cannot set your pretty little feet into this villainous mud."

"What is to be done, then?" demanded a small voice, sweet and flute-like.

"My dear maréchal," pursued the duke, "will you permit me to take your daughter in my arms? It will rejuvenate me by fourteen years; for, fourteen years ago this very day, my lovely goddaughter, I lifted you thus from your cradle. Come, fair dove," he continued, "come out of your ark."

And, taking the girl in his arms, he carried her at three strides into the interior of the great hall.

The title of dove, bestowed by the gallant Duc de Guise upon his goddaughter, of whom there was question of making his daughter-in-law, was not misplaced. It was, indeed, impossible to find a dove whiter, daintier, more alluring than the one which the duke bore in his arms and deposited on the damp flags of the inn.

The third person who descended, or, rather, who attempted to descend from the coach, was the Maréchal de Saint André. He called his page; but although the latter was only three steps distant, he did not hear.

True page that he was, his eyes were fondly fixed on his master's daughter.

"Jacques! Jacques!" reiterated the maréchal. "Where are you? Ah! you little rascal, will you come here?"

"Here I am!" cried the young page, speedily facing about. "Here I am, Monsieur le Maréchal!"

"*Morbleu!*" exclaimed the latter. "I see, indeed, that you are there; but there is not where you ought to be, clown! but here, here, at the foot of these steps. You know very well how helpless I am, just at present, you little knave! *Aïe! ouf! tonnerre!*"

"Pardon, Monsieur le Maréchal," said the confused page, presenting his shoulder to his master.

"Lean on me, Monsieur le Maréchal," said the duke, as he offered his arm to the gouty man.

The maréchal availed himself of the offer, and with the aid of this double support he, in turn, made his entrance into the inn.

He was at that time a man of fifty years, ruddy of cheek and florid of complexion, although somewhat pale, for the time being, on account of his indisposition; he had a red beard, fair hair, and blue eyes, and one felt at first sight that ten or twelve years before the period of which we write the Maréchal de Saint André must have been one of the handsomest cavaliers of his day.

He sat down with some difficulty in a kind of wicker armchair that seemed to have been placed for him at a corner of the fireplace; that is to say, in the corner opposite the one occupied by the captain from Gascony and the gentleman from Angoumois. For Mademoiselle Charlotte de Saint André, the duke placed the straw-bottomed chair, astride of which we saw the inn-keeper at the beginning of the preceding chapter, and, establishing himself on a tabouret, he ordered the landlord to make a big fire in the fireplace; for, notwithstanding it was midsummer, the dampness was such that the fire became a very needful accessory.

Just then the rain so increased, and fell in such torrents, that the water began to drive in at the open door as if through a breach in a dike or by a sluice that some one had forgotten to shut.

"*Holà*, landlord," cried the maréchal; "shut your door there! would you drown us alive?"

The inn-keeper handed his wife the fagot he was carrying, leaving to her, as to a modern vestal, the task of lighting the fire, and ran to the door to execute the maréchal's order. But just as he was exerting all his strength to swing the great barrier on its hinges a horse's quick galop was heard along the road.

Consequently the worthy man paused, fearing lest, should the door of the hostel be closed, the traveller might think it either full or deserted, and, on the one or the other supposition, pass by.

"Pardon, monseigneur," said he, thrusting his head through the gap of the door, "but I think a traveller is stopping."

In fact, a horseman halted before the inn, leaped from his horse, and tossed the bridle to the landlord, saying, —

"Take this animal to the stable, and spare neither bran nor oats."

And quickly entering the inn, where the fire was not yet lighted, he shook his hat, which was dripping with rain, without heeding that he was deluging every person in the room with streams of water.

The first victim of this shower was the Duc de Guise, who, quickly rising, made a single leap for the stranger, crying, —

"Hey! monsieur fool, can't you pay attention to what you are doing?"

At this apostrophe the new-comer turned around, and, as he turned, with a movement swift as thought he had his sword in hand. Doubtless Monsieur de Guise would have paid dearly for the words with which he had greeted the stranger, had he not recoiled, rather at sight of the face than of the sword.

"What! prince, is it you?" said he.

The person whom the Duc de Guise addressed as prince had only to glance at the illustrious leader from Lorraine to recognize him in turn.

"Why, yes, my very self, Monsieur le Duc," returned he, almost as much astonished to find the other installed in that paltry inn as the latter was astonished at seeing him there.

"Admit, prince, that the storm must indeed be a blinding one, since I could mistake Your Highness for a student from the Landi."

Then, bowing, he added, —

"I tender Your Highness a most sincere apology."

"Really, there is no occasion, duc," said the last arrival, with an air of grace and superiority habitual to him. "And by what chance do I find you here, whom I thought at your estate of Nanteuil?"

"I have, in fact, just come from there, prince."

"By way of Saint Denis?"

"We turned out of our way at Gonesse for a passing glance at the Fête du Landi."

"You, duc? It might answer for me, whose frivolity has become proverbial, thanks to my friends. But the serious, the stern Duc de Guise going out of his way to see a student's fête — "

"The proposition was not mine, prince. I was accompanying the Maréchal de Saint André, when his daughter, my goddaughter Charlotte, who is rather capricious, desired to see what the celebrated Fête du Landi was like, and, on being overtaken by the rain, we sought shelter here."

"Then the marechal is with you?" inquired the prince.

"He is there," said the duke, stepping aside and disclosing to view the two people whom the prince had indeed seen outlined in the half-light, but whose faces, by reason of the obscurity, he had not distinguished.

With an effort the maréchal arose, supporting himself by his chair.

"Maréchal," said the prince, advancing toward him, "pardon me for not having recognized you; but, in addition to the fact that this room is as dark as a cellar, or, rather, that this cellar is as dark as a dungeon, I am so blinded by the rain that, like Monsieur le Duc, I should be capable of confounding a gentleman with a clown. Happily, mademoiselle," continued the prince, — turning to the young girl and regarding her with admiration, — "happily, my sight is gradually returning, and I pity, with all my heart, the blind, who are deprived of the power of contemplating a face like yours."

This bold compliment caused a blush to overspread the girl's cheeks. She lifted her eyes to look at the one who had just addressed to her the first flattery, perhaps, that she ever received; but she lowered them as quickly, dazzled by the lightnings flashed from those of the prince.

What her impression was we do not know; but certainly it must have been very agreeable and full of charm, since it would have been difficult for a young girl of fourteen to find a more bewitching countenance than that of this cavalier of twenty-nine years, who was called prince, and styled Your Highness.

He was, indeed, an accomplished cavalier, this Louis I. of Bourbon, Prince de Condé.

Born on the seventh of May, 1530, he was, as we have said, just entering upon his thirtieth year at the time when our story begins.

He was short rather than tall, but of a wonderfully shapely figure. His auburn hair, cut short, shaded the lustrous brow on which a phrenologist of our time would have discovered all the bumps of superior intellect. His eyes, of a lapis-lazuli blue, were unspeakably soft and tender, and had not heavy eyebrows somewhat hardened the expression of a face which was still further softened by a fair beard, one might have taken the prince for a comely schoolboy, fresh from his mother's knee. And yet there were times when the beautiful eyes, limpid as the azure heavens, burned with fierce energy; the wits of the day compared them to waters that were inviting pools when lighted by the sun, forbidding whirlpools when troubled by storms. In a word, his face betrayed his ruling passions, — valor and love, both pushed to the extreme.

By this time, thanks to the closed door and the fire blazing in the chimney-place, the hall of the inn was aglow with fantastic beams, shedding divers and fanciful lights over the two groups occupying the corners, the one at the right and the other at the left; moreover, the tongues of flame that shot up the flue from time to time sent bluish lights flickering across the faces, giving to the youngest and most alive the aspect of beings from another world. This impression was so vivid that it even gained upon the inn-keeper, who, discovering that although it was barely seven o'clock in the evening night had already fallen, lighted a lamp, which he placed on the mantel above the group composed of the Prince de Condé, the Duc de Guise, the Maréchal de Saint André and his daughter.

Instead of abating, the rain redoubled; no one, therefore, could think of departing. The rain was reinforced by a wind which came from the river in such terrible gusts that the window-shutters slammed against the wall and the inn itself shook from ridge to foundation. Had the coach been on the road, it would, beyond doubt, have been carried away, horses and all, by the tempest. The travellers resolved, therefore, to remain at the inn as long as this dreadful hurricane raged.

Suddenly, at the very height of this terrible tumult of the elements, — the rain beating overhead, the shutters pounding the wall, the tiles wrenched from the roof and crashing on the ground, — a knocking was heard at the door, and a moaning voice entreated, in accents that grew fainter with each breath, —

"Open! open! In the name of Our Lord, open!"

Hearing the knock, the landlord rushed to open the door, thinking it the arrival of a new guest; but recognizing the voice he stopped midway of the room, and, shaking his head, called out, —

"You are at the wrong door, old hag. This is not the place for you to knock if you expect a door to be opened."

"Open, master landlord," repeated the plaintive voice; "surely it is a sin to leave an old woman outside in such weather as this."

"Turn your broom-handle another way, consort of

the devil!" returned the inn-keeper, through the door; "here is company too noble for you."

"But why," demanded the prince, shocked at the callousness of his host, — "why do you not open the door to the poor woman?"

"Because she is a witch, Your Highness, — the Witch of Andilly, — a miserable old woman who ought to be burned, as an example, in the middle of the Plain of Saint Denis, whose head runs on nothing but mischief, and whose predictions are always of thunder and hail. I am sure she is taking revenge on some poor peasant, and that she is the cause of this beastly weather."

"Witch or not," said the prince, "come, now, let her in. No human being must be kept at the door in such a storm."

"Since Your Highness desires it," yielded the host, "I will let the old heretic in; but I trust Your Highness may not repent it; for she brings bad luck wherever she goes."

Impelled to obey, in spite of his reluctance, the innkeeper unfastened the door; and there entered, or, rather, fell forward, an old woman with thin, gray, flowing locks, clad in a red woollen gown all in tatters, and a mantle as ragged, that came almost to her heels.

The Prince de Condé, true prince that he was, advanced for the purpose of assisting the old woman to rise, for he had the best heart in the world. But the inn-keeper interfered, and said, as he set the old woman on her feet, —

"Thank Monsieur le Prince de Condé, gammer; but for him, you can be very sure that, for the good of the neighborhood, I should have left you to die at the door."

The witch, without asking which was the prince, went directly to him, fell on her knees and kissed the hem of his mantle. The prince cast a compassionate glance upon the poor creature.

"Landlord," said he, "a pot of your best wine for this poor goodwife. Go and drink a little, dame," continued he; "it will warm you."

The old creature went and took a seat at one of the tables in the depths of the hall; she thus found herself facing the entrance, having at her right the princes, the Maréchal de Saint André and his daughter; at her left, the Gascon captain, the gentleman from Angoumois, and the page.

The gentleman from Angoumois had again fallen into a profound revery. The youthful page was lost in contemplation of the charms of Mademoiselle de Saint André. The Gascon captain alone had all his wits about him; he thought that, were the old woman but one-tenth the sorceress the landlord pretended, here would be a light, at least, to guide his steps in search of the position of which he had spoken to the gentleman from Angoumois and the young page, but of which they could give him no information.

Striding over his bench, therefore, he went and stationed himself in front of the sorceress, who was just drinking, with marked satisfaction, her first glass of wine, and, with his legs wide apart, his left hand resting on his sword-hilt, his head inclined over his breast, fixing on the old woman a glance expressive at once of shrewdness and of determination, he said, —

"Look here, witch! can you really read the future?"

"By the help of God, messire, yes, sometimes."

"Can you cast my horoscope?"

"I will try, if it is your desire."

"Well, it is my desire."

"Then I am at your bidding."

"See! there is my hand; for you gypsies read the hand, do you not?"

"Yes."

The sorceress took in her skinny black hands one of the captain's, almost as lean and black as her own.

"What would you have me tell you first?" demanded she.

"Tell me first whether I shall be successful."

The witch scanned long the Gascon's palm.

The latter, impatient that the witch did not speak out, tossed his head as he demanded, with a sceptical air,—

"How the deuce can you tell by a man's hand whether he will be successful?"

"Oh, very easily, messire! only, that is my secret."

"Tell us your secret."

"If I should tell you, captain," returned the witch, "it would no longer be my secret, but yours."

"You are right; keep it, but make haste! You tickle my hand, gypsy, and I do not like old women to tickle my hand."

"You will be successful, captain."

"Truly, witch?"

"Upon the cross!"

"Oh, *cap de Diou!* it is good news. And do you think success will come soon?"

"In a few years."

"*Diable!* I would rather it were sooner; in a few days, for example."

"I am able to tell the result of events, but not to hasten their march."

"And will it cause me much trouble?"

"No; but it will cost others much."

"What do you mean?"

"I mean that you are ambitious, captain."

"Ah! *per la crux Diou!* you speak the truth, gypsy."

"To reach your end, all roads will seem right to you."

"Yes; only put me in the one I must follow, and you shall see."

"Oh, you will take it of your own accord, full of horrors though it be."

"And what shall I come to, tell me, by following this dreadful road?"

"You will come to be an assassin, captain."

"*Sang du Christ!*" cried the Gascon; "you are but an old hag, and you can go and tell fortunes for those who are stupid enough to believe in them."

And casting at the old woman an indignant look he turned away, and sat down, grumbling, —

"Assassin! assassin! I! Be assured of one thing, witch, it would have to be for a very large sum!"

"Jacques," then said Mademoiselle de Saint André, who had observed the captain's proceedings, and who, her ears strained with the curiosity of fourteen years, had not lost a word of the dialogue between the witch and the Gascon, — "Jacques," — addressing herself to the page, — "go, now, and have your fortune told; it will amuse me."

The young man, addressed for the second time as Jacques, and who was no other than the page, arose without a word, and with the willing air of unquestioning obedience approached the sorceress.

"Here is my hand, good woman," said he. "Will you tell my fortune as you have just told the captain's?"

"Very willingly, my handsome lad," said she.

And taking the hand, white as a woman's, that the young man presented, she shook her head.

"Well, dame," inquired the page, "do you find nothing good in that hand?"

"You will be unhappy."

"Ah! poor Jacques," half in raillery, half in solicitude, exclaimed the fair girl who had evoked the prophecy.

The youth smiled sadly, and murmured, —

"Not 'will be,' — I am so."

"Love will cause all your misfortunes," pursued the old woman.

"Shall I die young, at least?" continued the page.

"Alas! yes, poor child, — at twenty-four."

"So much the better."

"Why, Jacques! 'so much the better'? What are you saying?"

"Since I must be unhappy, what is the use of living?" returned the youth. "But I shall at least die on the battlefield?"

"No."

"In my bed?"

"No."

"By accident?"

"No."

"How, then, shall I die, dame?"

"I cannot say just how you will die; but I can tell the cause of your death."

"And the cause?"

The old woman lowered her voice.

"You will be an assassin!" she said.

The young man became as pale as if the predicted event were already at hand, and with bowed head he regained his seat, saying, —

"Thanks, dame; what is to be will be!"

"Well," inquired the captain of the page, "what did that infernal old woman have to say, my young spark?"

"Nothing that I can repeat, captain," replied the latter. The captain turned to the Angoumois.

"Well, my friend," said he, "are not you, too, curious to try your fate? Come, true or false, good or bad, fortune-telling serves at least to while away the time."

"Pardon me," answered the gentleman, who appeared to start suddenly from his revery; "I have, on the contrary, a subject of great importance about which to consult this woman." And, rising, he advanced to the witch with the directness of movement that denotes in its possessor strength and tenacity of purpose.

"Magician," said he, in solemn tones, extending a nervous hand, "shall I succeed in my undertaking?"

The gypsy took the proffered hand; but after looking at it a second time she dropped it with a look of terror.

"Oh, yes," said she, "you will succeed, to your own destruction!"

"But I shall succeed?"

"At what cost, *Jesus Dieu!*"

"At the cost of my enemy's life; is it not so?"

"Yes."

"What matters it to me, then?"

And the gentleman returned to his seat, darting at the Duc de Guise a glance of unspeakable hatred.

"Strange! strange! strange!" muttered the old crone, — "assassins, all three!"

And she regarded with horror the group composed of the Gascon captain, the Angoumois gentleman, and the youthful page. This exhibition of chiromancy had been attentively followed by the eyes of the noble guests who occupied the opposite end of the room. We say by the eyes, because, not being able to hear all, they had at least been able to see all.

Now, however little we may believe in sorcerers, we are always curious to test the occult science called magic, whether it predicts for us a thousand blessings, and our verdict is in its favor, or foretells a thousand misfortunes, and we accuse it of lying. For the same reason, doubtless, the Maréchal de Saint André was impelled to question the old woman.

"I have but little faith in all this foolishness," said he; "but I must confess that in my infancy a gypsy woman foretold what would happen to me up to my fiftieth year; I am fifty-five, and I should not be loath to have another one, now, predict what will take place till the day of my death. Advance, then, daughter of Beelzebub," he added, addressing the old woman.

The sorceress arose and approached the group.

"Here is my hand," continued the maréchal; "now, then, speak, and speak boldly! what good can you tell me?"

"None, Monsieur le Maréchal."

"None? *Diable!* it is no great matter; and bad?"

"Do not ask, Monsieur le Maréchal."

"Nonsense, *parbleu!* I will ask. Come, tell me, what do you see in my palm?"

"An abrupt termination of the life-line, Monsieur le Maréchal."

"Which means that I have not long to live, eh?"

"Father!" murmured the girl, entreating him by a look to go no farther.

"Nonsense, Charlotte," said the maréchal.

"Hearken to that beautiful child," said the witch.

"Come, gypsy, proceed! Then I shall die soon?"

"Yes, Monsieur le Maréchal."

"Shall I die a violent death or a natural one?"

"A violent death. You will die on the battlefield, but not by the hand of an honorable enemy."

"At the hand of a traitor, then?"

"At the hand of a traitor."

"That is —?"

"You will be assassinated."

"Dear father!" murmured the girl, with a shudder, and pressing close to the maréchal.

"Have you any faith in all this witchcraft?" said the latter, kissing her forehead.

"No, father, and yet my heart throbs in my breast as if the predicted misfortune were about to overtake you."

"Child!" said the maréchal, shrugging his shoulders, "come, show her your hand, and let her predictions add as many days to your life as they cut off from mine.".

But the girl obstinately refused.

"I, then, will set you an example, mademoiselle," said the Duc de Guise, reaching forth his palm to the soothsayer.

Then, with a smile, he added, —

"I give you due warning, gypsy, that my horoscope has already been cast three times, and three times it has threatened disaster; for the honor of the black art, do not make it lie."

"Monseigneur," said the old woman, having examined the duke's hand, "I do not know what others have said; but this is what I myself predict."

"Let us hear!"

"Like the Maréchal de Saint André, you will be assassinated."

"It was nothing less," rejoined the duke, "and it is not to be avoided. There, take that, and go to the devil!"

And he tossed the witch a piece of gold.

"*Ah ça!* the gypsy must be warning us of a massacre of the nobility! I begin to repent having admitted her, duc; however, not to appear to be the only one to shirk his destiny, i' faith! it is my turn next, dame!"

"Do you, then, believe in witches, prince?" inquired the Duc de Guise.

"Faith! duc, I have seen so many predictions fail, so many horoscopes fulfilled, that I will say with Michel de Montaigne, 'What know I?' Come, good woman, here is my hand; what see you in it? Good or ill, tell me all."

"This is what I see in your hand, monseigneur: a life full of love, of battles, of pleasures, of dangers, terminated by a bloody death."

"Shall I, too, be assassinated?"

"Yes, monseigneur."

"Like Monsieur le Maréchal de Saint André,— like Monsieur de Guise?"

"Like them."

"Whether you speak truth or falsehood, good woman, since you have announced that I shall die in good company, take this for your trouble."

And he gave her, not one piece of gold, as the Duc de Guise had done, but his entire wallet.

"Please God, monseigneur," said the crone, as she kissed the prince's hand, "that the poor gypsy may be wrong, and her prediction unfulfilled!"

"And should it be fulfilled, good woman, in spite of your desire to see it miscarry, I promise you, thereafter, to believe in witches. True," he added, smiling, "it would be a little late."

There followed a moment of gloomy silence, during which the rain was heard gently falling.

"But," said the prince, "the storm has abated. I bid you good evening, Monsieur le Maréchal; Monsieur le Duc, good evening. I am due at the Hôtel Coligny at nine o'clock; I must set out."

"What, prince, in this storm?" demanded Charlotte.

"Mademoiselle," said the prince, "I thank you most sincerely for your solicitude; but, since I am to be assassinated, I have nothing to fear from the lightning."

And having bowed to his two companions, and rested on Mademoiselle de Saint André a look that compelled the girl to lower her eyes, the sound of a horse's swift gallop was heard on the road to Paris.

"Order the coach, little Jacques!" said the maréchal. "If the prince is due at the Hôtel Coligny by nine o'clock, we ourselves are due at the Palais des Tournelles at ten."

The coach came up. The Maréchal de Saint André, his daughter, and the Duc de Guise took their seats.

Let them follow the Prince de Condé on the road to Paris; we shall there meet them again later.

Let us merely note the names of the three whom the witch foretold were to be assassinated, and the names of the three whom she predicted were to be assassins: the Duc de Guise, the Maréchal de Saint André, the Prince de Condé; Poltrot de Méré, Baubigny de Mézières, Montesquieu.

It was undoubtedly with the purpose of giving each a warning, which to each alike was useless, that Providence had brought together these six men at the Red Horse Inn.

V.

THE TRIUMPHAL PROGRESS OF PRESIDENT MINARD.

On Tuesday, the eighteenth day of December, in the year fifteen hundred and fifty-nine, six months after the Fête du Landi, at about three o'clock in the afternoon, in the light of a setting sun as beautiful as one could wish to see so late in the year, there rode along the middle of the Vielle-Rue-du-Temple, astride upon a mule so sorry of aspect as to herald its owner's sordid avarice, Maître Antoine Minard, one of the parliamentary councillors.

Maître Antoine Minard, toward whom, for the time being, we direct the eyes of our readers, was a man of sixty years, fat and chubby, the fair locks of whose peruke were foppishly tossed to the breeze.

Ordinarily, his countenance must have expressed supreme beatitude. Of a certainty, no sorrow had ever clouded that polished brow, so glossy and free of wrinkles; no tear had left its furrow beneath those bulging eyes. In short, selfish indifference and vulgar enjoyment had alone spread their gloss upon the vermilion of that rubicund face, majestically propped by a triple chin.

But on that day the countenance of President Minard was far from being illumined by its usual halo. for, although he was not more than four hundred paces from his house. and the distance. as can be seen. was not great, he did not seem to be certain of reaching it. As a result, his face, reflecting the inner emotions by which it was agitated, was expressive of the keenest anxiety.

In fact, the rabble forming the worthy president's cortège was far from putting him into a good humor. From his starting out, he had been followed by an immense mob, which seemed to take real pleasure in abusing him; every brawler, shrieker, and scold in the capital of this truly Christian kingdom appeared to have gathered at the Place du Palais for the purpose of escorting him to his very door.

What, then, had roused the ire of the majority of his fellow-citizens against the worthy Maître Minard?

We are about to relate the cause as briefly as possible.

Maître Minard had but just condemned to death a man who, with good reason, was one of the most highly esteemed men in Paris, his own colleague in parliament, his brother in the sight of God, the virtuous councillor, Anne Dubourg.

What crime had Dubourg committed? That of Aristides, the Athenian. He was called the Just.

Here are the grounds of the trial, which had lasted six months, and had just ended so fatally for the poor councillor.

In the month of June, 1559, at the solicitation of Cardinal de Lorraine, and his brother, François de Guise, whom the French clergy had appointed as God's proxies for the defense and preservation of the Catholic religion, Apostolic and Roman, Henri II. had issued an edict constraining parliament to condemn all Lutherans to death, without mercy and without exception.

Now, a few councillors having, in spite of this edict, released a Huguenot from prison, the Duc de Guise and the Cardinal de Lorraine, satisfied with nothing less than the utter extermination of the Protestants, persuaded the king to go, on the tenth of June, and occupy his throne at the Augustine convent, where the court was then sitting, the Palais having been taken for the wedding festivities of King Philippe II. and Madame Elisabeth and of Mademoiselle Marguerite and Prince Emmanuel Philibert.

Three or four times a year all the chambers of the courts of justice united together and were called the "Grand Chamber," and this assembly was called *mercuriale* because of its being held, by preference, on Wednesday.

The king therefore repaired to the parliament on the day of the *mercuriale*, and opened the session by demanding why they had arrogated to themselves the right to set Protestants at liberty, and how it happened that they had not confirmed the edict condemning them to death.

Five councillors rose, impelled by the same sentiment, and, in behalf of himself and his colleagues, Anne Dubourg firmly answered, —

"Because that man was innocent, and because to liberate an innocent man, although a Huguenot, is to act according to the dictates of humanity."

The five councillors were Dufaur, La Fumée, De Poix, De la Porte, and Anne, or Antoine, Dubourg.

It was Dubourg, as we have said, who had taken it upon himself to answer. Then he added, —

"As for the edict, sire, I cannot advise the king to have it ratified; I beg, on the contrary, that the judgments it contains be suspended until the doctrines of those who are so hastily condemned receive mature consideration and be debated at length before a council.

At that moment President Minard interposed and asked for a special audience with the king.

"He was," say the "Memoirs of Condé," "a crafty, wily, sensuous, ignorant man, but a great leader of factions and intrigues. Eager to do anything that would be agreeable to the king and to the heads of the Church of Rome, and fearing that Dubourg's judgment carried greater weight than his own and that they must needs be influenced by it, he therefore gave the king to understand that the councillors of his court were nearly all Lutherans; that they wished to wrest from him his power and his crown; that they favored the Lutherans; that it was frightful to hear in what terms some of them spoke of the holy mass; that they paid no attention to the laws and royal ordinances; that they boasted aloud of disregarding them; that they dressed in black; that the majority of them went often to their meetings, but never to mass, and that, if he did not strike at the root of the evil, the Church, dating from this *mercuriale*, was forever lost."

In short, abetted by the Cardinal de Lorraine, he so excited, incensed, and bewitched the king that the latter, quite beside himself, sent for the Sieur de Lorges, Comte de Montgomery, captain of the Scotch guard, and Monsieur de Chavigny, captain of his regular guards, and commanded them to apprehend the five councillors and conduct them at once to the Bastile.

Scarcely had this arrest been made when every one foresaw its consequences: the Guises desired to terrify the Huguenots by some awful execution, and if not the five councillors, Anne Dubourg at least, the most important one of them, was regarded as lost.

Hence, on the morrow, this couplet, containing the

names of the five prisoners, so arranged as to hint at the fate in store for the chief of the Huguenot opposition, was going the rounds of Paris: —

"Par Poix, de la Porte du Faur,
J'aperçois du Bourg, La Fumée."[1]

However, the quintuple arrest, which had inspired some wit of the day with this bad distich, produced a sort of stupefaction throughout all Paris, and throughout every city in France, but especially in the provinces of the North. The arrest of this honest man, Anne Dubourg, may even be regarded as the chief cause of the Amboise conspiracy, and of all the uprisings and battles by which the soil of France was reddened with blood during forty years.

May we be pardoned, therefore, for dwelling, in this chapter, on these historical details which form the foundation on which is erected the entire framework of this new book, which we very humbly, but with the confidence habitual to us from their long indulgence, place before our readers.

Five days after this arrest, on Friday, the twenty-fifth of June, which was the third day of the tournament given by the king at the Château des Tournelles, near that same Bastile in which the imprisoned councillors heard the echoing clarions, trumpets, and hautboys of the fête, the king sent for the captain of the Scotch guard, that same Comte de Montgomery who, aided by Monsieur de Chavigny, had led the five councillors to prison, and gave him orders to make a raid at once upon the Lutherans in the country of Caux-les-Tournois.

[1] Which may be rendered: —

"From the pitch, through the furnace-door,
I can see Dubourg's smoke pour."

In this commission he had enjoined the Comte de Montgomery to put to the edge of the sword all who were attainted and convicted of heresy, to put them to the rack, to cut out their tongues, and then burn them at a slow fire; as for such as were merely suspected, they were to have their eyes put out.

Now, five days after Henri II. had given this commission to the captain of the Scotch guard, Gabriel de Lorges, Comte de Montgomery, struck King Henri with his lance and killed him.

This death made so great an impression that it certainly saved four of the five councillors, and arrested the execution of the fifth. One of the five was pardoned, three were fined. Anne Dubourg alone must pay with his life. Had he not acted as spokesman?

Now, although the Guises were the ardent promoters of these decrees, one of their most zealous executives was this hypocrite, President Antoine Minard, whom we have left riding a rebellious mule in the Vielle-Rue-du-Temple, assailed by vociferations, insults, and threats, inspired by the arrant hatred of indignant citizens.

And when we say that, although he was not more than a hundred paces from his own door, he was nevertheless not very certain of reaching home, we make out the situation to be no worse than it was, since, on the day before, in broad daylight, by a shot from a pistol thrust in his very face, a parliament clerk, Julien Fresne by name, had been killed; he was on his way to the palace, armed, it was said, with a letter from the Duc de Guise, in which the latter urged his brother, the Cardinal de Lorraine, to hasten the trial of Anne Dubourg.

Consequently this murder, whose perpetrator had not been found, was naturally present to the mind of the president, and the spectre of the poor clerk who had been assassinated only the morning before rode on the crupper behind him.

It was this fellow-traveller that occasioned the president's pallor and caused him to redouble the convulsive movements with which his heels belabored the obstinate animal that served as his mount, but was making no headway.

However, he arrived in front of his house safe and sound; I attest — and if he were still alive he too would attest — that it was high time.

In fact, goaded by his silence, which was merely the result of his agony, but was distrusted as a mark of his evil-mindedness, the crowd pressed closer and closer upon him, threatening to smother him in the end.

And, threatened as he was by the waves of that stormy sea, President Minard nevertheless reached his haven, to the great satisfaction of his family, who hastened, as soon as he was within, to close and bolt the door behind him.

He had been so agitated by his peril, the worthy man, that he forgot his mule at the door, — a thing he had never done on any other occasion, although, at a fair estimate, and rating her above her price, she was not worth twenty Paris sous.

And it was very fortunate for him that he forgot his mule; for the fickle Parisian populace, which turns so easily from threats to laughter, and from the sublime to the ridiculous, seeing that something was left to it, contented itself with what was left, and took the mule instead of the president.

What happened to the mule in the hands of the populace history does not relate: then let us leave the mule. and follow the master within doors.

VI.

THE BIRTHDAY OF PRESIDENT MINARD.

We are but slightly interested — is it not so, dear readers — in the alarm which the delay of the worthy President Minard had caused his family? We will concern ourselves, then, no longer about it, and following in the train of the family, while the latter follow their chief, with them we will enter the dining-room where the supper was served.

Let us cast a rapid glance at the guests, and we will then lend an ear to their conversation.

None of the guests about the table would, on first sight, have aroused the interest of an intelligent observer. They afforded a sample of the silly and insignificant countenances which are to be found in every class of society.

The thoughts by which he was agitated were reflected in the face of every member of the president's family. All their ideas were bewildered in the fogs of ignorance or stranded in the shallows of vulgarity.

With some it was interest, with others egotism; with these avarice, with those servility.

Thus, quite different from the mob which, like the slave behind the chariot of the Roman conqueror, had just cried to President Minard, "Remember, Minard, that you are mortal!" the members of this family, gathered together on the occasion of the president's anniversary, which was also his birthday, — all these people waited but for a cue from the councillor to congratulate him on the brilliant part which he had just taken at the trial of his colleagues, and to drink to the happy outcome of the trial, — that is, to the death sentence of Anne Dubourg; and when Minard, letting himself drop into his armchair, had said, while passing his handkerchief over his forehead, "Ah! faith! friends, we have had a stormy session to-day," all, as if they had waited only for this signal, burst into exclamations.

"Be quiet, noble man!" exclaimed a nephew, acting as spokesman. "Say not a word; recover from your fatigue, and permit us to stay the perspiration running from your noble brow. To-day is your birthday, — that grand day so glorious for your family and for parliament, of which you are one of the luminaries; we are assembled here to celebrate it, but let us wait a few moments longer. Regain your breath; drink a glass of this old Burgundy, and presently we ourselves will drink to the preservation of your precious days; but, in Heaven's name, do not arrest their course by any indiscretion! Your family entreats you to preserve yourself for its sake, to preserve for the Church its strongest prop, for France one of her most glorious sons."

At this little speech, antiquated in style even for that ancient date, President Minard, with tears in his eyes, endeavored to make reply; but the spare hands of the president's wife and the plump ones of his young daughters closed the president's mouth and hindered his utterance. Finally, after a few moments of rest, Monsieur Minard began to speak, and a prolonged "sh!" went forth among those present, so that the very servants standing at the doors should not lose a word of the eloquent councillor's response.

"Ah! friends," he began, "brothers, relatives, my esteemed and dearly beloved family, I thank you for your friendship and your kind praises; but I am in very truth deserving of them, O my loving family! for I can say without pride, or, if you prefer it, with a noble pride, I can say boldly that, but for me, but for my persistence and stubbornness, the heretic Anne Dubourg would at the present moment stand acquitted, like his accomplices,—De Poix, La Fumée, Dufaur, and De la Porte; but, owing to my energetic will, the day is won, and, thanks be to God," he continued, lifting his eyes in token of gratitude to heaven, "I have just pronounced the death-sentence of that wretched Huguenot."

"Oh, *vivat!*" cried the relatives with one voice, and raising their arms toward heaven. "Long live our illustrious kinsman! Long live the man who never yields! Long live the man who, on all occasions, puts down the enemies of the faith! May he live forever, the great President Minard!"

And the servants behind the door, the cook in the kitchen, the groom in the stable, gave back the echo:

"Long live the great President Minard!"

"Thanks, my friends, thanks!" said the president in unctuous tones,—"thanks! But two men—two great men—two princes, are entitled to their share in these praises you lavish upon me; without them, without their support, without their influence, I should never have carried out this glorious affair. Those two men, my friends, are Monseigneur le Duc François de Guise and His Eminence, the Cardinal de Lorraine. Having drank my health, let us now drink theirs, my friends, and may God prolong the days of those two great statesmen!"

They drank the health of the Duc de Guise and of the Cardinal de Lorraine; but Madame Minard observed that her gracious spouse merely touched the glass with his lips, and replaced it upon the table, while some memory flitted across his brain like a cloud, and darkened his face with its shadow.

"What is the matter, my dear," she asked; "what is the cause of this sudden sadness?"

"Alas!" said the president, "no triumph is complete, no joy unmixed! A melancholy recollection has just come to mind."

"And what melancholy recollection can you entertain, dear husband, in this the most beautiful hour of your triumph?" demanded his wife.

"Just as I was in the act of drinking to the prolongation of the days of Monsieur de Guise and his brother, the thought came to me that yesterday a man was assassinated whom they had done me the honor to despatch to me."

"A man?" cried the family.

"That is, a clerk," explained Minard.

"What! one of your clerks was murdered yesterday?"

"Ah! *mon Dieu!* yes."

"Can it be true?"

"You knew Julien Fresne, indeed?" returned the president.

"Julien Fresne?" cried one of the relatives. "Yes, of course we knew him!"

"A zealous Catholic," remarked a second.

"A very honest man," said a third.

"I met him yesterday in the Rue Barre-du-Bec, coming from the Hôtel de Guise, so he said, and on his way to the Palais.

"Well, this is the way of it: as he was nearing the bridge of Notre Dame, conveying to Monsieur le Cardinal de Lorraine from his brother, the Duc de Guise, a despatch which was to have been communicated to me, he was assassinated!"

"Oh," cried the president's wife, "how dreadful!"

"Assassinated!" reiterated the family in chorus,— "assassinated! One martyr more!"

"And has the murderer been arrested, at least?" demanded the president's wife of Minard.

"They do not know who he is," answered the latter.

"Have they any suspicion?" asked his wife.

"Better still, some certainty."

"Some certainty?"

"Yes; who should it be if not a friend of Dubourg's?"

"Of course it is a friend of Dubourg's," echoed the entire family; "who should it be, *pardieu!* if not a friend of Dubourg's?"

"Has any one been arrested?" pursued the president's wife.

"A hundred persons, nearly; I myself pointed out thirty of them."

"It will be very unfortunate," said a voice, "if the murderer is not found among the hundred persons."

"If he is not among them," said the president, "a hundred, two hundred, three hundred others will be arrested."

"The villains!" said a young gentlewoman of eighteen years; "they ought all to be burned together."

"It has been thought of," assented the president; "and the day when the extinction of the entire body of Protestants has been resolved upon will be a fine day for me."

"Oh, what a noble man you are, my dear!" exclaimed the president's wife, with tears in her eyes.

Monsieur Minard's two daughters advanced and kissed their father.

"And is it known what the duke's letter contained?" continued the president's wife.

"No," replied Minard. "That is what has so greatly concerned the court to-day; but it will be known to-morrow. Monsieur le Cardinal de Lorraine is to see his distinguished brother this evening."

"The letter was stolen, then?"

"Undoubtedly; it is even probable that poor Julien Fresne was assassinated because he was the bearer of that letter. The assassin having possessed himself of it and taken to flight, some archers have been sent in pursuit of him; the entire watch and all of Monsieur de Mouchy's men have been in the field ever since morning; but at five o'clock in the afternoon there was as yet no news."

Just then a servant entered, announcing to Monsieur Minard that a stranger, who had brought the letter snatched from Julien Fresne by the assassin on the day before, insisted upon speaking to him without delay.

"Oh, bring him in immediately!" cried the president, radiant with joy. "God is rewarding my zeal in his holy cause by permitting this precious document to fall into my hands."

Five minutes later the servant ushered in the stranger, and Monsieur Minard saw a young man of twenty-four or twenty-five years of age, with red hair, a fair beard, a keen, piercing glance, and a pale face; at the president's invitation he advanced to a seat near the opposite side of the table.

It was the same young man who, when leaving the river-bank, had told the murderers of his friend Médard that they would, perhaps, hear of him again.

It was Robert Stuart.

The young man accepted the invitation. Courteously, and with a smile upon his lips, he bowed to the entire company; he then seated himself, having the president in front of him and the door at his back.

"Monsieur," said Robert Stuart, addressing himself directly to the president, "is it, indeed, Monsieur le Président Antoine Minard whom I have the honor to address?"

"Yes, monsieur, certainly," returned the president, highly astonished that a man could be so ignorant of physiognomy as not to read in his face that he alone could be and was the renowned Minard. "Yes, monsieur, I am President Minard."

"Very well, monsieur," continued the unknown; "although I have asked a question which on the face of it must seem to you unnecessary, you will immediately see that it has arisen from my great desire to avoid any possibility of mistake."

"What do you mean, monsieur?" demanded the magistrate. "I was told that you desired to hand me the despatch that the unfortunate Julien Fresne was carrying when he was assassinated."

"It was somewhat misleading, perhaps, monsieur," said the young man, with infinite courtesy, "if it was announced that I would deliver that letter. I made no such promise, and I shall give it to you or I shall keep it, according to your answer to a request that I shall have the honor to make you; you understand, monsieur, that, to gain possession of so important a document, I have had to risk my life. A man does not risk his life, you are aware, — you who are skilled in reading the human heart, — without some great interest at stake. I have therefore the honor to repeat, in order that there may be no further misunderstanding, that I will not put you in possession of the despatch unless I am satisfied with the answer given to my request."

"And what is the request, monsieur?"

"Monsieur le Président, you know better than another, that in a well-conducted examination everything awaits its turn; therefore I can tell you that only in due season."

"However, you have this letter about you?"

"Here it is, monsieur."

And the young man drew from his pocket a sealed missive, which he showed to President Minard.

The latter's first impulse was, we must confess, an ignoble one; he was prompted to signal his cousins and nephews, who were listening to the conversation with a degree of surprise, to fall upon the unknown, seize the letter, and despatch him to the dungeons of the Châtelet, there to keep company with the hundred persons already arrested for the murder of Julien Fresne.

But, aside from the energy stamped on the young man's face, which bore every mark of a will that reached the height of obstinacy, and caused the president to be apprehensive lest he had not sufficiently reliable forces to wrest the parchment from him, he concluded that, thanks to his own extraordinary cleverness and skill, he would be more successful in employing a ruse than in displaying violence. He restrained himself, therefore, and as the young man's elegant figure and his careful though severe toilet justified, of themselves, the invitation which he thought of extending him, he begged him to draw up to the table and sup with them, that they might have an abundance of time for their interview.

The young man politely thanked him, but declined the invitation.

The president urged that he would at least refresh himself, but again the visitor declined with thanks.

"Speak, then, monsieur," said Minard; "and since you will accept nothing, I beg that you will allow me to proceed with my supper, for I frankly confess that I am perishing of hunger."

"Proceed, monsieur," replied the young man, "and a good appetite to you! The request I have to make is of such importance that, to be well understood, it demands a few preliminary remarks. Eat, Monsieur le Président; I will speak."

"Speak, monsieur; I will eat," returned the president.

Thereupon, with a sign to the rest of his family to follow his example, he fell to eating with an appetite that did not belie his statement.

"Monsieur," leisurely began the unknown, amid the clattering of knives and forks, which each did his best to subdue, that he might not lose a word of the conversation about to follow, — "monsieur, you must already have discovered, from my accent, that I am a foreigner."

"Indeed," remarked the president, with his mouth full, "you have something of an English accent."

"True, monsieur, and your usual clearsightedness is not at fault in my case. I was born in Scotland; I should be still there, had not an occurrence, which it is unnecessary for me to relate, compelled me to visit France. One of my fellow-countrymen, a fervent disciple of Knox — "

"An English heretic, was he not, monsieur?" queried President Minard, pouring for himself a glassful of Burgundy.

"And my beloved master," responded the unknown, inclining his head.

Monsieur Minard glanced around at his company with

an air that plainly said, "Listen, my friends, and you will hear some fine discourse!"

Robert Stuart continued: —

"One of my fellow-countrymen, an ardent follower of Knox, happened, a few days ago, to be at a house which I myself frequent; he there heard talk about sentencing the councillor, Anne Dubourg, to death."

The young man's voice trembled as he uttered these last words, and his face, already pale, blanched whiter still.

He continued, nevertheless, his voice no longer seeming to share the emotion expressed by his change of countenance; yet, as he felt every one's gaze to be fixed upon him, he said, —

"My compatriot, on the mere mention of Anne Dubourg's name, paled visibly, as I am doing perhaps at this moment, and he sought to learn from the persons who were discussing the sentence if it were possible that parliament would commit such an injustice."

"Monsieur," cried the president, who was nearly strangled by his food upon hearing such an unusual speech, "you must be ignorant of the fact that you are speaking to a member of parliament; is it not so?"

"Pardon me, monsieur," responded the Scotchman, "it was my compatriot who thus expressed himself; he, pray observe, was addressing, not a member of parliament, but simply a clerk of parliament, Julien Fresne by name, who was assassinated yesterday. Julien Fresne was then so imprudent as to say, in the presence of my fellow-countryman, —

"'I have in my pocket a letter from Monseigneur le Duc de Guise, in which Monsieur le Duc enjoins the king's parliament to make an end of the said Anne Dubourg, and despatch him quickly.'

"Upon hearing those words, my countryman shuddered, and from pale, as he had been, he became livid. He arose, approached Julien Fresne, and used every imaginable entreaty to prevent his delivering that letter, pointing out the fact that if Anne Dubourg was condemned, a share of the blame of this councillor's death would fall on him; but Julien Fresne was inexorable.

"My countryman took his leave, and went to await the clerk's departure from the house; thereupon, after permitting him to proceed a short distance, he overtook him.

"'Julien Fresne,' he said, in low tones and with infinite gentleness, but also with great firmness, 'I will grant you one whole night for reflection; but if to-morrow, by this hour, you have accomplished your purpose or have not abandoned it, you shall die!'"

"Oh! oh!" ejaculated the president.

"'And likewise,' continued the Scotchman, 'shall die every man, far and near, that has a hand in the death of Anne Dubourg.'"

Monsieur Minard shuddered, for it was impossible to divine, from the phrasing of this speech, whether these last words had been addressed to Julien Fresne by the Scotchman's fellow-countryman, or were aimed directly at Monsieur Minard.

"Why, your fellow-countryman is a *brigand*, monsieur!" he declared to Robert Stuart, on observing that his family were awaiting only a word from him to give vent to their indignation.

"An out-and-out *brigand!* a miserable *brigand!*" cried the relatives in chorus.

"Monsieur," returned the young man, quite unmoved, "I am a Scotchman, and I do not grasp the full import of the word you have just employed and your worthy relatives have repeated after you; therefore, I continue."

And bowing to the relatives, who returned his salute, although with visible reluctance, he continued, —

"My fellow-countryman returned to his lodgings, and, being unable to sleep, he arose and walked up and down before the house of Julien Fresne.

"He continued his promenade during the whole of that night and all of the next morning; he walked there until three o'clock in the afternoon without eating or drinking, sustained, as he was, by his determination to keep his word to Julien Fresne; for," continued the Scotchman by way of parenthesis, "while my countrymen may be *brigands*, Monsieur Minard, they possess the merit of never failing to keep their word when once it is given.

"Finally, at three o'clock, Julien Fresne emerged; my countryman followed him, and finding that he was bound for the palace, intercepted him at the corner of the bridge of Notre Dame, and said, —

"'Julien Fresne, have you reflected?'

"Julien Fresne grew very pale: the Scotchman seemed to have risen out of the ground, and he wore a most threatening aspect; but, to do the worthy clerk justice, he replied distinctly, —

"'Yes, I have reflected; but the result of my reflection is that I must execute the order given me by Monsieur le Duc de Guise.'

"'Monsieur de Guise is not your master, that he should give you orders,' returned the Scotchman.

"'Monsieur de Guise is not only my master,' replied the clerk, 'but, what is more, he is the master of France.'

"'How is that?'

"'Are you not aware, monsieur, that the Duc de Guise is the real king of the realm?'

"'Monsieur,' said my compatriot, 'a political discussion on this subject would lead us too far; I in no degree share your sentiments, and I return to the question that I put to you yesterday evening: Do you still intend to carry this letter to the parliament?'

"'I am going there for that purpose.'

"'Consequently, you have it about you?'

"'I have it with me.'

"'In the name of the living God,' cried my friend, 'I charge you to renounce your purpose of taking this letter to the executioners of Anne Dubourg!'

"'In five minutes it will be in their hands.'

"And Julien Fresne put out his arm to thrust my friend aside.

"'Well, since you will have it so,' cried the latter, 'neither you nor your letter shall reach the palace, Julien Fresne.'

"And drawing a pistol from under his cloak, he fired at Julien Fresne, who fell stone dead on the pavement; then, seizing the letter, the cause of the murder, my fellow-countryman went his way with an easy conscience; he had but killed a wretch in his efforts to save an innocent man."

It was the president's turn to change color; his purple faded to yellow and green. A thousand drops of perspiration beaded his forehead.

The profoundest silence brooded over the entire company.

"The heat is stifling here," remarked Monsieur Minard, turning alternately toward the two ends of the table. "Don't you find it so, my friends?"

Some one rose to open a window; but the Scotchman signed with both hands for all to keep their seats.

"Do not disturb yourselves, messieurs," said he. "I

am not eating, — I will open the window and give Monsieur le Président some air; but, as a draught would be bad for him," he added, having, in fact, opened the window, "I will close the door."

And giving the key in the door a turn he returned to his post opposite President Minard.

But, in executing the necessary movements, the Scotchman's cloak was brushed aside, and it could be seen that he wore underneath the cloak a coat of mail of linked steel as defensive armor, with two pistols in his belt and a short sword at his side as weapons of assault.

He appeared in nowise apprehensive as to what might or might not be seen, and as he resumed his place opposite to the president, from whom he was separated only by the width of the table, he asked, —

"Well, my dear Monsieur Minard, how do you feel?"

"A little better," replied the latter, much against his will.

"I am very glad of it, believe me," continued the young man.

And he resumed his narrative amidst a silence in which you could have heard a fly on the wing, had there been any flies in December other than the spies of Monsieur de Mouchy.[1]

[1] A play on the word *mouche*, which means both "fly" and "police-spy." — Tr.

VII.

PRESIDENT MINARD'S BIRTHDAY GIFT.

As we said in the foregoing chapter, the young man resumed his narrative where he had left off: —

"My countryman took the despatch, and, fearing pursuit, he fled through Grand-Rue-Montmartre, and gained the deserted quarter of the Grange-Batelière, where he could read at his leisure the despatch from Monsieur le Duc de Guise. Then only did he discover, as I myself discovered upon reading it, that the despatch from the Duc de Guise served only as a cover to an ordinance of King François II., as you yourselves will see, messieurs, when I have acquainted you with the contents of that letter; for, the missive being unsealed, my friend believed it justifiable that he should learn exactly whence it came, and to whom it was addressed, that he might himself, if he saw fit, deliver it to its address, with all the respect due to its subscriber."

Then, a second time, the Scotchman drew the parchment from his breast, unfolded it, and read as follows:

To our well-beloved and faithful, the President of the court of the Parliament of Paris, the advocates and attorneys of the court aforesaid: —

In the King's name,

Well-beloved and faithful, we are greatly displeased to behold such sloth in the prosecution and despatch of the trial pending in our court of parliament against the councillors held on a question of religion, and especially against the Councillor Dubourg; and we desire that it be brought to a speedy end. For which reason we put to this our hand and enjoin upon you very expressly that, every other matter being set aside, you do proceed forthwith, and expedite and conduct the trial of said suits, with the quorum of judges which has been and shall be advised by our said court, nor suffer nor allow them to be prolonged in greater tediousness, to the end that we may have other and greater cause for satisfaction than we have had hitherto.

Signed: FRANÇOIS.

And, underneath: LAUBESPINE.

"What, monsieur!" cried President Minard, growing valiant again during the reading of this letter, which so thoroughly justified the sentence that he had just passed, "have you detained such a letter in your possession since morning?"

"Since four o'clock in the afternoon of yesterday, monsieur; in the interests of truth, allow me to correct your impression."

"Have you kept such a letter in your possession since four o'clock in the afternoon of yesterday," resumed the president with the same intonation, "and delayed its delivery until this hour?"

"I repeat, monsieur," said the young man, re-installing the letter in his doublet, "that you are still ignorant as to the price I have paid for the letter, and of the terms on which I shall be willing to part with it."

"Then speak out," said the president, "and state what you desire in the way of reward for a deed which is, however, merely an act of simple duty."

"It is not so simple a duty as you suppose, monsieur," replied the young man; "the same reason which led my countryman to desire that this document should not reach parliament still holds good, and, whether Councillor Anne Dubourg is so near and dear to my friend that his death would be a great personal grief, or whether the injustice of parliament has seemed to him an odious crime and his retention of the letter was actuated only by the desire of any honest man to prevent the perpetration of an infamous act, or, at least, to delay it if he could not actually prevent it, he has in either case taken an oath that he would deliver the letter only when he should be assured of the acquittal of Anne Dubourg, and, what is more, that he would take the lives of all who stood in the way of his acquittal. It was for this reason he killed Julien Fresne; not that he could hold a being so insignificant as a clerk responsible, but, by his death, he wished to prove to some in loftier places than Julien Fresne's, that, as he had not hesitated at a petty existence, he would not hesitate at the lives of the great."

Here the president was strongly tempted to have the second window opened; every hair of his blonde wig was dripping with perspiration, as a willow branch drips with rain after the storm; but regarding it as an insufficient remedy for his indisposition, he contented himself with casting distracted glances around the table, his eye seeking advice from one and another as to what course he should pursue with respect to this Scotchman who possessed such a bloodthirsty friend; but the guests, not comprehending Monsieur Minard's pantomime, or refusing to comprehend for fear of calling down upon their heads a whole legion of Scotchmen, the guests, we say, lowered their eyes and maintained profound silence.

Yet a president of parliament, the man who had just been proclaimed the mainstay of the faith and the greatest statesman of France, could not let such threats pass unanswered; but what answer could he make? If he rose and went around the table, and, contrary to his usually pacific habit, prepared to apprehend that threatening Scot, he ran the risk of the latter's suspecting his design and drawing his sword from its sheath, or snatching the pistol from his belt; this could not fail to happen, judging from the determined expression of the Scotchman's visage. Now, if the idea of assailing his guest — a most disagreeable guest, we admit — flitted across the mind of President Minard, it passed away as swiftly as a cloud scudding before the wind, and that clear mind, if ever one was clear, saw from the very start that, in carrying out such a resolution, he had all to lose and very little to gain.

Now, among the things to lose, there was life, which was very sweet to this good President Minard, and he intended to preserve it as long as possible. He cast about, then, for an expedient by which to extricate himself from this embarrassing encounter, in which his instinct told him he had so much to fear that, avaricious as he was, he would have given fifty golden crowns to have had that accursed Scotchman on the other side of the door, instead of having him merely at the other side of the table. The expedient resolved upon was to deal with his unbidden guest as some people deal with ferocious dogs, that is, to cajole and to flatter him. With this determination, then, he appealed to the young man in accents which he endeavored to render sportive.

"Now, monsieur," said he, "from your mode of expression, from your face so full of intelligence, from your distinguished bearing, I can assume, without fear of mistake, that you are no ordinary person, and I will say even more, — that you reveal yourself to be a gentleman of good family."

The Scot bowed, but did not answer.

"Well," pursued the president, "since I am speaking to a gentleman, and not to a fanatic," — he felt a great desire to say, "and not to an assassin like your compatriot," but prudence, habitual to gentlemen of the long robe, prevented him, — "and not to a fanatic like your compatriot, permit me to say that no one man, from his single standpoint, has a right to condemn the actions of his fellowmen. Numerous considerations may lead him astray, and it is even because no one can judge of his own case that tribunals have been instituted. I admit, then, young man, that your countryman may have been perfectly conscientious in doing as he has done; but you will agree with me that, if each had the right of exercising jurisdiction, it would not be rational, — supposing, for example (it is but a supposition), that you share the opinions of your fellow-countryman, — it would not be rational for you, a well-bred, cool-headed man, to come here in the midst of my family and take my life, on the pretext that you do not approve of the condemnation of Councillor Dubourg."

"Monsieur le Président," said the Scot, who, during this parleying speech, detected the faintheartedness of Maître Minard peeping through, — "Monsieur le Président, permit me, as they say in parliament, to call you back to the question, just as if, instead of being president, you were a simple attorney."

"But, on the contrary, I am speaking to the question, it seems to me; we are even in open debate," replied Minard, regaining some of his assurance the moment that the dialogue assumed a form habitual with him.

"Excuse me, monsieur," retorted the Scotchman, "you appeal to me directly, and until now there has been no question of me; my friend alone is under discussion, since it is not in my own behalf, but in my friend's, that I have come to ask that you answer this question: 'Monsieur le Président Minard, do you think Monsieur le Conseiller Dubourg must be sentenced to death?'"

The answer was very simple, since Councillor Dubourg had been sentenced to death an hour before, and President Minard had already received his kinsmen's congratulations upon the subject.

But, as Maître Minard believed that, on his frankly confessing the existence of such a sentence, — a sentence, moreover, which would not be made known until the morrow, — he would receive from the Scotchman something else than congratulations, he continued to pursue the course he had deemed it prudent to adopt.

"What answer can you expect from me, monsieur?" he asked. "I could not give you the opinion of my colleagues; I could at best give you but mine."

"Monsieur le Président," said the Scotchman, "I hold your personal opinion in such high esteem that I do not ask for that of your colleagues, but for your own."

"Of what service can it be to you?" demanded the president, continuing to temporize.

"To know it will be of service to me," returned the Scotchman, who seemed determined to treat Maître Minard as the dog treats the hare, and follow him in all his doublings until he was run down.

"*Mon Dieu*, monsieur," said the president, forced to be explicit, "my opinion on the issue of the procedure was formed long ago."

The young man steadily regarded Monsieur Minard, who, in spite of himself, lowered his eyes and slowly continued, as if he comprehended the necessity of weighing every word.

"Certainly," he said, "it is to be regretted that a man should be sentenced to death who, along with other claims, must have merited public esteem, — a colleague, almost a friend; but you yourself see by this, the king's letter patent, the court of justice awaits but the termination of this unfortunate trial to take breath and pass on to others. It must end, therefore, and I doubt not that if parliament had received His Majesty's communication yesterday, the poor unfortunate councillor whom I am obliged to condemn as a heretic, but whom I regret as a man most sincerely, would have suffered his penalty to-day, or have been very near doing so."

"Ah! then my friend's having killed Julien Fresne yesterday was an advantage?" said the Scotchman.

"Not a great one," replied the president; "it will cause a delay, that is all."

"But, after all, a day's delay is at least twenty-four hours' respite accorded to an innocent man, and in twenty-four hours many things may change."

"Monsieur," said President Minard, who, little by little, in his character of the old advocate, was regaining his composure in the discussion, "you always speak of Councillor Dubourg as an innocent man."

"I speak from God's point of view, monsieur," returned the Scot, his finger impressively pointing to heaven.

"Yes," said the president; "but from man's point of view?"

"Think you, Maître Minard," demanded the Scot, "that even from man's point of view the proceedings can be considered quite fair?"

"Three bishops have condemned him, monsieur; three bishops have rendered the same decision, — three conformable decisions."

"Were not those bishops judges and prosecutors at once in the case?"

"Perhaps, monsieur; but how is a Huguenot to address Catholic bishops?"

"Whom would you have him address, monsieur?"

"It is a very grave question," said Maître Minard, "and bristles with difficulties."

"And so parliament has resolved to settle it."

"You have said it, monsieur," assented the president.

"Well, monsieur, my countryman was under the impression that to you belonged the glory of the conviction."

At this remark the president felt so ashamed of drawing back before one man, when he had just boasted in the presence of ten others of having secured the verdict in question, that after glancing around interrogatively at his kinsmen, and apparently gathering a degree of courage from their looks, he said,—

"Monsieur, truth forces me to acknowledge that, in this matter, I have in fact sacrificed to duty the very tender and very genuine friendship that I bore to my colleague, Dubourg."

"Ah!" exclaimed the Scot.

"Well, monsieur," demanded Maître Minard, who was beginning to lose patience, "to what is that a prelude?"

"To the end, and we are near it."

"Come, what does it matter to your compatriot whether I have or have not influenced the decision of parliament?"

"It matters much to him."

"In what way?"

"In this: my countryman assumes that, inasmuch as you have tied the knot, it is for you to untie it."

"I do not understand," faltered the president.

"It is very simple, however; instead of using your influence in favor of a conviction, use it in favor of an acquittal."

"But," interrupted one of the nephews, losing patience in turn, "since your Councillor Anne Dubourg is already convicted, how do you suppose my uncle can now have him acquitted?"

"Convicted!" cried the Scot; "did you, over there, say that Councillor Dubourg has been convicted?"

The president cast a look of dismay at his indiscreet nephew.

However, either the nephew did not see the look, or he did not heed it.

"Eh! yes, convicted," he said, — "convicted to-day, at two o'clock this afternoon — let me see, that is what you told us, uncle, or did I misunderstand?"

"You heard aright, monsieur," said the Scot to the young man, taking the president's silence for what it meant.

Then, turning to Minard, he demanded, —

"So to-day, at two o'clock, Councillor Dubourg was sentenced."

"Yes, monsieur," faltered Minard.

"But to what; to a fine?"

Minard did not reply.

"To prison?"

There was the same silence on the part of the president.

At each question from the Scot his face whitened; at the last his lips were livid.

"To death?" he finally demanded.

The president made a sign with his head.

Although full of hesitancy, the sign was, nevertheless. in the affirmative.

"Ah, well, so be it!" said the Scot. "After all, so long as a man is not dead, there is no occasion for despair; and, as my friend remarked, since you tied the knot, you can untie it."

"How is that?"

"By seeking from the king a reversal of the judgment."

"But, monsieur," said Maître Minard, who at every step he took in the matter seemed to stride across one chasm only to find himself on the brink of another, it is true, but who, each chasm cleared, became momentarily reassured, — "but, monsieur, should I desire to pardon Anne Dubourg, the king would never consent to it."

"Why not?"

"Why, because the letter you have read sufficiently indicates his desire."

"Yes, apparently."

"Why apparently?"

"For this reason: that letter of the king's was enclosed, as I have had the honor to tell you, in a letter from the Duc de Guise. Well, this letter from the Duc de Guise, which I have not read to you, I am about to read."

And the young man again drew the parchment from his breast; but this time, instead of reading the king's message, he read the letter of François de Lorraine.

It was couched in these terms: —

Dear Brother, — Here at last is His Majesty's message; I have secured it from him with great difficulty, and I was almost obliged to guide his pen in order to get these eight wretched letters composing his name. There must be some unknown friend of this accursed heretic near His

Majesty; make haste, then, lest the king should revoke his decision, or, the councillor being condemned, should pardon him.

Respectfully, your brother,
FRANÇOIS DE GUISE.

December 17, in the year of Our Lord 1559.

The Scotchman raised his head.

"Have you understood, monsieur?" he demanded of the president.

"Perfectly."

"Would you like me to read it again, lest some point may have escaped you?"

"It is unnecessary."

"Would you like to assure yourself that it is indeed in the handwriting and bears the seal of the Lorraine prince?"

"I have perfect confidence in you."

"Well, what is evident from that letter?"

"That the king hesitated to write, monsieur; but, in short, that the king did write."

"But he wrote reluctantly; hence, if a man like you, for instance, Monsieur le Président, should go to this crowned child who is called king, and say, 'Sire, we have condemned Councillor Dubourg for the sake of an example, but Your Majesty should pardon him for the sake of justice,' the king, whose hand Monsieur de Guise was obliged to guide to make him write the eight letters of his name, would grant a pardon."

"And if my conscience opposes my doing what you ask of me, monsieur?" said President Minard, with the evident intention of testing his ground.

"I shall entreat you, monsieur, to call to mind the oath that my friend the Scotchman took upon killing Julien Fresne, to kill in like manner all, far or near, who should be implicated in the conviction of Councillor Dubourg."

At that moment, assuredly, the clerk's shadow, like a shadow from a magic lantern, fell upon the dining-room wall; but of course the president did not turn his head to see it.

"Ah! that is madness!" he responded to the young man.

"Madness! why so, Monsieur le Président?"

"Why, because you are threatening me, a magistrate, in my own house, in the bosom of my family."

"It is that you may call up, out of consideration for your house and family, a sentiment of pity for yourself, which God has not placed in your heart for others."

"It seems to me, monsieur, that instead of exhibiting penitence and offering me an apology, you continue to indulge in threats."

"I have told you, monsieur, that the man who killed Julien Fresne has sworn to kill every man who stands in the way of Anne Dubourg's life and liberty, and that, lest his word should be doubted, he began with the clerk, less because he held the clerk culpable than because he desired by his death to give salutary warning to other enemies, however high their position. Will you ask the king for Anne Dubourg's pardon? In my friend's name, I demand an answer."

"Ah! do you demand an answer in the name of a murderer, in the name of an assassin, in the name of a thief?" cried the exasperated president.

"Understand, monsieur," said the young man, "that you are at liberty to answer me or not."

"Ah! I am at liberty to answer or not?"

"Undoubtedly."

"Well, then, tell your Scotchman," roared the president, beside himself at the very coolness with which he was interrogated, "tell your Scotchman that there is one man, Antoine Minard by name, a president of the court of justice, who has vowed, on his part, that Anne Dubourg shall die; that this president is as good as his word, and that he will prove it to-morrow."

"Well, monsieur," replied Robert Stuart, without a gesture or the display of a sign of emotion, and repeating almost the very words that had just been spoken, "know you that there is a Scotchman who has sworn that Monsieur Antoine Minard, a president of the court of justice, shall die; that this Scotchman is a man of his word, and will prove it to-day."

As he spoke the last words, Robert Stuart passed his hand within his cloak and detached one of his pistols, cocking it noiselessly, and before any one could even dream of staying him, so swift had been his movement, he had aimed at Monsieur Minard across the table, that is, almost in his very face, and fired.

Monsieur Minard fell over backwards, — he and his chair. He was dead.

Any family other than the president's would doubtless have attempted to seize the assassin, but they were very far from doing so; each of the dead man's guests thought only of his own safety: some fled into the pantry, shrieking in despair; others dived under the table, taking good care not to speak a word. It was a general rout, and Robert Stuart, finding himself somewhat lonely in this dining room, where all seemed to have disappeared through a trap door, retired slowly, after the manner of a lion, as Dante says, and without any man's having the least thought in the world of detaining him.

VIII.

AT THE SIGN OF THE SCOTCH THISTLE.

It was about eight o'clock in the evening when Robert Stuart left Maître Minard's, and, finding himself alone in the Vieille-Rue-du-Temple, — even more deserted after nightfall in those days than it now is, — he gave utterance to two significant words alluding to the men whom he had assassinated: —

"The second!"

He did not count the one on the banks of the Seine; that one was accredited to the account of his friend Médard.

Arriving opposite to the Hôtel de Ville, — that is, at the Place de Grève, where the condemned were executed, — his eyes mechanically wandered to the spot where the gibbet was usually erected; then he approached the place.

"It is here," he muttered, "that Anne Dubourg must undergo the penalty of his greatness, if the king does not pardon him. And how can the king be forced to pardon him?" added he.

And with these words he went on.

He turned into the Rue de la Tannerie and halted before a door over which creaked a sign bearing these words: —

THE SWORD OF FRANÇOIS I.

For a moment one might have supposed him to be about to enter, but suddenly he said, —

"It would be folly to enter the inn; within ten minutes the archers will be here. No, I will go to Patrick's."

He swiftly crossed the Rue de la Tannerie and the bridge of Notre Dame, flung a passing glance at the spot where, on the morning before, he had killed Julien Fresne, then, having cleared La Cité and the bridge of Saint Michel with rapid strides, he entered the Rue du Battoir-Saint-André.

There, as in the Rue de la Tannerie, he paused before a house bearing a sign like the first, but its legend ran: —

THE SCOTCH THISTLE.

"It is certainly here that Patrick Macpherson used to lodge," he mused, raising his head to look for the window. "Up there, under the roof, he had a little room where he used to come on the days when he was not on guard at the Louvre."

He made every effort to catch a glimpse of the garret window, but the projecting roof-cornice prevented.

Consequently he determined to push the door open, or, in case of its being locked, to knock with the pommel of his sword or the butt of his pistol, when suddenly the door swung back and gave egress to a man dressed in the uniform of the Scotch guard.

"Who goes there?" challenged the archer, almost running into the young man.

"'A Hielan' mon,'" answered our hero in the Scotch brogue.

"Oho! Robert Stuart?" cried the archer.

"It is even I, my dear Patrick."

"And what chance brings you into my street and to my door at this hour?" asked the archer, as he extended both hands to his friend.

"I have come to ask a favor, my dear Patrick."

"Speak, but be quick about it!"

"Are you in a hurry?"

"Much against my will; but, you know, it is roll-call at half-past nine at the Louvre, and nine o'clock has just sounded from the parish church of Saint André. Now, then, I am listening."

"Here is the case, my dear friend. The last edict has driven me out of my inn."

"Ah! yes, I see: you are a Protestant, and must have two Catholic sureties."

"I have no time to hunt them up, and perhaps I should not find them if I had it; now, I shall be arrested to-night if I am wandering about the streets of Paris. Will you let me share your room for two or three days?"

"For two or three nights, if you like, and for all the nights of the year, even, if that will serve you; but as for the days, — that is another matter."

"And why so, Patrick?" demanded Robert.

"Because," returned the archer, bridling with vanity, "since I last had the pleasure of seeing you, my dear Robert, I have been so lucky as to make a conquest."

"You, Patrick?"

"Does it surprise you?" inquired the archer, with a foppish air.

"By no means; but it happens awkwardly, that is all."

Robert seemed indisposed to push the subject further; but the vanity of his fellow-countryman did not take advantage of this discretion.

"Yes, my friend," he resumed, "the wife of a councillor of parliament has very naturally done me the honor to fall in love with me, and from one day to another, my dear friend, I am expecting to have the pleasure of entertaining her."

"*Diable!*" exclaimed Robert. "Then consider that I have said nothing, Patrick."

"But why? Do you take my confidence for a refusal? Grant that one day or another this virtuous dame, as Monsieur de Brantôme says, consents to ascend to my attic, — and, observe, this is but a supposition, — you can then be off; otherwise, you remain with me as long as it shall be agreeable to you; the matter could not be better arranged, you must acknowledge!"

"Really, my dear Patrick," said Robert, who was apparently very reluctant to give up his plan, "I accept your offer with gratitude, and await only the opportunity to render you a service, whatever its nature may be."

"Nonsense!" returned Patrick. "Is gratitude to be spoken of between friends and fellow-countrymen — between Scotchmen? It is as if — eh! but wait, now!"

"What is it?" asked Robert.

"Oh, an idea!" cried Patrick, as if struck by a sudden thought.

"What is it? Let us hear!"

"My dear fellow," said Patrick, "you *can* do me a great favor."

"A great favor?"

"An enormous favor."

"Speak! I am at your disposal."

"Thanks! yet — "

"Proceed."

"Do you think we are of the same height?"

"Nearly."

"Of the same size?"

"I think so."

"Come into the moonlight; let me look at you."

Robert did as his friend requested.

"Do you know that you have on a magnificent doublet?" continued Patrick, holding aside his friend's mantle.

"Magnificent is not the word."

"Quite new."

"I bought it three days ago."

"A trifle sober, it is true," mused Patrick; "but in that she will perceive my intent to escape observation."

"What are you driving at?"

"This, dear Robert: while my lady-love views me with favor, her husband bestows upon me a very different regard. So different that, whenever he sees an archer of the guard pass along, he turns very sour looks upon him; and you can imagine what sort of regard I should attract if he were to see this uniform ascending his stairs."

"Indeed, I can imagine it marvellously well."

"Now, the lady has advised me not to set foot in her house again dressed in my national costume. Consequently, ever since nightfall I have been puzzling over some honest means of gaining possession of a suit of clothes that could advantageously take the place of my own; it seems to me that your costume, although a trifle sober, and perhaps even because of its color, should answer my purpose. Be so kind, then, as to lend it to me for to-morrow; I will so arrange matters as to have no need of it after that."

The Scotchman's last words, betokening the perfect self-confidence his compatriots formerly possessed and yet retain, caused Robert Stuart to smile.

"My raiment, my purse, my heart are yours, my dear friend," returned he. "Yet, mind you, I shall probably be going out myself to-morrow, and, in that case, my clothes will be almost a necessity to me."

"*Diable!*"

"Like the ancient philosopher, my back carries all my possessions."

"By Saint Dunstan, but that is vexatious!"

"And I am in despair."

"Because, really, the more I look at your doublet, the more it seems to have been made for me," cried Patrick.

"Miraculously so," assented Robert, who seemed bent on forcing his friend into making some suggestion.

"Is there then no way of encompassing the matter?"

"I see none; but you are a man of expedients,—set yourself about it."

"There is a way!" exclaimed Patrick.

"Name it."

"Unless, that is, your mistress's husband entertains the same horror of messieurs the archers of the Scotch Guard as does my mistress's husband."

"I have no mistress, Patrick," said Robert, gravely.

"Well, then," said the archer, who was merely pursuing the realization of his scheme, and was concerned about nothing else, "in that case you must be indifferent as to your costume."

"Quite indifferent," said the young man.

"Then, as I am taking your clothes, do you take mine."

This time Robert Stuart repressed a smile.

"What do you mean?" he asked, as if he did not quite understand.

"You have no objection to donning the Scotch uniform?"

"None at all."

"Well, if any imperious necessity compels you to go out, you can wear my uniform."

"You are right; nothing, in fact, could be simpler."

"Moreover, it carries with it the freedom of the Louvre."

Robert thrilled with joy. "The height of my ambition," he remarked with a smile.

"Very well; good-by till to-morrow!"

"Till to-morrow!" returned Robert, taking his friend's hand.

Patrick detained him.

"You are forgetting something," said he.

"What?"

"True, it is not of much consequence, — the key of my room."

"Faith, you are right," said Robert. "Give it to me!"

"There it is. Good-night, Robert!"

"Good-night, Patrick!"

And the two young men, after again clasping hands, went each his separate way, Patrick to the Louvre, Robert to Patrick's door.

Let us leave the former to pursue his course to the Louvre, where he will be just in time to answer at the evening roll-call, and follow Robert Stuart, who, after having fumbled about two or three doors, at last found the key-hole of Patrick's.

The remains of a still blazing fagot quite illuminated the young guard's room. It was a tidy retreat, rather like the small chambers of the students of our day.

It was furnished with a bedstead well fitted up, a small chest of drawers, two straw-bottomed chairs, and a table upon which, in a little, long-necked earthen jar, the wick of a tallow candle was still smoking.

Robert took a firebrand, and by dint of blowing succeeded in eliciting a blaze, at which he lighted the candle.

After that he seated himself at the little table, and

burying his forehead in his hands fell to thinking deeply.

"I have it!" he said at last, passing his hand through his hair as if to relieve his head of some terrible weight. "I have it, — I will write to the king."

And he arose.

On the mantel-piece he discovered a full inkstand and a pen; but in vain he searched and rummaged the table drawer and the three drawers of the chest, — he found not so much as a shadow of paper or parchment.

He renewed his search, but without success; his comrade had, beyond doubt, used up his last leaf in writing to Madame la Conseillère.

He sat down again in despair.

"Oh," said he, "shall I not, then, for want of a bit of paper, be able to try this last expedient?"

In fact, ten o'clock was striking. The merchants in those days did not, as in ours, keep open doors until midnight; the difficulty therefore was real.

Suddenly he remembered the king's letter which he had with him; he drew it forth from his breast and resolved to write to the king on the back of that sheet.

He took down the pen and ink, and wrote the following letter: —

"SIRE, — The conviction of the councillor, Anne Dubourg, is iniquitous and ungodly. Your Majesty has been blinded, and made to spill the purest blood in the kingdom.

"Sire, a man cries to you from the midst of the multitude that you open your eyes and behold the blazing funeral piles that ambitious men are kindling around you all over France!

"Sire, open your ears and hearken to the plaintive groans breathed forth on the Place de Grève, and rising toward the Louvre.

"See and hear, sire! When you have seen and heard, surely you will pardon."

The Scotchman reread his letter and folded it inversely, — that is, in such a manner that the front page on which the king's letter was written became the back of his own letter to the king, and the back on which his letter was written preceded the page of the king's letter.

"Now," he mused, "how can I get this letter within the Louvre? Shall I wait until to-morrow for Patrick? That will be too late. Besides, poor Patrick would be arrested as my accomplice. I am already exposing him quite enough in accepting his hospitality. What shall I do?"

He went to the window in search of an idea. In desperate circumstances one consults exterior objects willingly enough.

We have said that the day had been a magnificent one for December.

Robert sought counsel of the fresh air, the starry sky, the silent night, as to what was to be done.

From Patrick's attic window, at the very top of the house, he could see the towers of the king's palace.

The wooden tower erected at the end of the palace, nearly opposite to the Tour de Nesle, and uplifting itself between the river and the inner court of the Louvre, suddenly loomed up before him, magnificently outlined in the fantastic moonlight.

At sight of this tower, Robert seemed to discover the means he sought for getting his message to the king; for, returning the parchment to his breast, he extinguished the candle, put on his hat, wrapped himself in his mantle, and quickly descended the stairs.

An ordinance had been issued only a few days before, prohibiting all passengers and boatmen from crossing the Seine after five o'clock in the afternoon.

It was ten o'clock in the evening; hence to take a boat was not to be thought of.

The only course possible for Robert was to retrace his steps and go back over the route he had taken in coming from the Grève.

He went back then toward the bridge of Saint Michel, leaving the Rue de la Barillerie at his left so as not to encounter the palace sentinels, and, crossing the bridge of Notre Dame, he returned through the net-work of streets leading to the Louvre.

The Louvre had been a litter of stones, gravel, and timbers ever since the reign of François I.

It reminded one of the interior of a quarry, or of one of those unfinished palaces fallen in ruins before being completed, rather than of the residence of the king of France.

It was therefore easy enough to steal along among the blocks of stone by which the Louvre was obstructed, without as well as within.

From rock to rock, from ditch to ditch, skirting the bank of the Seine, Robert Stuart arrived within a hundred paces of the great front of the Louvre facing the river, which in extent covered all the space now occupied by the quay; he then followed the structure as far as the New Tower, and, seeing two lighted windows, he picked up from one of the ditches a stone, which he enveloped in the parchment, detached the cord from his hat, tied the parchment around the stone, and, retreating two or three steps to gain impetus, he calculated the distance, taking aim as if about to throw a ball, and flung both stone and parchment through one of the lighted windows of the first story.

The sound of breaking glass and the stir that ensued in the room immediately after the crash, assured him that his missive had made its way, and that if it failed to reach the king it would not be for want of messengers.

"Capital," he said. "And now, let us wait; we shall certainly know by to-morrow whether my letter has produced any effect."

As he withdrew, he looked about on all sides to assure himself that he had not been observed, and saw only the sentinels in the distance walking with the sentinel's slow and measured tread.

Evidently the sentinels had remarked nothing.

Robert Stuart then regained the Rue de Battoir-Saint-André by the same route over which he had come, convinced that he had been neither seen nor heard by any one.

He was deceived: he had been seen and heard by two men, who, at about fifty paces from him in one of the angles of the New Tower, hidden in its shadow, were conversing with such animation as not to see and hear, or at least to give no sign of so doing.

These two personages were the Prince de Condé and the Admiral de Coligny.

Let us say what topic of conversation could engross these two illustrious personages to such a degree that they did not appear to be concerned about the stones that were flung through the windows of the Louvre at that advanced hour of the night.

IX.

AT THE FOOT OF THE NEW TOWER.

"Now," says Brantôme, in his book of the "Capitaines Illustres," "we are about to speak of a mighty captain, if ever was one."

We say with Brantôme; only, let us be more just toward Gaspard de Coligny, Seigneur de Châtillon, than was the courtier of the Guises.

In two other books of ours we have already dwelt upon the illustrious defender of Saint Quentin; but our readers may have forgotten "Marguerite de Valois," and they may not yet be familiar with "The Page of the Duke of Savoy." We deem it necessary, therefore, to say a few words as to the birth, family, and antecedents, as they say to-day, of the *Admiral.*

We italicize this word because it was rare, indeed, that he was spoken of by the name of Gaspard de Coligny, or was styled Seigneur de Châtillon, his title of "admiral" having prevailed.

Gaspard de Coligny was born on the seventh day of February, 1517, at Châtillon-sur-Loing, the seigniorial residence of his family.

His father, a nobleman of Bresse, had established himself in France after his province was annexed to the kingdom; he occupied a high rank in the king's army, and took the name of Châtillon, having become the proprietor of that seigniory.

He had espoused Louise de Montmorency, sister of the constable, whom we have very often had occasion to mention, and particularly in "Ascanio," "The Two Dianas," and "The Page of the Duke of Savoy."

The four sons of the Seigneur de Châtillon — Pierre, Odet, Gaspard, and Dandelot — were, therefore, the constable's nephews. The first, Pierre, died at five years of age; the second, Odet, was then looked upon as destined to uphold the honor of the name.

Twenty years later a cardinal's hat was at the disposal of the constable. None of his own sons desired it; he then offered it to his sister's sons: Gaspard and Dandelot, both possessed of warlike temperaments, refused the gift; Odet, of a quiet and contemplative nature, accepted it.

Gaspard then found himself the head of the family, especially as his father had been dead since the year 1522.

We have elsewhere related how his early exploits had been achieved in the companionship of François de Guise, and what friendship bound these two young people together up to the time when, in connection with the battle of Renty, in which each had won great distinction for valor, a coolness intervened between them. The Duc Claude de Lorraine being dead, and the Duc François and his brother the cardinal having placed themselves at the head of the Catholic party and seized upon the affairs of state, the coldness turned to hatred outright.

During this time, in spite of his hatred of the Guises, young Gaspard de Châtillon had become one of the most distinguished men of his time, and had sprung into fame and renown. Dubbed knight by the Duc d'Enghien, as was his brother Dandelot, and that, too, on the very battlefield of Cérisoles, where each had captured a flag, he had been made colonel in 1544, and, three years later, colonel-general of the infantry, and finally admiral.

It was then he resigned the post of colonel-general in favor of his brother Dandelot, whom he dearly loved, and who dearly loved him.

About the year 1545 the two brothers wedded two daughters of the noble Breton house of Laval.

In "The Page of the Duke of Savoy" the admiral will be found at the siege of Saint Quentin, and it will be seen with what admirable faithfulness he defended the town, stone by stone, and was taken at the final assault, weapons in hand.

It was during his captivity at Antwerp that, a Bible having fallen into his hands, he changed his religion.

For six months his brother Dandelot had already been a Calvinist.

The admiral's importance naturally pointed him out as the military leader of the reformed religion.

However, as there had as yet been no rupture between the two parties, and but few persecutions, Dandelot and his brother occupied at court the position to which the rank of each entitled him.

"But," says a historian of that day, "the court had not a more formidable enemy."

Gifted with extraordinary coolness, courage, and insight, he seemed born to become, what he in fact became, the real leader of the Calvinist party. He possessed both perseverance and indomitable energy, and although often vanquished he nearly always became more formidable after his defeats than his enemies after their victories.

Counting his rank as nothing, and his life for so little that he was ready at all times to sacrifice it in the defence of the realm or for the triumph of his faith, he added to a warlike genius the solid virtues of the greatest citizens.

During those stormy times the sight of that unruffled brow was restful to the eyes; it resembled the great oaks that stand upright amid the tempests; it was like the lofty mountains whose crests remain undisturbed amid the storms, because they are above the lightnings.

That oak's rugous bark the rain will not harm, the wind will not bow its head; to uproot it will require the hurricane that sweeps away all.

That mountain will become a volcano, and at every eruption the throne will tremble, shaken almost to its very foundation; and to destroy the crater, to stanch the lava, there must occur one of those great cataclysms that change the face of empires.

And the Prince de Condé, an active, enterprising, and ambitious genius, will support him in battle after battle with the king's armies for the period of ten years.

As we have said, the Prince de Condé was talking with the admiral. With this illustrious young man, Coligny, lost in the shadow outlined by the New Tower, was conversing on that night between the eighteenth and the nineteenth of December.

By sight, at least, we know the Prince de Condé; we saw him enter the Red Horse Inn, and from a few remarks made by him we were able to form some estimate of his character.

Permit us to give a few details, which we deem indispensable, as to his character and the position held by the prince at court.

Monsieur de Condé had not yet given proof of what he was; but one felt a presentiment of what he might be, and this presentiment foreshadowed great importance for the handsome young man, known until that time chiefly for his follies and fickle amours, and who, like his contemporary, Don Juan, had enrolled in his vast catalogue the names of the most renowned ladies of the court.

He was twenty-nine years of age at that time, we think we have said. He was the fifth and last son of Charles of Bourbon, Comte de Vendôme, the modern stock of all the branches of the house of Bourbon.

His elder brothers were Antoine de Bourbon, King of Navarre and father of Henri IV.; François, Comte d'Enghien; Cardinal Charles de Bourbon, Archbishop of Rouen; and Jean, Comte d'Enghien, who had been killed only two years previously in the battle of Saint Quentin.

Louis de Condé, therefore, was at this time but a younger son, whose entire fortune consisted of his cloak and sword.

And the sword, moreover, was of greater value than the cloak.

That sword the prince had gloriously drawn in the wars of Henri II., as well as in a few private quarrels, which had gained him a reputation for courage almost equal to that he had acquired for luck, and especially for inconstancy, in love.

This axiom seemed to have been made purposely for the Prince de Condé: "Possession slays love."

When once the prince possessed, he loved no longer.

This was very well known among the *Belles Dames* whose gallant history Brantôme has given us, and yet, strange to say, it did not appear to damage in their eyes the young prince, who was so loving, so gay, that some one made him the subject of the following quatrain in the form of a prayer:—

"Ce petit homme tant joli,
Qui toujours chante et toujours rit,
Qui toujours baise sa mignonne,
Dieu gard' de mal le petit homme!"

As may be seen, the intention of the poet who originated these four lines was better than his verse; yet, as they convey a sufficiently exact idea of the sentiment of sympathy inspired at court by Louis de Condé, we venture to quote them.

Besides, our book is signed Alexandre Dumas, — not Richelet.

Between the admiral and the young prince this sympathy was strong: still young, being forty-two years of age, the admiral loved Louis de Condé as he might have loved one of his own young brothers; and, on his side, the Prince de Condé, of a chivalric and adventurous temperament, naturally much more given to studying the mysteries of love than to troubling himself over the triumphs and defeats of religion, careless Catholic as he was at that time, — the Prince de Condé, like a pupil with a beloved master, listened to the serious admiral, while his eye followed the gallop of a beautiful amazon returning from the chase, or the ditty of a maiden on her way from the fields.

Now, this is what had happened an hour before.

The admiral, on coming out of the Louvre, where he had been paying his court to the young king, had, with the eye of a captain trained to the darkness, distinguished at the foot of the New Tower a man, who, enveloped in a mantle and his head raised toward a balcony that overhung two lighted windows, seemed to be waiting either to receive a signal or to give one. The admiral, not naturally curious, was proceeding toward the Rue de Béthisy, in which he lived, when it occurred to him that but one man could have the hardihood to stand in front of the king's palace, within a hundred yards of the sentinels, at an hour when all passers-by were usually arrested if they in the least approached the Louvre, and that this man must be the Prince de Condé.

He went toward him, and as the man, the nearer the admiral approached, shrank back as far as possible into the shadow, when within twenty paces he called out to him, —

"Hey! Prince!"

"Who is it?" demanded the Prince de Condé; for it was he, in fact.

"A friend," answered the admiral, continuing to advance, and smiling at the fact that his acuteness had this time, as ever, divined aright.

"Aha! that voice belongs to the admiral, if I mistake not," said the prince, advancing a few steps to join the person who had accosted him.

The two men met at the verge of the shadow; the first drew the admiral toward him, so that both stood in the gloom.

"How the devil," asked the prince, after having affectionately, and with an air of respect, pressed the admiral's hand, — "how did you know that I was here?"

"I guessed it," said the admiral.

"Ah! it was well guessed, *par exemple!* How did you go about it?"

"Oh, very simply!"

"Come, let us hear."

"Seeing a man here within range of the sentinels, I told myself that there was but one knight in France capable of risking his life for the sake of seeing the wind toss the curtain of a pretty woman's window, and that that man was Your Highness."

"My dear admiral, permit me, first of all, to thank you for the excellent opinion you entertain of me, and, next, to pay you a very sincere compliment. More wonderful sagacity than yours it were impossible to possess."

"Ah!" exclaimed the admiral.

"I am, in fact, watching the window of a room where dwells, not a pretty woman, — since she who draws me here was, six months ago, still a child, and is to-day barely a girl, — but a bewitching being of matchless beauty."

"You are speaking of Mademoiselle de Saint André," remarked the admiral.

"Precisely. Better and better, my dear admiral," rejoined the prince; "and that leads me to explain the motive that has impelled me to take you into my confidence."

"Then you are impelled by a motive?" inquired the admiral, laughing.

"Yes, and a tremendous one."

"What was it? Make me your confidant, prince."

"It was that, if I did not have you for a friend, Monsieur l'Amiral, I should perhaps have you for an enemy, and in that case I should have an invincible enemy."

The admiral shook his head at this flattery, emanating from a man whom he was on the point of reproaching, and contented himself with saying, —

"You are doubtless ignorant, prince, that Mademoiselle de Saint André is affianced to Monsieur de Joinville, the eldest son of the Duc de Guise."

"Not only am I not ignorant of the fact, Monsieur l'Amiral, but, worse still, it was on learning the news of the match that I fell madly in love with Mademoiselle de Saint André; consequently, I can boldly state that my love for Mademoiselle de Saint André arises chiefly from my hatred of the Guises."

"Well! well! but this is the first time, prince, that I have heard this amour spoken of; your love affairs usually sing on the wing like the lark. This, then, is a new-born passion, since it has as yet made no stir."

"Not so new, my dear admiral; on the contrary, it is six months old."

"Nonsense! is it truly?" queried the admiral, accompanying his question with a look that expressed his amazement.

"Six months, yes, almost to a day, i' faith! Do you not remember the horoscopes read by an old woman to Monsieur de Guise, the Maréchal de Saint André, and your servant, at the Fête du Landi? It certainly seems to me that I related the incident to you."

"Yes, I recall it perfectly. It happened at an inn on the road from Gonesse to Saint Denis."

"The very place, my dear admiral. Well, from that hour dates the discovery of my love for the charming Charlotte, and it may be that the death then predicted has given me a singular taste for life; but from that day forth I have lived only in the hope of winning the love of the maréchal's daughter, and I have enlisted every resource of my brain toward achieving that end."

"And if I may ask, without indiscretion, prince," demanded the admiral, "is your love requited?"

"No, cousin, no; that is why you find me here kicking my heels."

"And waiting, gallant knight that you are, to receive a flower, a glove, a word?"

"*Ma foi*, waiting not even for that."

"For what are you waiting, then?"

"For the light to go out, and for Monsieur le Prince de Joinville's fiancée to go to sleep, so that I, in turn, may go and put out my own light and sleep also, if I can."

"And this undoubtedly is not the first time, my dear prince, that you have waited for the young lady's bed-time?"

"It is not the first time, cousin, nor will it be the last. It will soon be four months that I have devoted myself to this innocent amusement."

"Unknown to Mademoiselle de Saint André?" inquired the admiral, with an air of doubt.

"Unknown to her, I begin to think."

"But this is more than love, dear prince; this is absolute worship, adoration like that of the Hindoos for their invisible divinities, which certain navigators tell us about."

"Your word is very apt, my dear admiral; it is absolute worship, and I must needs be the good Christian that I am not to abandon myself to this idolatry."

"Idolatry is the worship of images, my dear prince, and you do not happen to possess even an image of your goddess, do you?"

"Faith, no, not even her image," said the prince; "but," continued he, with a smile, and carrying his hand to his heart, "her image is here, and graven so well that, on my word, I have need of no other picture than the one that lives in my memory."

"And what limit do you assign to this monotonous exercise?"

"None. I shall come as long as I love Mademoiselle de Saint André. I shall love her, according to my wont, as long as she grants me nothing; and as, in all probability, she will not very soon grant me what must be granted before my love begins to wane, it is probable that I shall love her a long time."

"What a strange fellow you are, my dear prince!"

"What would you have? I am so constituted; it is something I do not myself understand. As long as a woman bestows nothing upon me, I am madly in love, capable of killing her husband, her lover, of killing her, of killing myself, of making war for her sake, as did Pericles for Aspasia, Cæsar for Eunoë, Antony for Cleopatra; then, if she yields—"

"If she yields?"

"Then, my dear admiral,—unfortunately for her, unfortunately for me!—the damper of satiety is turned on my folly, and it is extinguished."

"But what the deuce do you find of pleasure, now, in watching here by the light of the moon?"

"Under the window of a pretty maid? An enormous pleasure, dear cousin. Oh, you don't understand; you, a grave, austere man, who stake your whole happiness on the winning of a battle or the triumph of your faith! With me, Monsieur l'Amiral, it is another matter: with me, war is but an interregnum between two loves, the old love and the new. I really believe that God put me into the world only to love, since I am good for nothing else. Besides, it is God's law. God has commanded us to love our neighbor as ourselves. Well, excellent Christian that I am, I love my neighbor more than myself. Only, I love the most beautiful half, in its most agreeable form."

"But where, then, have you seen Mademoiselle de Saint André since the Fête du Landi?"

"Ah! my dear admiral, it is a very long story, and, unless you are prepared, in spite of my trivial tale, to bear me company for at least a good half-hour, like the indulgent kinsman you are, I advise you not to insist, but to leave me to my reveries and my communion with the moon and stars, which are to me less luminous than the light you see shining from the windows of my divinity."

"My dear cousin," said the admiral, laughing, "I have future designs on you that you do not even suspect. It is to my interest, then, to study your every aspect; what you are showing me to-day seems not only a face but a façade. Come, open every portal! When I would deal with the true Condé, with the mighty captain, show me the one at which I must enter; and when, instead of the hero I seek, I find only a Hercules spinning at the feet of Omphale, a Samson sleeping at the knees of Delilah, show me the one by which I must go out."

"Then I am to tell you the whole truth?"

"The whole."

"As to a confessor?"

"More frankly."

"I warn you that it is a veritable eclogue."

"Virgilius Maro's most beautiful verses are nothing else than eclogues."

"Then I will begin."

"I am all attention."

"Will you stop me when you have had enough?"

"I promise you that; but I do not think that I shall stop you."

"Ah! great and sublime politician that you are!"

"Do you know, my dear prince, it looks to me as if you were jesting."

"I? Ah! *par exemple*, you know that such a speech plunges me into despair."

"Proceed, then."

"It was during the month of last September, after the hunt given to all the court by the Messieurs de Guise in the forest of Meudon."

"I remember hearing about it, although I was not there."

"Then you will also remember that after the chase Madame Catherine repaired with all her maids of honor, her flying squadron as they are called, to Monsieur de Gondy's château at Saint Cloud; you remember that, do you not, as you were there?"

"Perfectly."

"Well, there, as you further recall, unless your attention was bestowed upon graver matters, during the collation a young girl, on account of her beauty, won the attention of the court, and especially mine: it was Mademoiselle de Saint André. Afterwards, during the excursion on the water, a young girl, by means of her wit, excited the admiration of all the guests, and especially mine: it was Mademoiselle de Saint André. Finally, in the evening, at the ball, all eyes, and especially mine, were fixed upon a dancer whose peerless grace won smiles from every lip, murmured flattery from very tongue, looks of admiration from all eyes: again it was Mademoiselle de Saint André. Do you recall all that?"

"No."

"So much the better! for, had you remembered it, it would not have been worth while for me to tell it. You can well understand how the fire, feebly burning in my heart at the Red Horse Inn, became at Saint Cloud a devouring flame. As a result, having retired, when the ball was over, to the room assigned me on the first floor, instead of going to bed and closing my eyes in sleep, I sat at the window, and, thinking of her, I fell into a gentle revery. I yielded myself up to it wholly, for how long a time I do not know, when, through the veil which thoughts of love had cast before my eyes, I seemed to see a living creature moving along, as ethereal as the passing breeze that tossed my hair. It seemed a thing as light as mist, — a pink and white shade, which floated down the walks of the park, and came to a halt just under my window, and leaned against the trunk of a tree whose foliage swept my closed jalousies. I recognized, or rather divined, that the beautiful nocturnal fairy was no other than Mademoiselle de Saint André, and I should most probably have jumped through the window to reach her as speedily as possible, and fallen at her feet as promptly, when a second shadow, less pink and white than the first, but almost as airy, cleared the space between the two sides of the walk. This shade was evidently of the male sex."

"Ah! ah!" murmured the admiral.

"That is just the exclamation I permitted myself to make," said Condé. "But the baleful doubts arising in my mind as to Mademoiselle de Saint André's virtue were not of long duration; for the two shades began to babble, and the sound of their voices reached me through the branches of the tree and the openings of the jalousies, so that, just as I had recognized the actors in the scene played twenty feet below me, I heard what they were saying."

"And who were the actors?"

"They were Mademoiselle de Saint André and her father's page."

"And what were they talking about?"

"They were simply discussing a fishing excursion for the next morning."

"A fishing excursion?"

"Yes, my dear cousin; Mademoiselle de Saint André is an enthusiastic angler."

"And it was for the purpose of arranging a fishing excursion that, at midnight, or one o'clock in the morning, a girl of fifteen and a page of nineteen appointed a rendezvous in the park?"

"Like you, my dear admiral, I had my suspicions, and I must say that the page seemed very much disappointed when, having eagerly hastened to meet her, inspired, doubtless, by some other hope, he learned from Mademoiselle de Saint André's own lips that she had made the rendezvous merely to request that he would secure two lines, one for herself and one for him, with which she invited him to meet her on the bank of the canal at five o'clock in the morning. The page himself could not help exclaiming, —

"'But, mademoiselle, if it was merely for the sake of asking me to get you a line that you arranged for me to meet you, it was unnecessary to make so great a mystery of so simple a matter.'

"'There is where you are wrong, Jacques,' replied the girl; 'ever since the fête began, I have been so flattered, so attended, so hemmed in by admirers and lovers, that, had I asked you for a line, and by any mischance my purpose had become known, in the morning, at five o'clock, I should find three-fourths of the lords of the court, including Monsieur de Condé, waiting for me on the bank, and you very well know that would scare away the fish, so that I could not catch the smallest gudgeon. Now, that is not what I wish; I intend to have some fine sport in the morning, with only you for company, ingrate that you are.'

"'Ah! yes, mademoiselle,' said the page, 'yes, I am an ingrate.'

"'So it is arranged, Jacques, for five o'clock.'

"'I will be there at four, mademoiselle, with two lines.'

"'But you will not fish before I come, and without me, Jacques, will you?'

"'Oh, I promise to wait for you!'

"'Very well. Stay; for your trouble, there is my hand.'

"'Ah! mademoiselle,' cried the youth, falling upon the coquettish hand and covering it with kisses.

"'Gently!' said the girl, withdrawing her hand. 'I meant that you might kiss, not devour, my hand. Come, that will do! good-night, Jacques! On the bank of the great canal at five o'clock.'

"'Ah! come when you will, mademoiselle, I shall be there, I promise you.'

"'Be off, be off!' bade Mademoiselle de Saint André, waving him away with her hand.

"The page instantly obeyed, without reply, like a genie obeying the magician who has conjured him. In less than a second he had disappeared.

"Mademoiselle de Saint André lingered behind for a moment; then, having assured herself that nothing disturbed the stillness of the night nor the solitude of the garden, she in turn disappeared, believing that she had been neither seen nor heard."

"Are you sure, my dear prince, that the sly puss did not suspect you were at your window?"

"Ah! my good cousin, thus would you rob me of my illusions!"

Then, drawing nearer to the admiral, he said, —

"Well, profound politician that you are, there are moments when I would not take my oath upon it."

"Upon what?"

"That she had not seen me, and that the line, the fishing party, and the rendezvous at five in the morning, had not been a comedy."

"Come, now!"

"Oh, I never deny, when feminine trickery is in question," said the prince; "and the younger and more naïve the woman, the less I deny; but agree, my dear admiral, that if such were the case, she is a very clever person."

"I do not say the contrary."

"You can easily imagine that at five o'clock the next morning I was in ambush in the neighborhood of the great canal. The page had kept his word. He was there before daylight. As for the lovely Charlotte, she came, like the dawn, a moment before the sun, and with her rosy fingers took from the hands of Jacques a line already baited. For a second, I asked myself why she need have brought a fishing squire; but I soon discovered that such charming fingers could not touch the hideous creatures with which she would have been obliged to bait her hook, or those even that she must have unhooked if the page had not been there to spare her the repugnant office; as it was, of the fishing, which lasted until seven o'clock, there remained to the beautiful and refined girl only the pleasure, and it must have been very great, for, by my faith, the young people caught between them a magnificent fry."

"And what did you catch, my dear prince?"

"A very severe cold from getting my feet wet, and a fever of love, the effects of which you witness."

"And you think the little jade was unaware of your presence?"

"Eh! *mon Dieu!* cousin, perhaps she knew I was there; but, really, she curved her arm so gracefully when landing her fish, and held up her dress so coquettishly while advancing to the edge of the canal, that the arm and the ankle made me pardon all, since, if she knew me to be there, it was for me she practised all those charming poses, and not for the page, as I was at her right, and it was the right arm she curved and the left ankle that was displayed. To sum up, my dear admiral, I love her, if she is artless; but, if she is coquettish, so much the worse, — I adore her! You see that in either case I am very ill."

"And since that time?"

"Since then, cousin, I have seen the charming arm, I have seen the ankle again, but only from afar, never being able to join the mistress of those fascinating treasures, who, when she perceives me in one direction, — I must do her this justice, — flits away in the other."

"And what is to be the *dénouement* of this mute infatuation?"

"Eh! *mon Dieu!* ask a wiser man than I, my dear cousin; for if my infatuation is dumb, as you suggest, it is blind and deaf as well, — which means that it hears no counsel and does not see, and, more than that, does not wish to see beyond the present hour."

"But yet, my dear prince, you must hope at some future time to receive some recompense for this exemplary servitude."

"Naturally; but it is a future so distant that I dare not contemplate it."

"Well, believe me, it is not to be contemplated."

"Why do you say that, Monsieur l'Amiral?"

"Because you would see nothing there, and you would be disheartened."

"I fail to comprehend."

"Eh! *mon Dieu!* it is, nevertheless, quite comprehensible."

"Speak out, Monsieur l'Amiral."

"Expect but one thing, my dear prince."

"When Mademoiselle de Saint André is in question, I expect everything."

"I will tell you the truth frankly, prince."

"Monsieur l'Amiral, I have for a long time entertained for you the respectful tenderness one cherishes for an elder brother, and the tender devotion one feels for a friend. You are the only man in the world whose right to advise I should recognize. Let me tell you that, far from deprecating the truth from your lips, I humbly solicit it. Speak!"

"Thanks, prince!" responded the admiral, like one who understood the powerful influence that love affairs must exert over such a temperament as Monsieur de Condé's, and who, consequently, attached grave importance to a matter which, in any but the brother of the King of Navarre, he would have regarded as a trifle, — "thanks! and since you grant me such liberty, here is the plain truth: Mademoiselle de Saint André does not love you, my dear prince; Mademoiselle de Saint André will never love you."

"Are you not something of an astrologer, Monsieur l'Amiral? And, prior to such a sorry prediction, have you not, peradventure, questioned the stars in my behalf?"

"No. But do you know why she will not love you?" added the admiral.

"How can you expect me to know that, since I am making every effort to win her love?"

"She will never love you, because she will never love any one, the little page no more than you; she has a hard heart, an ambitious soul. I have known her from her earliest childhood, and, without any knowledge of the science of astrology, as you just now implied, I have, for my part, predicted that she would one day play a rôle in this great theatre of debauchery before us."

And with a gesture of utter contempt the admiral indicated the Louvre.

"Aha!" ejaculated Monsieur de Condé, "that is a point of view from which I have not considered her."

"She was not eight years old before she was playing the consummate courtesan, Agnes Sorel or Madame d'Étampes: her little playmates would place a cardboard crown upon her head, and escort her about the hôtel, crying, 'Long live the little queen!' Well, all through her girlhood she has retained the memory of that childish royalty. She professes to love Monsieur de Joinville, her fiancé. She lies! It is only a pretence; do you know why? It is because Monsieur de Joinville's father, Monsieur de Guise, my friend of old, my inveterate enemy to-day, will, if he is not interfered with, be King of France before very long."

"Ah! *diable!* are you convinced of that, cousin?"

"Perfectly, my dear prince; from which I conclude that your love for the queen's beautiful maid of honor is a hopeless attachment, and one of which I advise you to rid yourself as soon as possible."

"That is your advice?"

"And I give it from the bottom of my heart."

"As for me, dear cousin, I hasten to assure you that I receive it as it is given."

"Only, you will not follow it."

"What can I do, my dear admiral? a man is not his own master in such matters."

"Yet, my dear prince, judge the future by the past."

"Ah! well, yes, I confess that so far she has not given proof of any really ardent sympathy for your humble servant."

"And you think such a state of things will not continue. Ah! I know you have a good opinion of yourself, my dear prince."

"Well, really, it would be giving others very good grounds for despising us if we despise ourselves. But it is not that at all. The tenderness which she does not feel for me, you cannot, unfortunately, prevent my cherishing for her. That makes you shrug your shoulders. How can it be helped? Am I free to love or not to love? Suppose I were to say to you: 'At the siege of Saint Quentin you held out, for three weeks, with two thousand men, against the fifty or sixty thousand Flemish and Spanish troops of Emmanuel Philibert and Philip II.; well, now it is your turn to make the siege; there are thirty thousand men in the place, and you have but ten thousand;' would you refuse to besiege Saint Quentin? No; is it not so? Why? Because you have learned from experience in war that no place is impregnable to the valiant. Ah, well, my dear cousin, perhaps I am boasting, but I think I have gained the same experience in love as you in war, and I say, 'No place is impregnable.' You have set me an example in war, my dear admiral; permit me to set you an example in love."

"Ah! prince! prince! what a great leader you would have made," said the admiral, sadly, "if, instead of love's filling your heart with carnal desires, a loftier transport had thrust the sword into your hand."

"You mean religion?"

"Yes, prince; would that God had willed you to be one of us, and, consequently, one of His own!"

"My dear cousin," said Condé, with his habitual gayety, but revealing beneath that gayety the decision of a man who, without seeming to do so, has often reflected upon the subject, "you will not believe it, perhaps, but in matters of religion I have ideas as settled, at least, as in those of love."

"What do you mean?" demanded the astonished admiral.

The Prince de Condé's smile vanished from his lips, and he continued seriously: —

"I mean to say, my dear admiral, that I have my own religion, my own faith, my own charity; that to honor God I need no exhortation, and, so long as you fail to prove, my dear cousin, that your new doctrine is preferable to the old one, suffer me to adhere to the religion of my fathers, — unless I take a fancy to change it for the sake of playing a trick on Monsieur de Guise."

"Oh, prince! prince!" murmured the admiral, "is it thus you dispense the treasures of strength, youth, and intelligence bestowed on you by the Almighty, and will you not learn how to use them in advancing some great cause? Is not this instinctive hatred you feel for the Guises a providential warning? Rouse yourself, prince, and if you do not fight the enemies of your God, at least fight those of your king."

"Good!" said Condé; "but you are forgetting, cousin, that I have a king of my own, as well as a God of my own, — true, my king is as small as my God is great. My king, dear admiral, is my brother, the King of Navarre. He is my real king. The King of France is but my adopted king, a suzerain lord."

"Now you are evading the question, prince; you have fought for this king, however."

"But that is because I fight for any king, according

to my whim, as I love any woman, according to my fancy."

"Is it, then, impossible, my dear prince, to speak seriously with you upon any of these matters?" asked the admiral.

"By no means," answered the prince, with a degree of gravity; "let us speak of them on some other occasion, cousin, and I will give you an answer. Believe me, I should regard myself as a great wretch and a contemptible citizen, were I to consecrate my whole life to the sole service of dames. I know that I have duties to fulfill, Monsieur l'Amiral, and that intelligence, courage, and skill, the precious gifts that I hold from the Lord, have not been given me merely for the purpose of humming serenades under balconies. But have patience, my good cousin and excellent friend; allow the first fires of youth a chance to burn out. Why, the devil! consider, I am not yet thirty years old, Monsieur l'Amiral; and, in the absence of war, I must employ my pent-up energies in some way. Pardon me, then, even this adventure; and, as I do not accept the counsel you have proffered, be so kind as to give me that I shall ask for."

"Speak, foolish soul," said the admiral, in a fatherly way, "and God grant the advice I am to give may profit you in some manner!"

"Monsieur l'Amiral," said Monsieur le Prince de Condé, taking his cousin's arm, "you are a great general, a great strategist, beyond contradiction the first soldier of the day. Tell me how you would go about it, if you were in my place, for instance, to gain access at this hour, almost midnight, to Mademoiselle de Saint André, in order to tell her that you love her?"

"I see, indeed, my dear prince," said the admiral,

"that you will not be cured until you know the woman with whom you have to deal. It is, therefore, doing you a service to humor your madness, until madness gives place to reason. Well, in your place — "

"Sh! " said Condé, retreating into the shadow.

"And why?"

"Because it strikes me that something like a second lover is approaching the window."

"That is true," said the admiral.

And, following Condé's example, he shrank back into the darkness of the shadow cast by the Tower.

Then, motionless, and holding their breath, the two watched Robert Stuart's approach; they saw him pick up the stone, fasten a note to it, and throw the whole, stone and note, through the lighted window.

Next they heard the sound of breaking glass.

Then they saw the unknown, whom they had taken for a lover, — and who was no less, to do him justice, — take flight and disappear, after having assured himself that the missile which he had thrown had reached its destination.

"Ah! by my faith," said Condé, "without letting you off from the advice for some other time, I excuse you from giving it to-night."

"How is that?"

"Because my course is clear."

"In what respect?"

"Eh! *pardieu!* it is simple enough; that broken window belongs to the Maréchal de Saint André, and certainly it was not broken with good intent."

"Well?"

"Well, — I was coming out of the Louvre; I heard the crash of their broken window; I feared there might be some mischief afoot against the maréchal, and, i' faith, despite the advanced hour of the night, such is my regard for him, I could not refrain from entering to learn whether any harm has been done."

"Mad! mad! thrice mad!" exclaimed the admiral.

"I asked your advice, my friend; have you any better to offer?"

"Yes."

"And that is?"

"Do not go in."

"But, you know, that was your first advice, and I told you I did not mean to follow it."

"Ah, well, so be it! Let us go to the Maréchal de Saint André's."

"Then are you coming with me?"

"My dear prince, when one cannot keep a madman from committing mad acts, and when one loves the madman as I love you, one must needs half enter into his folly in order to get him out of it as well as possible. Come, to the maréchal's."

"My dear admiral, tell me by what breach I must mount, what arquebusade I must pass in order to follow you, and, at the first opportunity, I will take the lead instead of following after."

"Come, to the maréchal's."

And both directed their steps toward the great entrance of the Louvre, where, after giving the pass-word, the admiral entered, followed by the Prince de Condé.

X.

THE SIREN.

ARRIVED at the door of the apartment occupied at the Louvre by Monsieur le Maréchal de Saint André in his capacity of king's chamberlain, the admiral knocked; but the door, slightly pushed, yielded under his touch, and opened into the antechamber.

In the antechamber stood a valet, very much frightened.

"Friend," said the admiral, addressing the valet, "is Monsieur le Maréchal visible, notwithstanding the lateness of the hour?"

"Certainly, Monsieur le Maréchal would always be visible to Your Excellency," replied the valet; "but an unexpected occurrence has just compelled him to go to the king."

"An unexpected occurrence?" repeated Condé.

"It is an unexpected occurrence, also, which brings us to him," said M. de Coligny, "and it is probably the same one. Is it not that a stone has broken one of his windows?"

"Yes, monseigneur; it fell at the feet of Monsieur le Maréchal just as he was passing from his office to his bedroom."

"You see that I know of the occurrence, my friend, and as I can, perhaps, place Monsieur le Maréchal on the culprit's track, I should like to confer with him upon the subject."

"If Monsieur l'Amiral will wait," answered the valet, "and go, meanwhile, to Mademoiselle de Saint André, Monsieur le Maréchal will not be long in returning."

"But perhaps Mademoiselle de Saint André is not awake at this moment," said the Prince de Condé; "and for nothing in the world would we be willing to intrude."

"Oh, monseigneur," replied the valet, who had recognized the prince, "Your Highness may be reassured. I have just seen one of mademoiselle's women, who said that she would not go to bed until her father returned and she understood the meaning of that letter."

"What letter?" asked the admiral.

The prince touched his elbow.

"It is very plain," said he, — "the letter which was probably attached to the stone." Then, under his breath, he added, to the admiral, —

"It is a kind of correspondence that I have more than once carried on successfully, cousin."

"Well," said the admiral, "we accept your invitation, my friend; ask Mademoiselle de Saint André if she will receive Monseigneur le Prince de Condé and myself."

The lackey departed, and in a brief space of time returned to announce that Mademoiselle de Saint André awaited the two seigneurs.

Then, preceded by the valet, they directed their steps down the corridor leading to Mademoiselle de Saint André's apartment.

"Confess, my dear prince," said the admiral, in an undertone, "that you are engaging me in pretty work."

"My dear cousin," said Condé, "you know the saying, — 'No work is undignified,' especially if one engages in it heartily."

The valet announced His Highness, Monsieur le Prince de Condé, and His Excellency, Admiral Coligny.

Then Mademoiselle de Saint André was heard to say, most graciously, —

"Show them in."

The valet withdrew, and the two seigneurs entered Mademoiselle de Saint André's apartment, in the centre of which glittered the five-branched candelabrum at whose lights the prince had been gazing for the last three months through the young girl's curtained windows.

It was a tiny boudoir, hung with pale blue satin, where Mademoiselle de Saint André, pink and white and fair, looked like a naiad in a blue grotto.

"Eh! *mon Dieu!* mademoiselle," exclaimed the Prince de Condé, as if he were too excited to pause for ordinary compliments, "what has just happened to you, or to Monsieur le Maréchal?"

"Ah!" said Mademoiselle de Saint André, "you already know of the incident?"

"Yes, mademoiselle," rejoined the prince. "We were leaving the Louvre, Monsieur l'Amiral and I; we were just under your windows, when a stone whizzed over our heads. At the same instant we heard a great crash of breaking glass, which so alarmed us both that we immediately re-entered the Louvre, and have taken the liberty to come and inquire of your lackey whether anything has happened to the maréchal. The good fellow very imprudently told us that we could learn from you; that, in spite of the advanced hour of the night, in view of the motive which brings us, you might, perhaps, permit us to enter. Monsieur l'Amiral hesitated. My interest in Monsieur le Maréchal and the other members of his family caused me to insist, and, i' faith, mademoiselle, indiscreet or not, we are here."

"It is really very kind of you, prince, believing us to be in danger, thus to inconvenience yourself on our account. But the danger, if it exists, threatens loftier heads than ours."

"What mean you, mademoiselle?" quickly interposed the admiral.

"The stone that broke the window was wrapped in an almost threatening letter to the king. My father picked up the missive, and has taken it to the king."

"But," demanded the Prince de Condé, by a sudden inspiration, "has the captain of the guard been notified?"

"I do not know, monseigneur," returned Mademoiselle de Saint André; "but, in any event, if it has not been done, it should certainly be attended to."

"Undoubtedly; there is not a moment to lose," pursued the prince.

And, turning to Coligny, Condé demanded, —

"Your brother Dandelot commands the Louvre this week, does he not?"

"He does, my dear prince," returned the admiral, catching Condé's meaning on the wing; "and I will myself go and tell him, at all events, to double the watch and change the password as precautionary measures."

"Go, my dear admiral," cried the prince, highly delighted at being so readily understood; "and God grant that you arrive in time!"

The admiral smiled and retired, leaving the Prince de Condé alone with Mademoiselle de Saint André.

With a look of amusement on her face, the girl watched the grave admiral's retreat.

Then, turning to the prince, she said, —

"And let them now pretend to say that Your Highness is not as attached to the king as to your own brother!"

"But who has ever questioned my devotion, mademoiselle?" demanded the prince.

"The whole court, monseigneur, — I, particularly."

"Nothing is simpler than that the court should doubt it; the court belongs to Monsieur de Guise, while you, mademoiselle —"

"I do not yet belong to him, but I shall; it is the difference between what is and is to be, monseigneur, nothing more."

"So this incredible match is still in prospect?"

"More than ever, monseigneur."

"I do not know why," said the prince, "but I have an idea in my head, in my heart I should say, that it will never take place."

"Really, I should be afraid, prince, if you were not so poor a prophet."

"*Bon Dieu!* Who, then, has been injuring my reputation with you for astrological knowledge?"

"You yourself, prince."

"And how is that?"

"By predicting that I should love you."

"Did I really predict that?"

"Oh, I see you have forgotten the day of the miraculous fish."

"To forget it, mademoiselle, I must first break the meshes of the net in which you caught me that day."

"Oh, prince, you might indeed say the net in which you caught yourself! I have never, thank God, cast any net for you!"

"No; but you have lured me on like one of the sirens Horace speaks of."

"Oh," said Mademoiselle de Saint André, familiar with Latin, like all the ladies of that epoch, who were almost as learned in letters as in love, "'*desinit in piscem*,' says Horace. Look at me; do I end in a fish?"

"No, and you are but the more dangerous, since you have the voice and the eyes of the ancient enchantresses. You have drawn me, without knowing it, innocently, perhaps; but now, and I swear it, I am irretrievably ensnared."

"If I could place the least faith in your words, I should pity you sincerely, prince; for to love without return seems to me the cruellest pain that a sensitive heart can experience."

"Pity me, then, with all your soul, mademoiselle, for never has a lover been less loved than I."

"You will at least render me this justice, prince," said Mademoiselle de Saint André, with a smile: "I warned you in time."

"I beg your pardon, mademoiselle; it was already too late."

"And from what era do you date the birth of your love, — from the Christian or the Mohammedan era?"

"From the Fête du Landi, mademoiselle; from that day, happy or unhappy, when, all muffled up in your mantle, I first saw you, your hair unknotted by the storm, and curling in blond ringlets about your swan-like neck."

"But you scarcely spoke to me that day, prince."

"Probably I was gazing too intently, and sight destroyed speech. We never speak to the stars; we gaze at them, and dream, and hope."

"Why, know you not, prince, that is a metaphor of which Monsieur Ronsard might be envious?"

"Poets, mademoiselle, are the echoes of nature; nature sings and the poets repeat her songs."

"Better and better, prince. I see you are slandered when it is said that you have nothing but wit. You have, in addition, it seems to me, a splendid imagination."

"I have your image in my heart, and that radiant image sheds lustre even on my least word. The merit you impute to me is therefore to be ascribed to yourself alone."

"Ah, well! prince, heed me, close your eyes, do not look at my image. I could wish you happier."

As radiant in her victory as Monsieur de Condé was humiliated by his defeat, Mademoiselle de Saint André advanced a step toward him, and, extending her hand, said, —

"Come, prince, this is the way I treat the vanquished."

The prince seized the girl's hand, white, but cold, and ardently pressed it to his lips.

In this miscalculated movement, a tear, which had trembled in the corner of the prince's eye, and the fever of pride had in vain endeavored to dry, fell on that marble hand, where it quivered and glistened like a diamond.

Mademoiselle de Saint André both felt and saw it.

"Ah! upon my word! I believe that you are really weeping, prince," she cried, bursting into a laugh.

"'T is the drop of rain after the storm," returned the prince, with a sigh. "What is there amazing in that?"

Mademoiselle de Saint André fixed an eye of flame on the prince, seeming to hesitate a moment, between coquetry and pity. At last, although we are unable to say by which of the two sentiments she was impelled, — perhaps she was influenced by a mingling of both sentiments, — she drew from her pocket a fine batiste handkerchief, scented with the perfume that she usually dispensed, and, tossing it to the prince, she said, —

"There, monseigneur, if you happen to be subject to the malady of weeping, take my handkerchief to dry your tears."

Then, with a glance that certainly leaned to the side of coquetry, she said, —

"Keep it in memory of an ingrate."

And, as light as a fairy, she disappeared.

The prince, half crazed with love, caught the handkerchief in his hand; and, as if fearful lest the precious gift should be withdrawn, he ran down the stairs, unmindful that the king's life was threatened, forgetting that his cousin, the admiral, would return to Mademoiselle de Saint André's apartment for him, and aware of but one purpose in his heart, — to rain passionate kisses upon that precious handkerchief.

XI.

THE VIRTUE OF MADEMOISELLE DE SAINT ANDRÉ.

Not until he had reached the river-bank did Condé pause, as if he thought that nothing less than the hundred yards he had just placed between himself and Mademoiselle de Saint André could assure him of undisputed possession of the precious handkerchief.

Then only did he remember the admiral and his promise to wait for him. He waited therefore about a quarter of an hour, pressing the handkerchief to his lips, and straining it to his bosom, like a sixteen-year-old school-boy in his first love affair.

Now, was he in reality waiting for the admiral, or was he lingering there purely and simply for the sake of hovering longer near the light that had the fatal power of attracting him, the brilliant moth, until he should be consumed?

For that matter, he was already on fire, poor prince, and that perfumed handkerchief fanned the flame amazingly.

He was far from believing himself vanquished, the haughty champion of love, and could the girl, hidden behind her window-curtain, have seen in the moonlight a second tear, a tear of happiness, glistening on the edge of the prince's eyelid, she would doubtless have been convinced that the handkerchief, instead of drying tears, had the power to make them spring, and that the tears of regret had been washed away by tears of joy.

After a few moments of these transports and frenzied kisses, one of the prince's unoccupied senses, out of revenge, no doubt, for the neglect to which its master had abandoned it, started out of its sleep at a sudden sound. It was the sense of hearing.

The sound evidently came from the folds of the handkerchief. It recalled the dance of dead leaves at the first breath of the autumn wind, or a colony of insects returning in a swarm to their hollow in the tree after a day's outing, or, again, the melancholy plash rising from the drops of a fountain as they fall into its basin.

It was, in short, a slight rustling such as a silken robe yields under a touch of the hand.

Whence did it come?

Apparently, this charming little handkerchief of batiste was able, by itself and of its own accord, to emit a very decided sound.

Astonished, the Prince de Condé carefully unrolled the handkerchief, which innocently yielded up its secret.

He came upon a tiny, folded paper which, without doubt, had inadvertently found its way into the folds of the handkerchief.

The billet not only seemed to be perfumed with the same fragrance as the handkerchief, but perhaps even the charming fragrance emanated not from the handkerchief but from the billet.

Monsieur de Condé was preparing to seize the tiny note between his thumb and forefinger with as much precaution as a child displays in picking up by its wings a butterfly poised on a flower; but as the butterfly eludes the child, so the billet, swept away by a puff of wind, escaped from Monsieur de Condé.

Monsieur de Condé saw it float away into the night like a snow-flake, and he ran after it with an eagerness very unlike the child's when chasing his butterfly.

Unfortunately, the paper had fallen among stones hewn for the construction of the palace, and, being of nearly the same color as the stone, it was difficult to distinguish in the rubbish.

The prince began a desperate search. Had it not gradually dawned upon him, — lovers are indeed strange creatures! — that Mademoiselle de Saint André had espied him beneath her windows, that she had beforehand written the little note to give him whenever an opportunity offered, and that, the opportunity afforded, she had delivered it.

The little billet probably contained an explanation of her conduct; that gift of the handkerchief had been merely a way of posting the note.

To lose such a note was very bad luck, it must be acknowledged.

But Monsieur de Condé swore the note should not be lost, if he had to wait until the next morning.

Meanwhile he searched, but in vain.

For an instant he entertained the idea of running to the guard of the Louvre to borrow a lantern with which he could return and search for his note.

Yes; but should in the mean time a gust of wind by some ill chance arise, what assurance had the prince that he would find the billet where he had left it?

The prince was in the very midst of his cruel perplexity, when he saw the night-patrol coming toward him, preceded by a sergeant carrying a lantern in his hand.

It was all that he could for the moment desire.

Calling the sergeant, he made himself known, and borrowed the lantern for a short time.

After a ten minutes' search, he gave a cry of joy, — he had caught sight of the blessed paper!

This time it did not even attempt to fly away, and with unspeakable delight the prince placed his hand upon it.

But, just as his own hand touched the paper, he felt another's laid on his shoulder, while a familiar voice demanded in accents of astonishment, —

"Why, what the devil are you doing there, my dear prince? Do you happen to be looking for a man?"

The prince had recognized the admiral's voice.

He quickly returned the sergeant's lantern, and gave the soldiers the two or three pieces of gold which he had about him, and which for the time being probably comprised the entire fortune of the poor younger son.

"Ah!" said he, "I am looking for something quite as important to a lover as, in a different way, a man is to a philosopher; I am hunting for a woman's letter."

"And have you found it?"

"By good luck, yes! for had I not persevered, it is likely that an estimable lady of the court would to-morrow have been frightfully compromised."

"Ah! the deuce! here is a discreet cavalier. And this billet —?"

"Is of importance only to me, my dear admiral," said the young prince, thrusting the hand that held it into the side-pocket of his doublet. "Tell me, now, while I escort you back to the rue Béthisy, what it was that the Maréchal de Saint André carried to the king."

"Faith! something very strange, — a letter of remonstrance relative to the execution of Councillor Dubourg, announced for the twenty-second."

"*Ah ça!* my dear admiral," said the Prince de Condé laughing, "that has every appearance of proceeding from some madman whose head has been turned by Protestantism."

"I am afraid it is so, upon my word," said Coligny; "I suspect it settles the poor councillor's affairs. Why ask for a pardon now? The king can only reply, 'No; for, if the councillor is not put to death, I shall be thought afraid.'"

"Well," said Condé, "think over this grave question, my dear admiral, and I have no doubt that, thanks to your wisdom, you may see some way to settle the matter."

Then, as they had reached the church of Saint-Germain-l'Auxerrois, and, in order to regain his hôtel, he was obliged to cross the Seine by the Pont aux Meuniers, the prince, when one o'clock of the morning was proclaimed by the night-watch thirty feet away, pleaded the place, the distance to traverse, the advanced hour of the night, as excuses for leaving the admiral and regaining his own hôtel.

The admiral, for his part, was too preoccupied to retain him.

So that nothing hindered the departure of Monsieur de Condé, who, once out of sight of the Seigneur de Châtillon, took to his heels, still clutching the precious billet in his doublet pocket, lest he should again lose it. But this time there was no danger!

To reach his home, to mount the fifteen or eighteen steps leading to his apartment, to have the wax-candles lighted by his valet de chambre, to dismiss him saying that he had no more need of his services, to fasten the door, to draw near the light and extricate the paper from his pocket, — all was a matter of barely ten minutes.

But, as he was on the point of unfolding and reading the charming love-letter, for a billet so perfumed could be nothing less, a haze swept over his eyes and his heart beat so violently that he was forced to lean against the chimney-piece.

At last, the prince regained his self-control. The cloud passed away and his eyes were able to fix themselves upon the billet and read the following lines, which, in the sweet illusion into which he had fallen, were very far from being what he had expected.

And you, dear readers, are you waiting for the contents of the note inadvertently enveloped in the handkerchief that Mademoiselle de Saint André had flung at her despairing adorer?

You who know the human heart, have you a good opinion of this young girl who loves neither that pretty page, nor this handsome prince, and who grants a rendezvous to the one to ask him for a fishing-line, and throws her handkerchief to the other to help him dry the tears that she has caused to flow, — all this just as she is about to marry a third?

Does nature really produce hearts of stone which the most highly tempered blade cannot cut? Do you doubt it?

Look upon the contents of the note and you will doubt no more: —

"Do not fail, dear love, to repair to-morrow, an hour after midnight, to the Salle des Métamorphoses. The room in which we met last night is too near the apartments of the two queens; our confidante will see that the door is open."

There is no signature; the writing is unknown.

"Ah! the perverted creature!" cried the prince, striking the table with his fist and dropping the paper.

And, after the first explosion coming from the depths of his heart, the prince stood for a moment rooted to the spot.

But speech and motion very soon returned to him, and, striding up and down the room, he exclaimed as he went, —

"So the admiral was right!"

Then he observed the note which he had let fall on a chair.

"And," he continued, becoming more and more excited, "I have been the toy of an arrant coquette, and she who has played with me is a child of fifteen years! I, the Prince de Condé, the man who, above all others, pass at court as knowing the hearts of women, I, — I have been the dupe of a little girl's trickery! *Sang du Christ!* I am ashamed of myself! I have been scorned like a school-boy, and have wasted three months of my life, — three months of an intelligent man's life sacrificed, lost, thrown to the winds aimlessly, unreasonably, uselessly, ingloriously. I have wasted three months, madly in love with a hussy! I! I!"

Full of wrath he picked it up.

"Ah! yes; now that I know her," he continued, "two can play! We will play it to the end. You know my game, *belle demoiselle;* and now I know yours. Ah! I will learn the name, I promise you, of the man who was unable to taste delight undisturbed."

The prince crumpled the letter, thrust it into the space between the hollow of his hand and his glove, resumed his sword, put on his hat and prepared to go out, when suddenly a thought struck him.

He rested his elbow against the wall, and his forehead on his hand, and pondered deeply. Then, after a moment's reflection, he removed his hat, sent it flying across the room, reseated himself at the table, and for the second time read the letter that had just wrought such a fearful revolution in his mind.

"Detestable race!" said he when he had finished reading; "she-hypocrite and liar! You repelled me with one hand and drew me on with the other. You employed against me, a man honest even to simpleness, every resource of your infernal duplicity, and I saw nothing, understood nothing. I, loyal myself, was stupid enough to believe in loyalty; I, an upright man, to bow down before falsehood! Ah! yes, I wept; I wept from vexation; I wept for joy! Now, flow, flow, tears! tears of shame and rage! Flow and efface the stains this unworthy love has left! Flow and carry away, as a torrent does dead leaves, the last illusions of my youth, the last faith of my soul! —"

And, in fact, that strong soul, that lion-hearted man, sobbed like a child.

Then, his sobs exhausted, a third time he read the letter, but this time without bitterness.

His tears had not swept away the illusions of youth, the soul's beliefs which only they who have never had them lose, but, on the contrary, his anger and bitterness. True, they left in their place disdain and scorn.

"Nevertheless," he said after a pause, "I have sworn that I will learn this man's name; I will know it. It shall not be said that any man with whom she has laughed at my ridiculous infatuation shall have laughed and live! But," continued the prince, "who can he be?"

And again he read the note.

"I know the handwriting of almost every gentleman of the court, from the king's to Monsieur de Mouchy's, and I do not recognize this handwriting. Upon study, one would think it a woman's hand, — disguised writing. 'An hour past midnight,' 'the Salle des Métamorphoses.' Wait till to-morrow. It is Dandelot's week at the Louvre. Dandelot will help me, and, in case of need, so will Monsieur l'Amiral."

And this resolution formed, the prince again took three or four turns up and down the room and ended by casting himself, dressed as he was, upon his bed.

But the conflicting emotions he had just experienced had thrown him into a fever that would not permit him to close his eyes for a moment.

Never had he passed such a night on the eve of any battle, however bloody it was likely to prove.

Happily the night was already far advanced; the watchmen were proclaiming three o'clock when the prince cast himself upon his bed.

At dawn, the prince rose and went out; he was going to the admiral's.

Monsieur de Coligny was an early riser, and the prince found him already up.

At sight of Monsieur de Condé, the admiral was alarmed by his pallor and agitation.

"*Mon Dieu!*" cried he, "what is the matter, my dear Prince? what has happened?"

"Last night," responded the prince, "you found me hunting for a billet among the stones at the Louvre. Do you remember?"

"Yes, and you even had the luck to find it."

"Luck! I believe, indeed, that is very like the word I used."

"From a woman, was it not?"

"Yes."

"And the woman?"

"As you said, cousin, she is a monster of hypocrisy."

"Aha! Mademoiselle de Saint André; she, it seems, is the one in question."

"Here, read it. This is the note I had lost, the wind having snatched it from the handkerchief she had given me."

The admiral read.

Just as he was concluding Dandelot entered, on his way from the Louvre where he had spent the night.

Dandelot was of about the same age as the prince and strongly attached to him.

"Ah! my dear Dandelot," cried Condé, "I came to Monsieur l'Amiral's especially hoping to meet you here."

"Well, prince, here I am."

"I have a favor to ask of you."

"I am yours to command."

"Here is the point: for a certain reason which I am not at liberty to reveal, I must gain entrance to the Salle des Métamorphoses about midnight. Have you any reason for keeping me out?"

"Yes, monseigneur, to my great regret."

"Why?"

"Because His Majesty last evening received a threatening letter, in which some person declares that he has the means of gaining access to the king, and the king has given the strictest orders forbidding admission to the Louvre, after ten o'clock in the evening, to all gentlemen who are not in waiting."

"But, my dear Dandelot, such a measure cannot concern me. I have had the freedom of the Louvre at all hours, until now, and, unless the order has been directed against me personally —"

"Of course, monseigneur, the order cannot have been directed against you personally; but as it is directed against everybody, you find yourself included with the rest."

"Well, Dandelot, an exception must be made in my favor for reasons which are known to the admiral, reasons entirely foreign to what has happened. For a wholly personal motive, I must enter the Salle des Métamorphoses at midnight, and it is a matter of necessity, moreover, that my visit be kept secret from every one, even from His Majesty."

Dandelot hesitated, quite abashed at having to refuse the prince anything.

He turned to the admiral with a questioning look as to what he should do.

The admiral gave a nod equivalent to the words, "I will answer for him."

Dandelot yielded gracefully enough.

"Then, monseigneur," said he, "confess that a love affair counts for something in your expedition, so that, if I am reprimanded, it shall at least be in a cause that a gentleman may espouse."

"Oh! as regards that, I will conceal nothing from you, Dandelot. On my honor, a love affair is my sole reason for asking this favor of you."

"Very well, monseigneur," returned Dandelot, "the matter is settled, and at midnight I will conduct you to the Salle des Métamorphoses."

"Thanks, Dandelot!" exclaimed the prince holding out his hand; "and if ever you are in need in a matter of this kind or in any other, do not look, I beg, for any supporter other than myself."

And having shaken hands first with one and then with the other of the two brothers, Henri de Condé rapidly descended the stairs of the Hôtel de Coligny.

XII.

THE SALLE DES MÉTAMORPHOSES.

RECALL, dear readers, the feverish hours you have slowly counted, one after the other, while awaiting the moment of your first rendezvous; or, better still, call to mind the sharp pangs that have seized your heart while awaiting the fatal instant that must bring you proofs of unfaithfulness in the woman you love, and you will have some idea of the tedious and melancholy manner in which that day dragged itself along, seeming like an eternity to the poor Prince de Condé.

He therefore tried to put into practice that prescription of physicians and philosophers of all ages, — to fight weariness of mind with bodily fatigue. He ordered his fastest horse, mounted him, gave him the rein, or thought he did so, and at the end of fifteen minutes, horse and rider found themselves at Saint Cloud, to which place, however, Monsieur de Condé had entertained no intention of going when he started from his hôtel.

He wheeled his horse in the opposite direction. In an hour, he found himself on the same spot. The château of Saint Cloud was to him the magnetic mountain of the sailors in "The Thousand and One Nights," to which their vessels, vainly striving to get away, repeatedly returned.

The prescription of philosophers and physicians, infallible for others, produced no effect, it would seem, on the Prince de Condé. In the evening he found himself bruised in body, it is true, but as preoccupied in mind as he had been in the morning.

Just as the evening was coming on, he returned home, pale, dejected, worn out.

His valet brought him three letters, which he recognized as letters from the first ladies of the court, — he did not even open them. The same valet announced that a man had presented himself at the hôtel, six times during the day, saying that he had most important communications for the prince, but refusing in spite of all entreaties to give his name, and the prince paid no more attention to the news than if he had said: "Monseigneur, it is a fine day," or "It is raining, monseigneur."

He ascended to his bed-chamber and mechanically opened a book. But what book could dull the pain of the viper-fangs buried in his heart?

He cast himself on the bed; but, badly as he had slept on the preceding night, worn out as he was by the fatigue of the day's hard riding, he called in vain upon the friend named Sleep, that, like other friends, is at our side in our days of prosperity, but stands aloof in our greatest need, that is, in adversity.

At last, the expected hour arrived; the clock struck twelve; the watchman passed, crying, —

"Midnight!"

The prince donned his mantle, girded on his sword, secured his poniard, and went out.

It is unnecessary to ask what direction he took.

At ten minutes past midnight, he reached the gates of the Louvre.

The sentinel had his orders, the prince had only to give his name, — he entered.

A man was walking along the corridor upon which opened the door of the Salle des Métamorphoses.

Condé hesitated a moment. The man's back was turned; but at the noise made by the prince, he faced about, and our lover recognized Dandelot, who was waiting for him.

"Here I am," said he, "ready, according to my promise, to abet you against any lover or husband in your way."

Condé, with a feverish hand, took that of his friend.

"Thanks!" he answered; but I have nothing to fear that I am aware of. I am not the man that is loved."

"Then, why the devil do you come here?" asked Dandelot.

"To find out who is loved. — But, hush! some one is coming."

"Where? I see no one."

"But I heard steps."

"*Morbleu!*" said Dandelot, "what acute ears a jealous man has!"

Condé drew his friend into a recess, and from there they saw moving along like a shadow some one who, having reached the door of the Salle des Métamorphoses, paused an instant, listened, looked about, and, hearing nothing, seeing nothing, pushed open the door and entered.

"That is not Mademoiselle de Saint André!" murmured the prince; "this one is a head taller than she."

"Then you are waiting for Mademoiselle de Saint André?" demanded Dandelot.

"Waiting for, no; lying in wait for, yes."

"But why Mademoiselle de Saint André?"

"Hush!"

"However, —"

"Come, my dear Dandelot, to set your conscience at rest, take this billet; guard it as the apple of your eye;

read it at your leisure, and if by chance I do not discover this evening what I am in search of, try among all the handwritings that you know to find a mate for this one."

"Can I communicate the contents to my brother?"

"He has already seen it; do I have any secrets from him? Ah! I would give much to know who wrote that note."

"To-morrow, I will return it to you."

"No, I will come for it. Leave it with your brother; perhaps I shall have something to tell you myself — but, stay, there is the same person coming out."

The shadowy apparition that had entered the room was, in fact, leaving it, and was at this time advancing in the direction of the two friends. Fortunately, and probably intentionally, the corridor was badly lighted, and the recess in which they stood kept them out of the way and concealed them in its darkness.

But, by the quick and assured tread with which the apparition walked in spite of the obscurity, it was easily seen that the path pursued was a familiar one.

Indeed, just as it passed the two friends, Monsieur de Condé seized Dandelot by the hand.

"Lanoue!" he murmured.

Lanoue was one of Catherine de Médicis's maids. Of all her women, she was said to be the queen-mother's favorite and one in whom she placed the utmost confidence.

What had she come there for, if not in the interests of the rendezvous indicated in the billet?

Besides, she had not closed the door, but had left it ajar; consequently, she meant to return.

There was not a moment to lose; the next time the door would probably be closed.

All these reflections passed like a flash through the

prince's brain. Again he seized Dandelot's hand, and then he darted off toward the Salle des Métamorphoses.

Dandelot made a movement to detain him, but Condé was already far away.

As he had expected, the door yielded to a slight pressure and he found himself in the room.

This chamber, one of the finest in the Louvre before the *petite galerie* was commenced by Charles IX., borrowed its mythological name from the tapestries which covered its walls.

In fact, legends of Perseus and Andromeda, of Medusa, of the god Pan, of Apollo, and of Daphne formed the principal subjects of these pictures in which the needle more than once engaged in victorious contest with the brush.

But the tapestry that especially attracted the attention, says a historian, represented the story of Jupiter and Danaë.

The Danaë was fashioned by a hand so delicate and was so skillfully wrought, that one saw the rapture in her face on feeling, hearing, and beholding the golden shower.

She, as if queen of the other tapestries, was lighted up by a silver lamp, carved, not cast in a mold, we are assured, by Benvenuto Cellini himself. And, indeed, who but the Florentine sculptor would have delighted in converting a block of silver into a vase of flowers from which luminous blossoms themselves issued the flames?

The tapestry of Danaë covered the walls of an alcove, and the lamp, at the same time that it lighted up the immortal and pictured Danaë, was destined to shine on all the real and mortal Danaës who, in the bed which it overhung, waited for the golden shower of the Jupiters of that terrestrial Olympus called the Louvre.

The prince looked all around him, lifting curtains and portières to assure himself that he was really alone; then, after this careful inspection, he bestrode the balustrade, crouched on the floor, and slipped under the bed.

For those of our readers who are unfamiliar with the furniture of the sixteenth century, let us explain what the balustrade was.

The railing made by the small posts framing a gallery was called a balustrade, and this was placed around beds to shut off the alcoves, as one sees them to-day in church or chapel choirs, and in the bed-chamber of Louis XIV., at Versailles.

We had thought in digressing from Monsieur de Condé to the balustrade as abruptly as we have just done, that we should be acquitted by the reader from recording his thoughts, but on reflection, we prefer, instead of shirking the difficulty, to go bravely ahead.

And so, crouching on the floor, the prince, we said, slipped under the bed.

Eh! yes, without doubt, it was a ridiculous position, a position unworthy of a prince, especially when that prince is called the Prince de Condé. But what would you have! It is not my fault if the Prince de Condé, young, handsome, and in love, was so jealous that he placed himself in a ridiculous position; and as I find the fact chronicled of the prince in history, I may not be more fastidious than the historian.

And your observation, dear reader, is so true, so sensible, that barely was he under the bed, before the prince made the very reflections that you have just indulged in, and, reprimanding himself most severely, he asked himself what sort of a figure he would cut if discovered there under the bed, were it only by a valet. What a series of jests and pasquinades he would furnish to his enemies!

what disgrace he ran the risk of incurring in the eyes of his friends! He went even so far as to fancy that he saw the admiral's wrathful countenance emerge from the depths of the hangings; for when, child or man, we find ourselves in an equivocal situation, the person of whom we first think, and most dread to have appear and reproach us for our folly, is always the one whom we most love and respect, because that one is at the same time the one whom we most fear.

The prince, therefore, administered to himself — we beg the scrupulous reader to be persuaded of this — every rebuke that a man of his character and condition could formulate under such circumstances; but the result of all his self-controversy was that he advanced twenty centimetres, as they say to-day, further under the bed, and there established himself as comfortably as he was able.

Besides, he had indeed something else to think about.

He had to map out the line of conduct he was to pursue, when once the two lovers came in sight.

What seemed to him the simplest course was to rush forth abruptly, and without preamble to cross swords with his rival.

But this line of action, apparently so simple, seemed to him on second thought to involve in danger, not only his person, but his honor. This companion, whoever he might be, was, it is true, an accomplice of Mademoiselle de Saint André's coquetry, but a very innocent accomplice.

Therefore he rejected his first plan, and resolved to observe and to listen coolly to the events about to take place within sight and hearing of a rival.

He had just achieved this great act of renunciation, when the bell of his watch, which was very sonorous, suddenly awakened him to a danger which he had not foreseen. At that period, — the occupation of Charles V. at Saint Just proves it moreover, — at that period, watches and mantel-clocks were not only articles of luxury, but they were also capricious ones which worked much less in harmony with the mechanic's intention than in accordance with their own whim. The result was that Monsieur de Condé's watch, which was half an hour slower than the time of the Louvre, began to strike the hour of midnight.

Monsieur de Condé, as we have already seen, was the victim of an unusual degree of impetuosity. Fearing lest, having finished striking, the watch might take a fancy to begin again, and that the tell-tale bell would denounce him, he took the indiscreet jewel in the hollow of his left hand, placed over it the hilt of his dagger, firmly pressed the hilt against the dial-plate, and, under the pressure which broke its double case, the innocent watch yielded up its last sigh.

Man's injustice was satisfied.

This execution was barely ended when the door of the room again opened. Its noise drew the prince's attention, and Monsieur de Condé saw Mademoiselle de Saint André with watchful eyes and listening ears following on tip-toe the odious creature called Lanoue.

XIII.

THE TOILET OF VENUS.

When we say, following on tip-toe the odious creature called Lanoue, we err, not with regard to Lanoue, but to Mademoiselle de Saint André.

Once within the Salle des Métamorphoses, Mademoiselle de Saint André no longer followed Lanoue, she preceded her.

Lanoue remained behind to close the door.

The young girl stopped in front of a dressing-table, on which stood two candelabra, which required, in order to shine forth in all their glory, but the touch of fire that must give them life.

"Are you sure we have not been seen, my dear Lanoue?" she asked, in the sweet voice that, having thrilled the prince's heart with love, now thrilled it with anger.

"Oh! fear nothing, mademoiselle," answered the go-between. "On account of the threatening letter addressed to the king yesterday, the strictest orders have been issued, and, since ten o'clock this evening, the gates of the Louvre have been shut."

"Against every one?" demanded the girl.

"Against every one."

"Without exception?"

"Without exception."

"Even against the Prince de Condé?"

Lanoue smiled.

"Against the Prince de Condé especially, mademoiselle."

"Are you quite certain of it, Lanoue?"

"Positive, mademoiselle."

"Ah! because — "

The young girl stopped.

"Why are you afraid of monseigneur?"

"For many reasons, Lanoue."

"For many reasons?"

"Yes, and for one above all others."

"And that is — ?"

"Lest he should follow me here."

"Here?"

"Yes."

"Into the Salle des Métamorphoses?"

"Yes."

"But how should he know that mademoiselle is here?"

"He knows it, Lanoue."

The prince, as may be expected, listened with both ears.

"Who can have told him?"

"I, myself."

"You?"

"Yes, fool that I was."

"Oh! *mon Dieu!*"

"Imagine that last night, just as he was leaving me. I was so imprudent as to follow up a jest by tossing him my handkerchief; in that handkerchief was the little note you had just brought me."

"But the note was not signed."

"No, fortunately."

"It is very fortunate, indeed, *Jesu Maria!*"

The go-between crossed herself devoutly.

"And," pursued she, "did you not ask for your handkerchief again?"

"Yes, indeed; Mézières went to his house for me six times during the day. The prince had gone out in the morning, and at nine in the evening he had not returned."

"Aha!" murmured the prince, "it was the fisherman page who came to speak to me, and so strongly insisted on seeing me."

"Have you confidence in the youth, mademoiselle?"

"He is passionately devoted to me."

"Pages are very indiscreet; there is a proverb about them to that effect."

"Mézières is not my page; he is my slave," said the young girl, in the accents of a queen. "Ah! Lanoue, that detestable Monsieur de Condé! worse will never happen to him than I wish."

"Thanks! most beautiful of beauties," murmured the prince. "I will remember your kindly sentiments with regard to me."

"Well, mademoiselle," returned Lanoue, "you can be at ease for to-night. I know the captain of the Scotch guard, and I will commend monseigneur to him."

"In whose behalf?"

"My own! Be at ease, that will suffice."

"Aha! Lanoue!"

"Why not, mademoiselle! while arranging the affairs of others, there is no harm in arranging one's own."

"Thanks, Lanoue; for that idea alone spoiled the pleasure I had promised myself to enjoy to-night."

Lanoue prepared to depart.

"Oh! Lanoue!" exclaimed Mademoiselle de Saint André, "before going, light these candles, I beg of you.

I cannot remain in this dim light. All these great half-naked figures frighten me; they seem to be leaving their tapestry and coming toward me."

"Ah! should they come," said Lanoue, lighting a taper at the fire burning in the fireplace, "be reassured. They will come to adore you as the goddess Venus."

She lighted the five branches of the candelabra, leaving the beautiful girl, with a nimbus of flame, revealed to the prince's gaze.

She was adorable, reflected thus in the mirror of the dressing-table, robed in a transparent gauze, through which shone the pink-tinted flesh.

She had in her hand a spray of myrtle-bloom; she arranged it in her hair like a crown.

A priestess of Venus, she had decked herself with the sacred flower.

Alone, then, or, at least, believing herself to be alone in the room, the girl gazed coquettishly and tenderly at her reflection in the glass, while the pink finger-tips arched the black, velvety eyebrows, and the palm of her hand patted her golden sheaf of hair.

Thus adorned, and standing negligently before the mirror, in an attitude that set off her slender and supple figure, a fair creature, fresh as the water from a spring, rosy as a morning cloud, serene as maidenhood, as full of life and as tender as the earliest shoots of springtime, that, in their eagerness for life, pierce the late snows, she resembled Venus Cytheræa, as Lanoue had said, — but Venus, in her fourteenth year, on the morning when, standing on the shore, ready to ascend to the celestial court, she regarded herself a last time in the mirroring sea, still cool from its recent touch.

Having arched her brows, smoothed her hair, restored to her face by a moment's rest the rose tints which an anxious and hurried walk had too warmly flushed, the young girl's eyes wandered from the image of her face, reflected by the mirror, to her person; they descended to her neck, to her shoulders, and seemed to seek her breast, lost in the billows of fluffy lace, as light as the vaporous clouds that the first puff of wind drives from the sky.

She was so beautiful thus, with limpid eyes, blushing cheeks, half-open mouth, and teeth shining like twin rows of pearls in a coral casket, — she was so complete an image of voluptuousness, that the prince, forgetful of her coquetry, his own hatred, his threats, was, at the moment, on the point of leaving his retreat, and throwing himself at her feet, crying, —

"For the love of Heaven! girl, love me for an hour, and take my life in return for an hour of love!"

Fortunately, or unfortunately for him, — we have not weighed the advantages and disadvantages that he must have experienced had he followed up that sudden impulse, — the girl turned toward the door, murmuring, in broken accents, —

"Ah! heart's beloved, are you not coming?"

At that exclamation all the prince's wrath returned, and Mademoiselle de Saint André again seemed to him the most hateful creature on earth.

She went to the nearest window, drew aside the thick curtains, and tried to open the heavy casement; but her delicate, tapering fingers lacking the strength for such a task, she contented herself with leaning her head against the thick glass.

The sensation of coolness communicated to her forehead made her open her eyes, which were drooping in languor. For an instant they remained vague and sightless; then gradually they began to distinguish objects, and finally became fixed upon a man enveloped in a cloak, and standing motionless, at the distance of a stone's throw from the Louvre.

The sight of that man caused Mademoiselle de Saint André to smile, and, without doubt, had the prince seen the smile, he would have guessed the wicked thought that prompted it.

Besides, had he been near enough to see the smile, he would have been near enough, also, to hear the words that came in triumphant accents from the girl's lips, —

"It is he!"

Then, in indescribably sarcastic tones, she added, —

"Proceed with your walk, dear Monsieur de Condé. I wish you great joy of your promenade."

Evidently Mademoiselle de Saint André took the man in the cloak for the Prince de Condé.

And the mistake was quite natural.

Mademoiselle de Saint André knew perfectly well of the visits which the prince had paid, incognito, under her window every evening for the last three months, but Mademoiselle de Saint André had taken great care not to speak of the matter to the prince; for, to say that she had seen him was to confess that for the last three months she had secretly entertained a thought which, on the contrary, she had disclaimed openly.

Mademoiselle de Saint André therefore believed it was the prince whom she saw at the water's edge.

Now, the sight of the Prince de Condé walking on the bank of the river, when she had been trembling in dread of meeting him in the Louvre, was the most reassuring sight that the moon, that pale and melancholy friend of lovers, could reveal to her.

However, to our readers, who know perfectly well that the prince, not being endowed with the gift of ubiquity, could not be within and without the palace at the same time, under the bed and on the bank of the river, let us hasten to declare who this man was, wrapped in his mantle, and taken by Mademoiselle de Saint André for the prince, whom she supposed to be shivering on the bank.

This man was our Huguenot of the day before, — our Scotchman, Robert Stuart, — who, instead of receiving the response to his letter that he expected, had learned that messieurs, the councillors of parliament, had so arranged everything during the day, that the execution of Anne Dubourg would take place on the next day, or the day following. It was Robert Stuart, who had resolved to risk a second attempt.

It was in virtue of this resolution that, just as that wicked smile overspread the maiden's lips, she saw the man on the bank draw his arm from under his cloak, make a gesture, which she took for a threatening one, and set off at full speed.

At the same time she heard a crash like that of the evening before, that is, of a shattered window-pane.

"Ah!" she cried, "it was not he."

And the roses of her smiling lips immediately vanished under the tints of the violets.

Oh! this time she really trembled, no longer with delight but with terror; and, letting the window-curtain fall, she returned, tottering and pale, and leaned upon the back of the sofa, on which, a few moments before, she lay so languidly extended.

As on the night before, a pane had been broken in one of the Maréchal de Saint André's windows.

But this time it was a window on the side at right angles to the Seine; yet that window, likewise, belonged to her father's apartment.

If, as on the night before, the maréchal, whether still sitting up or already gone to bed, and awakened with a start, should go and knock at his daughter's door and receive no response, what would happen?

There she stood, fearing, trembling, half-fainting, to the great amazement of the prince, who, without being able to divine its cause, had perceived the sudden change wrought on the face of the girl, who was in that stage of prostration in which any certainty is preferable to uncertainty. Then the door opened, and Lanoue hurriedly entered.

Her countenance was almost as disconcerted as the girl's.

"Oh! Lanoue," said the latter, "do you know what has just happened?"

"No, mademoiselle," replied the maid; "but it must be something very dreadful, for you are as pale as a corpse."

"Very dreadful, indeed, and you must take me at once to my father's apartment."

"And why, mademoiselle?"

"Do you not know what happened yesterday at midnight?"

"Does mademoiselle refer to the stone that was tied in a paper, which threatened the king?"

"Yes. Well, the same thing has just happened again, Lanoue. A man, the same, doubtless, that I took for the Prince de Condé, came, as he did last night, and threw a stone, breaking one of the maréchal's windows."

"And you are afraid?"

"I am afraid, — pray understand, Lanoue, — I am afraid that my father will go and knock at my door, and that, receiving no answer, he may, from suspicion or uneasiness, open it, and find the room empty."

"Oh! if that is your only fear, mademoiselle," said Lanoue, "be reassured."

"Why?"

"Your father is with Queen Catherine."

"With the queen, at one o'clock in the morning?"

"Ah! mademoiselle, a serious accident has happened."

"What is it?"

"Their Majesties were out hunting to-day."

"Well?"

"Well, mademoiselle, the horse of the little queen," — thus was Marie Stuart spoken of, — "the horse of the little queen stumbled, Her Majesty fell, and, as she has been with child for three months, it is feared that she is injured."

"Ah! *bon Dieu!*"

"And so the entire court is astir."

"I should think so, indeed."

"And all the maids of honor are in the antechamber or with the queen-mother."

"And you did not come to tell me, Lanoue?"

"I learned the news this very moment, mademoiselle, and took time only to run and assure myself of its truth."

"Then you have seen him?"

"Whom?"

"Him!"

"Certainly."

"Well?"

"Well, mademoiselle, the affair is postponed; you can well understand that he could not be absent at such a moment."

"And postponed to what time?"

"Till to-morrow."

"Where?"

"Here."

"At the same hour?"

"At the same hour."

"Then, come away quickly, Lanoue."

"Ready, mademoiselle; only let me extinguish the candles."

"Really," cried the young girl, "one would think some evil genius at work against us."

"Nonsense!" said Lanoue, blowing out the last candle; "quite the contrary."

"How quite the contrary?" demanded Mademoiselle de Saint André from the corridor.

"Certainly; this accident gives you the greater freedom."

And she followed the footsteps of Mademoiselle de Saint André, — footsteps whose echo was very soon lost in the depths of the corridor, as was that of her companion's.

"To-morrow, then!" declared the prince, in turn, as he emerged from his retreat, and cleared the balustrade, quite as ignorant of his rival's name as he had been the day before. "To-morrow, the day after to-morrow, every day, if needs be; but, by the soul of my father! I will follow to the end."

And he, too, left the Salle des Métamorphoses, proceeded down the corridor, in the direction opposite to that taken by Mademoiselle de Saint André and Lanoue, crossed the court, and gained the street, without any one's dreaming, amid the confusion into which the Louvre had been thrown by the two incidents mentioned by us above, of asking whither he went or whence he came.

XIV.

TWO SCOTCHMEN.

ROBERT STUART, whom Mademoiselle de Saint André had seen from the window of the Salle des Métamorphoses, so quickly and so strangely returned to the darkness, — Robert Stuart, whom the girl had so maliciously apostrophized as the Prince de Condé, after casting his second stone, and by that means causing a second letter to reach the king, had, as we have said, taken to flight, and disappeared.

As far as the Châtelet, he had hastened his steps; but having reached that point, he felt himself beyond pursuit, and, apart from encountering two or three cutthroats on the bridge, who kept their distance at sight of the sword tapping his heels, and the pistol suspended from his belt, he had returned quietly enough to the quarters of his friend and compatriot, Patrick.

Once there, he had gone to bed with an appearance of composure that he owed to self-control; but his self-control, great as it was, had no power over sleep. Consequently, for three or four hours he turned and tossed in his bed, or, rather, in his compatriot's bed, without securing the repose that had deserted him for three nights.

Only at daybreak did the mind, vanquished by fatigue, seem to forsake the body and allow Sleep to come and take its place for a brief space of time. And then the body so completely succumbed to Sleep, the brother of Death, that any one might have thought him a corpse, so profound was his lethargy.

Until evening, moreover, of the preceding day, faithful to his word, he had waited for his friend Patrick; but the archer, detained at the Louvre by his captain, who had been ordered not to allow a single man to leave the palace, — the reason of this order is known, — the archer, we say, had not been able to profit by Robert Stuart's clothes.

Having no news of his friend by seven o'clock in the evening, Robert Stuart had proceeded to the Louvre, and there he had learned of the strict orders that had been issued, and the cause of them.

After that, he had wandered about the streets of Paris, where he had heard a hundred different versions — not one being correct — of the assassination of President Minard, whose death had rendered him more illustrious than any act of his life.

Taking pity on the ignorance of some and the curiosity of others, Robert Stuart had in turn related — on hearsay, but from a reliable source he assured them — the story of that death in all its veracious details, and with the actual circumstances attending it; but it is unnecessary to add that his hearers would not consent to believe a single word of his narration.

We have no reason to assign for their incredulity save that this account was the only truthful one.

He had, moreover, learned of the promptness and severity which the parliament was prepared to exercise with regard to the judgment rendered in the case of Councillor Dubourg, whose execution, he was assured, would take place at the Grève within forty-eight hours.

Then Robert Stuart had seen no other remedy for

this obstinacy on the part of the judges than to renew still more pointedly his appeal to the king.

At the end of his watch, his friend Patrick, having at last been released from the Louvre, had come with all the speed of his legs, had climbed his ladder, as he called it, had invaded the room, shouting, —

"Fire!"

He had decided that this was the only way to awaken Robert Stuart, since the noise he had made in shutting the door, and moving the chairs, and shifting the table were insufficient to rouse him from his slumber.

The yell given by Patrick, much more than the sense of his words, at last awakened Robert; the sound reached him, but not the idea. His first thought was that men were coming to arrest him, and he reached for his sword, which stood between his bedside and the wall, and drew it half out of its sheath.

"Eh! there, there!" cried Patrick, laughing; "you seem to wake in a disputatious mood. Come, easy now! and wake up, it is time."

"Ah! it is you," said Stuart.

"Of course it is I. I will lend you my room again, depend upon it, that you may kill me when I return!"

"Come! I was asleep."

"So I see, and that is what amazes me; you were asleep —?"

Patrick went to the window and drew the curtains.

Broad daylight flooded the room.

"There," said he, "look."

"What time is it?" asked Stuart.

"Past ten o'clock by all the steeples of Paris," said the archer.

"I waited for you all day yesterday, and even all night I may say."

The archer shrugged his shoulders.

"How can I help that?" said he. "A soldier is only a soldier, if he is a Scotch bowman. We were stationed at the Louvre all day and all night; but, to-day, as you see, I am at liberty."

"Which means that you come to reclaim your room."

"No, to claim your clothes."

"Ah! true; I had forgotten Madame la Conseillère."

"Happily she has not forgotten me, as can be proved by this game-pie standing here on the table and waiting the good pleasure of our appetites. Is yours on hand? As to mine, it was at its post two hours ago, answering, — present!"

"But to come back to my clothes — "

"All right! Well, you understand that my conseillère does not come all at once to my fourth story. No, this pie is only a messenger; it was the bearer of a letter saying that I shall be expected from noon, the hour when our councillor sets sail for the Parliament, until four o'clock, when he makes the conjugal port again. At five minutes past twelve I shall be with her, and I will reward her devotion by presenting myself in a costume that cannot compromise her, — if, that is, you are still in the same mind with regard to your friend."

"My clothes are at your disposal, my dear Patrick," said Robert; "laid out on the chair, as you see, and waiting only for an owner. Give me yours in exchange, and do what you like with those."

"All in good time; but, let us first discuss this pie. It is not necessary for you to rise in order to engage in the discussion; I will carry the table over to the side of your bed. There! does that suit?"

"Wonderfully, my dear Patrick."

"Now," — Patrick drew his poniard and presented it, handle first, to his friend, — "now, while I go to look for something to wash him down, disembowel that fellow, and tell me whether Madame la Conseillère is a woman of taste."

Robert obeyed the command as promptly as the Scotch archer himself could have obeyed one from his captain; and when Patrick returned to the table, caressing, with both hands, the plump belly of a jug full of wine, he found the dome of the gastronomical edifice completely carried away.

"Ah! by Saint Dunstan!" said he, "a hare lodged in a nest of six partridges! What a fine country, this, where feathers and fur live in such sweet harmony! The 'Land of Cocagne,' does not Messire Rabelais call it? Robert, my friend, follow my example: make love to a lawyer's dame, my dear fellow, instead of a soldier's, and we shall not need to see seven fat kine in a dream, as Pharaoh did, in order to foretell a bounteous harvest of the good things of heaven and earth. Let us profit by them, my dear Stuart, or we shall prove unworthy of possessing them."

And, adding example to precept, the archer took his place at the table, and transferred to his plate a first ration of the pie that did credit to what he called the advance-guard of his appetite.

Robert ate also. At twenty-four a man always eats, whatever may be the mind's preoccupation.

He ate, therefore, more silently, more abstractedly, indeed, than his friend, — but he ate.

Besides, the thought of visiting Madame la Conseillère rendered Patrick gay enough and talkative enough for two.

Half-past eleven sounded.

Patrick rose from the table in all haste, crunched in his teeth, as white as those of his Highland wolf, a last morsel of the meat-pie's golden crust, drank a last glass of wine, and began to put on the clothes of his compatriot.

Dressed thus, he presented the odd and stiff appearance the soldiers of our day also have when they exchange their uniforms for the citizen's dress.

A soldier's face and bearing, indeed, always contract something from his uniform, which betrays him wherever he may go, and in whatever costume he may appear.

The archer, thus arrayed, was nevertheless a handsome cavalier, with blue eyes, red hair, and fresh, lively color.

As he regarded himself in the fragment of mirror, he seemed to be saying, —

"If Madame la Conseillère is not pleased, by my faith, she is very hard to suit!"

However, having some misgivings, perhaps, or wishing, possibly, to hear Robert second his own opinion, he turned to his companion and demanded, —

"How do I look, comrade?"

"Why, the very perfection of face and figure; and I have no doubt that you will make a profound impression on Madame la Conseillère."

It was exactly what Patrick wished, and he was served to his heart's desire.

He smiled, settled his neck, and, holding out his hand to Robert, said, —

"Well, I must hasten to reassure her, for she must be worried to death, poor woman! she has not seen me nor had news of me for two days!"

He moved toward the door; but, arresting himself, he added. —

"By the way, I need not tell you that my uniform does not condemn you to stay within doors. You are not confined to my fourth floor, as I was yesterday at the Louvre. You can circulate freely throughout the city in the broad sunshine, if there is any, or in the shade if there is not, and, provided that you get into no serious quarrel while in my uniform, — and I caution you against this for two reasons: first, because you would be arrested, conducted to the Châtelet, and recognized; secondly, because I, your innocent friend, should be punished for having abandoned my uniform, — provided, I repeat, that you get into no serious quarrel while in my old clothes, you are as free as a house-sparrow."

"You have nothing to fear on that score, Patrick," answered the Scotchman; "I am not naturally of a very quarrelsome disposition."

"Ah! ah!" exclaimed the archer, shaking his head, "I would not be too sure of it. You are a Scotchman, or as good as one, and, like every man reared on the other side of the Tweed, you must have moods when it is not safe to look black at you. Besides, you understand, I am giving you advice, that is all. I say, pick no quarrels; but, if others pick one with you, by my patron saint, don't shirk it! The deuce! the honor of the uniform is then at stake, and if you cannot kill them fast enough, you have there, mark it well, a dirk and a claymore that will leap from the sheath of themselves."

"Rest easy, Patrick; you will find me here as you have left me."

"Why, no, no! I do not wish you to be bored," insisted the obstinate Highlander. "You will die of inanition in this room, from which the view is not disagreeable in the evening, because you do not see it, but where nothing is to be seen in the daytime but roofs and steeples, and those only when the smoke and fog do not interfere."

"Still, it is as good as our own blessed country, where it always rains," remarked Robert.

"Nonsense!" said Patrick, "and when does it snow, then?"

And, satisfied with having set the Scotchman right as to his meteorology, Patrick at last decided to depart; but on the landing he stopped, and, opening the door again, he said, —

"That was all a joke; go, come, run, dispute, quarrel, fight; if only you return with no holes in your skin, and, consequently, in my doublet, all will be well. But, my dear friend, I have one serious injunction to impress on you, only one, but, ponder it well."

"What is it?"

"My friend, in view of the gravity of the times in which we live, and the threats that the infamous Baptists take the liberty of addressing to the king, I am obliged to be at the Louvre exactly at eight o'clock; roll-call this evening comes an hour earlier."

"You will find me here on your return."

"Then, God bless you!"

"And joy go with you!"

"Useless," said the archer, moving off with the air of a conquering lover; "it awaits me."

And this time he departed, as gay and vanquishing as the handsomest courtier, humming one of his native airs that must have dated back to the days of Robert Bruce.

The poor soldier was certainly much happier at that moment than the cousin of the French king, the brother of the King of Navarre, the young and handsome Louis de Condé.

We shall know in a moment, however, what the

prince was doing and saying just at this time; but we are obliged to remain a little longer in the company of Master Robert Stuart.

The latter had, as he had assured his friend, two serious subjects for reflection, so that he did not suffer from ennui until four o'clock in the afternoon; he therefore kept his word by waiting for him.

From four o'clock to five he still waited, but with greater impatience.

It was the hour at which he had intended to wait at the door of parliament to gain fresh news, not of the sentencing of Councillor Dubourg, but of the decision reached with regard to his execution.

At half-past five he could endure it no longer, and went out, in turn, leaving a note, however, for his compatriot, telling him not to be uneasy, and that at seven in the evening, punctually, his uniform should be returned.

Night was beginning to fall; Robert ran all the way to the entrance of the Palais.

There was an immense gathering in the square; parliament was still sitting.

This explained the absence of his friend Patrick; but it did not tell him what was the subject of discussion within.

Not until six o'clock did the councillors disperse.

The news that reached Robert as to the result of the session was inauspicious.

The mode of punishment was determined, — the councillor must die at the stake.

However, it was not known whether the execution would take place on the next day, the day after, or the day following.

Perhaps there would even be a delay of several days,

so that the poor queen, Marie Stuart, who had been injured the day before, could be present.

But this would happen only in case the injury were slight enough to delay the execution not more than a week.

Robert Stuart left the Place du Palais, intending to return to the Rue du Battoir-Saint-André.

However, in the distance he saw a Scotch bowman, who, in advance of the time for roll-call, was returning to the Louvre.

Thereupon, the idea occurred to him to enter the Louvre in his friend's costume, and there, from a reliable source, gain news of the young queen, whose health was to have such a terrible influence over the life of the condemned.

He had almost two hours before him; he turned in the direction of the Louvre.

He met with no difficulty, at either the first or the second entrance. He found himself, therefore, in the court.

He was barely within, when a messenger from the parliament was announced.

The messenger from the parliament desired, in the name of the illustrious body which he represented, to speak with the king.

Dandelot was summoned.

Dandelot went to receive the king's commands.

Ten minutes later he returned, himself, charged to bring in the councillor.

Robert well knew that after the councillor had gone, with a little patience and skill he could learn what he desired to know. He therefore waited.

The councillor remained for nearly an hour with the king.

Robert had already waited so long that he was resolved to wait till the end.

Finally, the councillor departed.

Dandelot, who was accompanying him, looked very sad, more than sad, — gloomy.

In a low voice he spoke a few words in the ear of the captain of the Scotch guard, and retired.

The words evidently had some connection with the councillor's embassy.

"Messieurs," said the captain of the Scotch guard to his men, "you are notified that on the day after to-morrow you are detailed for special duty at the Grève, on the execution of Councillor Anne Dubourg."

Robert Stuart had learned what he wished to know. He therefore took a few rapid strides toward the door, but he undoubtedly thought better of it, for he stopped suddenly, and, after some moments of profound meditation, he turned, and became lost among his companions, — an easy matter, considering the number of men and the darkness of the night.

XV.

WHAT MAY HAPPEN UNDER A BED.

When entering the Salle des Métamorphoses, the Prince de Condé had arranged to meet Dandelot at the house of his brother, the admiral, at noon of the next day.

The prince was so impatient to relate the events of the night to Coligny, and especially to Dandelot, younger and less serious than his brother, that he reached the Rue Béthisy before the stated hour.

Dandelot, for his part, had preceded the prince. Since one o'clock, he had been with Coligny, and the love affair of Mademoiselle de Saint André had been more seriously considered by these two grave minds than it had been by the prince and Dandelot.

The alliance of the Maréchal de Saint André with the Guises was not only an alliance of family with family, but it was, moreover, a religious and political league formed against the Calvinist party; and the way in which they were proceeding with regard to the councillor, Anne Dubourg, showed that they were not disposed to deal leniently with reformers.

The two brothers had grown weary over Mademoiselle de Saint André's note. They had racked their memories in vain, but neither had recognized the handwriting, and they had sent it to Madame l'Amirale, shut up in her room, where she was performing her devotions, to see if her memory was more reliable than her husband's and her brother-in-law's.

Under any other circumstances, Dandelot, and more especially Coligny, would have opposed their cousin, the Prince de Condé, in his pursuit of this venturesome folly; but the most upright hearts make certain capitulations of conscience when they think themselves obliged to yield to stress of circumstances.

Now, it was very important to the Calvinist party that Monsieur de Joinville should not espouse Mademoiselle de Saint André; and, unless Mademoiselle de Saint André's rendezvous was with Monsieur le Prince de Joinville, which was improbable, it was more than certain that Monsieur de Condé, granting that he made a discovery, would create so great a stir about it that the scandal would reach the ears of the Guises, and a rupture ensue.

More than this, according to all probability, from such indiscretion on the part of the prince, some humiliation must arise for him; then, wavering between the Catholic and the Calvinist faiths, the prince, drawn on by Coligny and Dandelot, would perhaps decide in favor of Protestantism.

Often a man is worth more to a party than a victory.

Now, he was not only a man, but a victorious one, was this handsome, brave young prince.

Therefore they awaited him at the Hôtel Coligny with an impatience that he himself was far from suspecting.

He arrived, as we have said, before the appointed hour, and, on the invitation of the two brothers to make a general confession, he began a recital, in which, let us say in honor of his veracity, he concealed from his hearers nothing of what had happened to him.

He related all he had seen and heard, without omitting a single detail, even confessing from what vantage-ground he had seen and heard what he was relating.

Like a man of spirit, the prince had begun by laughing at himself, in order to forestall the others, since they, finding it already done, would be the less likely to laugh at his expense.

"And now," demanded the admiral, when the prince had concluded his recital, "what do you intend to do?"

"*Pardieu!*" said Condé, "a very simple thing, in which I rely on you more than ever, my dear Dandelot, — to renew my expedition."

The two brothers glanced at each other.

The prince was concurring in their plans; however, Coligny believed himself in honor bound to raise a few objections.

But at the first word he ventured toward dissuading the prince, the latter placed his hand on his friend's arm, saying, —

"My dear admiral, if you are not of my mind on this subject, let us talk of something else, as my determination is fixed, and it would cost me too great an effort to engage in a determined struggle against the man I love more and respect more than any one else in the world, that is, against you."

The admiral bowed his head like a man who is resigned to what he feels himself powerless to combat; but, at the bottom of his heart, he was enchanted with his cousin's obstinacy.

It was then agreed that on this night, as on the preceding one, Dandelot should facilitate the prince's entrance to the Salle des Métamorphoses.

Their rendezvous was set for a quarter of an hour before midnight, in the same corridor as on the preceding night.

The pass-word was confided to the prince, that he

might enter without difficulty. He then claimed his note.

Thereupon, the admiral confessed to the prince that, neither he nor his brother having been able to recognize the handwriting, he had sent the billet to Madame l'Amirale, upon whom he did not dare intrude at that hour, as she was at her devotions.

Dandelot took it upon himself to demand it of his sister-in-law on that same evening, at Queen Catherine's levee, and the admiral charged himself with advising his wife that she was to take the billet with her to the Louvre.

These several points settled upon, Dandelot and the prince took leave of the admiral, Dandelot to return to his post, the prince to return home.

The remainder of the day passed as slowly and intolerably to the latter as had the previous day.

At last the hours wore away, one after the other, and half-past eleven came in its turn.

We know the evening's topic of conversation from having followed the course of Robert Stuart three hours before the prince's entrance to the palace.

Nothing was talked of but the execution of Councillor Dubourg, which the king had set for the day following the morrow.

The prince found Dandelot greatly depressed; but, as this execution was, on the whole, indisputable evidence of the power which Monsieur de Guise, the avowed persecutor of Anne Dubourg, enjoyed with the king, Dandelot was only the more desirous of witnessing the accomplishment of the humiliation with which Monsieur de Joinville was threatened, and of raising, at least, the laugh of ridicule in the very midst of his enemies' bloody triumph.

As on the preceding night, the corridor was plunged in gloom; as before, the Salle des Métamorphoses was lighted only by the silver lamp; and again the candelabra awaited but a command to illuminate afresh the fascinating beauty upon which they had shone the night before.

But this time the balustrade of the alcove was open. That was a bit of confirmatory evidence that the rendezvous had not been countermanded.

And, believing that he heard footsteps in the corridor, the prince quickly dived under the bed, without taking the trouble to engage in the same reflections on that evening as on the night before, — which goes to prove that one gets accustomed to everything, even to hiding under beds.

The prince was not deceived. He had, indeed, heard footsteps in the corridor, and the footsteps were certainly in quest of the Salle des Métamorphoses; for they paused at the entrance, and the prince heard a slight creaking of the door as it turned on its hinges.

"Excellent!" he thought. "Our lovers are more eager than yesterday, — which is quite simple: they have not seen each other for twenty-four hours."

The steps advanced lightly, as of a person who enters by stealth.

The prince craned his neck, and saw the two bare legs of an archer of the Scotch guard.

"Oh! oh!" thought the prince; "what does this mean?"

And, by craning his neck a little further, above the legs he saw the body.

He had made no mistake, for it was really an archer of the Scotch guard who had just entered.

But the new-comer seemed quite as much at a loss as

he himself had been on the night before. As the prince had done, he lifted curtains and table-covers; but, in all probability, none of these affording him a refuge sufficiently safe, he approached the bed, and, like the prince, considering the hiding-place a good one, he crept in under the side opposite to that under which Monsieur de Condé himself had just crept.

However, before the Scotchman had found time to make himself at home under the bed, he felt the point of a dagger pressed against his heart, while a low voice said in his ear, —

"I do not know who you are, nor what purpose brings you here, but, not a word, not a move, or you are a dead man!"

"I do not know who you are, nor what purpose brings you here," retorted the new-comer in the same tone; "but I accept conditions from no man. Therefore thrust in your dagger, if it suits you; it is in the right place. I am not afraid to die."

"Ah! ah!" exclaimed the prince, "you appear to be a brave man, and brave men are always welcome with me. I am the Prince de Condé, monsieur, and I restore my weapon to its sheath. I hope you will return my confidence and tell me who you are."

"I am a Scotchman, monseigneur; my name is Robert Stuart."

"The name is unknown to me, monsieur."

The Scotchman was silent.

"Will you be kind enough," pursued the prince, "to tell me your purpose in coming to this room, and why you are hiding under the bed?"

"You have set the example of frankness, monseigneur; would it not be worthy of you to continue and tell me why you are here yourself?"

"Faith, monsieur, it is a simple matter," responded the prince, as he settled himself in a more comfortable position than he had at first assumed. "I am in love with Mademoiselle de Saint André."

"The maréchal's daughter?" asked the Scot.

"Quite right, monsieur, with her. Now, having indirectly learned that she had a rendezvous here this evening with a lover, I was seized with a culpable curiosity to learn who the happy mortal may be that enjoys the good graces of the estimable demoiselle, and I have poked myself under this bed, where I am very uncomfortable, I confess. Your turn, monsieur."

"Monseigneur, it shall not be said that a stranger has less confidence in a prince than the prince in a stranger. I am the man who, last night and the night before, wrote to the king."

"Ah! *morbleu!* and posted your letters through the window-panes of the Maréchal de Saint André's apartment?"

"The very man."

"Your pardon!" said the prince; "but you then — "

"Well, monseigneur?"

"If I rightly recall, in that letter, in the first one at least, you threatened the king?"

"Yes, monseigneur, if he refused to set Councillor Dubourg at liberty."

"And, to render your threat the more alarming, you added that it was you who had killed President Minard," continued the prince, disconcerted enough at finding himself cheek by jowl with a man who had written such a letter.

"I did, indeed, monseigneur, kill President Minard," replied the Scotchman, without the other's remarking the least change in his tone.

"Perhaps you would dare do violence to the king."

"I am here for that purpose."

"For that purpose?" cried the prince, forgetting where he was, and the danger of being overheard.

"Yes, monseigneur; but I would remind you that Your Highness speaks rather loud, and that our hazardous position demands that we speak low."

"You are right," returned the prince.

"Yes, *morbleu!* monsieur, let us speak low; for we are talking of things that sound ill in a palace like the Louvre."

And, in fact, lowering his voice, he continued, —

"*Peste!* it is very fortunate for His Majesty that I chance to be here, although I came on other business."

"Then you purpose interfering with my plan?"

"I should think so! A pretty business, that you should attack a king to prevent a councillor's being burned!"

"This councillor is the most upright man on earth."

"It does not signify!"

"This councillor, monseigneur, is my father!"

"Ah! that is another thing. Well, then, it is very fortunate, not only for the king, but for yourself, that we have met."

"Why?."

"You shall see — Pardon, but did I not hear —? No, I mistake. — Do you ask why our meeting is fortunate?"

"Yes."

"I will tell you. First, however, you must swear, on your honor, to make no attempt against the king."

"Never!"

"But, if I pledge you my word as a prince to obtain the councillor's pardon myself?"

"If you pledge your word, monseigneur?"

"Yes."

"Then I say, with you, that is another thing."

"Well, on my word as a gentleman, I will do my best to save Monsieur Dubourg."

"Then, on the word of Robert Stuart, monseigneur, if the king grants you that pardon, the king shall be sacred to me."

"Two men of honor need but to pledge their word. We have pledged ours, monsieur; let us talk of something else."

"I think, monseigneur, it would be better for us not to talk at all."

"Did you hear a noise?"

"No; but at any moment —"

"Nonsense! they will leave us time enough for you to tell me how you got here."

"That is very simple, monseigneur. I entered the Louvre by the aid of this disguise."

"You are not an archer, then?"

"No, I have taken the uniform of one of my friends."

"And you are doing that friend a pretty turn."

"I should have told you that the uniform was taken without his knowledge."

"And what if you had been killed without having had time to make such a statement?"

"A paper would have been found in my pocket, declaring him innocent."

"Come, I see that you are a methodical man; but all that does not tell me how you have been able to penetrate this far, nor how you came to poke yourself under a bed in this room, where His Majesty does not set foot perhaps four times a year."

"Because His Majesty comes here to-night, monseigneur."

"You are certain of that?"

"Yes, monseigneur."

"And how did you learn it? Come! speak."

"A moment ago I was in a corridor, — "

"Which one?"

"I do not know. I am in the Louvre for the first time."

"Well, but you are not doing badly for the first time! And so you were in a corridor?"

"Hidden behind the portière of an unlighted room, when I heard whispering two steps away. I listened, and overheard this conversation carried on by two women: — "

"'It is still for to-night, is it not?'

"'Yes.'

"'In the Salle des Métamorphoses?'

"'Yes.'

"'At one o'clock precisely the king will be there. I will leave the key.'"

"Did you hear that?" cried the prince, with a formidable outburst, again forgetting his surroundings.

"Yes, monseigneur," replied the Scotchman; "otherwise, what occasion have I to be in this room?"

"True," remarked the prince.

And he muttered under his breath, —

"Ah! it was the king!"

"What did you say, monseigneur?" inquired the archer, thinking himself addressed.

"I ask, monsieur, how you managed to find this room, as you declared yourself to be unacquainted with the Louvre.

"Oh! very easily, monseigneur. I held the portière

partly open, and watched the person who went to leave the key. The key in place, she continued her way, and disappeared at the end of the corridor. Then, I was about to venture forth in turn, when I heard approaching steps; I again hid behind my curtain, and a man went by me in the dark. When he was past, I watched him also, and saw him stop at the door of this room, push it open, enter. Then I said to myself, 'That man is the king!' I took only time enough to commend my soul to God. I had but to follow the path which the man and the woman each in turn had just shown me. I not only found the key in the door, but, more than that, the door was ajar. I pushed it and entered; seeing no one, I concluded that I had mistaken, that the man who appeared to be familiar with the Louvre had gone into some neighboring room. I looked for a place of concealment. I saw a bed, — you know the rest, monseigneur."

"Yes, *morbleu!* I know the rest; but — "

"Silence, monseigneur!"

"Why?"

"Because this time they are coming."

"I have your word, monsieur."

"And I yours, monseigneur."

The hands of the two men met.

A light step, a woman's, timidly trod the carpet.

"Mademoiselle de Saint André," said the prince, in an undertone, "here, at my left."

Just then a door opened at the other end of the apartment, and a youth, a boy almost, entered.

"The king!" whispered the Scot; "here, at my right."

"*Morbleu!*" murmured the prince; "that one, I confess, I was very far from suspecting!"

XVI.

THE QUEEN-MOTHER AND HER POETS.

The apartment that Catherine de Médicis occupied at the Louvre had brown hangings, and was bordered with wainscotings of sombre-hued oak. The trailing robe of mourning which, as a widow of a few months, she was wearing at that moment, and which she wore, moreover, all the rest of her life, produced, at first sight, a melancholy impression; but a glance above the dais upon which she was seated would have sufficed to assure the beholder that he was not within a necropolis.

In fact, above this dais glowed a rainbow bearing a Greek device, which the king had bestowed on his daughter-in-law, and which might be translated, as we think we have already said elsewhere, by these words: "I bring light and peace."

Moreover, if the rainbow, like a bridge spanning the chasm between the past and the future, between a funeral and a fête, had not sufficed to reassure the stranger suddenly ushered into this apartment, he would have needed but to lower his eyes and look beneath it upon the dais, where, surrounded by seven young women known as the Royal Pleiades, was seated in the arm-chair the truly beautiful creature called Catherine de Médicis.

Born in the year 1519, Lorenzo's daughter was already entering upon her fortieth year; and, although the color of her garments suggested death in all its cold rigidity, her keen, piercing eyes, beaming with supernatural lustre, revealed life in all its vigor, in all its beauty.

Catherine de Médicis.

THE HOROSCOPE, 186.

Then, too, the ivory whiteness of her brow, the brilliancy of her complexion, the purity, the nobility, the severity of the lines of her face, the pride of her look, the immobility of her countenance, ever at variance with the restless eyes, all made that head seem the mask of a Roman empress, and, in profile, with the eye fixed, the lips motionless, one might have taken it for an antique cameo.

Yet her brow, habitually gloomy, had just lighted up; her lips, usually unmoved, were just parting, and, when Madame l'Amirale entered, the latter had, with difficulty, repressed an exclamation of surprise upon seeing that woman smile who smiled so seldom.

But she very soon divined under whose breath that flower had bloomed.

Near the queen was Monseigneur le Cardinal de Lorraine, Archbishop of Rheims and of Narbonne, Bishop of Metz, of Toul and Verdun, of Thérouanne, of Luçon, of Valence, Abbé of Saint Denis, of Fécamp, of Cluny, of Marmoutiers, and the rest.

The Cardinal de Lorraine, we repeat, who has already engaged our attention almost as many times as Queen Catherine herself, on account of the important place occupied by him in the history of the end of the sixteenth century; the Cardinal de Lorraine, the man upon whom all the ecclesiastical favors known and unknown in France were showered at once, — the man, in short, who, when sent to Rome in 1548, had created such a sensation in the pontifical city by his youth, his beauty, his grace, his stately figure, his magnificent retinue, his affable manners, his wit, his love of science, to whom all these gifts received from nature, finished and refined by education, had justified the gift of the Roman purple, with which the pope, Paul III., had honored him a year before.

Born in 1525, he was at this time thirty-four years of age. He was a cavalier, prodigal and magnificent, lavish and luxurious, repeating with his co-sponsor, Catherine, when they were accused of squandering the finances, —

"Let us live to the glory of God; but let us live."

His "gossip," Catherine, to give her this familiar title, was, in fact, his gossip in every sense of the word; at that period, she would not have taken a step without consulting Monsieur le Cardinal de Lorraine. This intimacy is explained by the influence which the cardinal exercised over the mind of the queen-mother, and gives one to understand the unlimited sway, the absolute power of the house of Lorraine over the French court.

Therefore, on seeing the Cardinal de Lorraine leaning over Catherine's arm-chair, Madame l'Amirale had an explanation of the queen-mother's smile; doubtless the cardinal had just related some story in that spirit of raillery which he possessed in the highest degree.

The other august personages surrounding the queen-mother were François de Guise and his son, the Prince de Joinville, Mademoiselle de Saint André's fiancé; the Maréchal de Saint André himself; the Prince de Montpensier; his wife, Jacqueline of Hungary, so celebrated for her influence over Catherine de Médicis; and the Prince de la Roche-sur-Yon.

Behind these stood the Seigneur de Bourdeilles, — Brantôme, — Ronsard, and Baïf, "as bad a poet as he was good fellow," says the Cardinal Duperron-Daurat, "a fine wit, an ugly poet, and the Pindar of France," say his contemporaries.

Then Remi Belleau, somewhat known for his bad translation of Anacreon and his poem on the diversity of precious stones, but celebrated for his brilliant lyric on the month of April; Pontus de Thiard, mathematician, philosopher, theologian, and poet, "the man," says Ronsard, "that introduced the sonnet into France;" Jodelle, the author of "Cléopâtre," the first French tragedy, — God forgive him in heaven as we forgive him on earth! — author of "Dido," the second tragedy, of "Eugène," a comedy, and of a host of sonnets, songs, odes, and elegies in vogue at that period, unknown to ours, — in short, the Pleiades entire, less Clément Marot, dead in 1544, and Joachim du Bellay, called by Marguerite of Navarre the French Ovid.

The occasion of the assembling at the queen-mother's, on that evening, of all these poets, who ordinarily made little effort to enjoy one another's society, was the accident that had befallen the little queen, Marie Stuart, on the day before.

That, at least, was the pretext of which each had made use; for, to speak the truth, the young wife's beauty, youth, grace and wit, paled before the queen-mother's majesty and might. And so, after a few hackneyed condolences on an event which, however, must have terrible consequences, the loss of an heir to the crown, the cause of the visit had been forgotten in the remembrance of the pardons, benefits, or favors that were to be asked for their friends or for themselves.

They had even spoken of the two threatening letters sent, one after the other, to the King of France by way of the Maréchal de Saint André's windows; but the subject, not seeming to be endowed with sufficient interest, had fallen flat of itself.

On the arrival of the admiral's wife, all those smiling faces began to frown, and the conversation, lively as it had been, became cold and serious.

One would have supposed that an enemy had arrived in a camp of allies.

In fact, because of her religious severity, Madame l'Amirale acted as a cloud upon the seven stars that surrounded Catherine. Like the seven daughters of Atlas, this brilliant galaxy felt ill at ease in the presence of that steadfast virtue which they had so often sought to impeach, and which, through the impossibility of bringing aught of truth against it, they were reduced to slandering.

Amidst the very significant silence which, however, she appeared not to remark, the admiral's wife advanced to kiss Queen Catherine's hand, and returned to seat herself on a tabouret at the right of Monsieur le Prince de Joinville, and at the left of Monsieur le Prince de la Roche-sur-Yon.

"Well, gentlemen of Parnassus," said Catherine after Madame l'Amirale was seated, "have none of you a new chanson to recite, a new triolet, or a good epigram? Come, Maestro Ronsard, *Monsou* Jodelle, *Monsou* Remi Belleau, it is your duty to entertain us; a fine thing, to have birds around you if the birds do not sing! *Monsou* Pierre de Bourdeilles has just delighted us with a fine tale; come, enliven us, some one, with a beautiful poem."

The queen spoke with the half French, half Italian pronunciation that lent such a piquant charm to her conversation when it was sprightly, and yet which could, like the tongue of Dante, assume such a terrible accent when it took a gloomy turn.

And, as Catherine's look had rested upon Ronsard, he it was who advanced, and, in response to the appeal, said, —

"Gracious queen, all that I have done has come to

Your Majesty's knowledge; and as for what may be unknown to you, I would not be so bold as to make it known."

"And why, maestro?" demanded Catherine.

"Why, because they are love verses, composed for private circles, and because Your Majesty is much too imposing for one to dare sing before you the love songs of the shepherds of Cnidus and Cythera."

"Nonsense!" exclaimed Catherine; "am I not from the land of Petrarch and Boccaccio? Proceed, proceed, Maître Pierre, if, however, Madame l'Amirale permits."

"The queen is queen here as elsewhere; she commands, and her commands are obeyed!" responded Madame l'Amirale, bending low.

"You see, maestro," said Catherine, "you have full license. Come! we are listening."

Ronsard took a step forward, passed his fingers through his beautiful flaxen beard, lifted his eyes, full of sweet gravity, a moment, toward heaven, as if to invoke memory where he sought inspiration, and, in a charming voice, he repeated a love-song, which more than one of our contemporaneous poets might have envied.

After him, Remi Belleau recited, at Queen Catherine's request, a villanelle on a young turtle-dove mourning her mate. It was a malicious bit, aimed at Madame l'Amirale de Coligny, who was accused by malignant tongues at court of a tender passion for the Maréchal de Strozzi, killed the year before, by a musket shot, at the siege of Thionville.

The company clapped their hands, to the great confusion of Madame l'Amirale, who, whatever self-control she might possess, could not prevent the blood from mounting to her cheeks.

When quiet was somewhat restored, Pierre de Bourdeilles, Seigneur de Brantôme, was invited to recite one of his gallant anecdotes. It ended amid screams of laughter; some were gasping for breath, others were writhing and twisting, or clinging to a neighbor, in order not to fall. Shouts issued from every mouth, tears streamed from every eye, and each drew his handkerchief, crying, —

"Oh! enough, Monsieur de Brantôme; for pity's sake! enough! enough!"

Madame l'Amirale, like the rest, had been seized with the nervous and irresistible spasm called laughter, and had, like the rest, with violent, convulsive movements, drawn her handkerchief from her pocket.

Now, it happened that in getting her handkerchief, she at the same time drew forth the billet which she had brought for Dandelot.

But, as she carried the handkerchief to her eyes, the billet fell to the floor.

The Prince de Joinville, as we have said, was beside Madame l'Amirale. While he was laughing and writhing, and holding his sides, the young prince saw the note fall, — a perfumed, carefully-folded note, an unmistakable billet-doux, issuing from the pocket of the admiral's wife. Monsieur de Joinville had drawn his handkerchief, like the rest. He dropped it over the note, and gathered them up together, note and handkerchief.

Then, having assured himself that the one contained the other, he put both into his pocket, reserving the reading of the note for a more opportune moment.

That opportune moment was the one following Madame l'Amirale's departure.

Like all paroxysms of joy, grief, or laughter, the noisy outburst of the royal company was succeeded by a few moments of quiet, during which midnight sounded. The striking of the clock and the hour of the night reminded the admiral's wife that it was time for her to give the billet to Dandelot, and return to the Hôtel de Coligny.

She fumbled in her pocket in search of the note.

The note was no longer there.

She fumbled successively through all her pockets, in her purse, in her bosom, all in vain. The billet had disappeared, either taken or lost, — lost, in all likelihood.

Madame l'Amirale still held her handkerchief in her hand. . The thought struck her that in taking out her handkerchief she had pulled out the billet.

She looked down, — the note was not there. She moved her stool, — no note!

The admiral's wife felt that she was changing color.

Monsieur de Joinville, who was following all these proceedings, could not contain himself any longer.

"What is the matter, Madame l'Amirale?" he inquired. "You seem to have lost something."

"I? No — unless — nothing — nothing — I have lost nothing," stammered Madame l'Amirale, rising.

"Ah! *Mon Dieu!* dear friend," demanded Catherine, "what has happened then? You are changing from white to red."

"I am indisposed," plead the confused wife of the admiral, "and, with Your Majesty's permission, I will withdraw."

Catherine caught Monsieur de Joinville's eye, and gathered from his look that it was expedient to excuse the admiral's wife.

"Oh! my dear," said she, "God forbid that I should detain you, suffering as you are! Return home, and take good care of your health; you are so dear to us all."

Half suffocated, the admiral's wife inclined without reply, and withdrew.

With her departed Ronsard, Baïf, Daurat, Jodelle, Thiard, and Belleau, who accompanied her, still fumbling in her pockets, to her sedan; then, having seen the bearers set off toward the Hôtel de Coligny, the six poets gained the quay, and, discoursing of rhetoric and philosophy, returned to the Rue des Fossés-Saint-Victor, in which stood Baïf's house, a sort of ancient academy where poets gathered on certain days, or rather on certain nights, to discuss poetry or other literary or philosophical matters.

Let us leave them, for their paths lead away from the clue that guides us through the labyrinthine intrigues of love and politics which we are pursuing, and let us return to Catherine's apartment.

XVII.

MARS AND VENUS.

MADAME L'AMIRALE had barely taken her departure, when everybody, suspecting that something extraordinary had just taken place, cried, —

"Why, what was the matter with Madame l'Amirale?"

"Ask *Monsou* de Joinville," rejoined the queen-mother.

"What! you?" demanded the Cardinal de Lorraine.

"Speak! prince, speak!" entreated all the women.

"Faith, mesdames," returned the prince, "I do not yet know what to tell you. But," he added, extracting the billet from his pocket, "here is something that will speak for me."

"A billet!" was exclaimed on all sides.

"A billet! warm, perfumed, satin-like, and fallen from whose pocket?"

"Oh! prince — "

"Guess."

"No; tell us quickly."

"From the pocket of our straitlaced enemy, Madame l'Amirale."

"Ah!" said Catherine, "then is that why you gave me a signal to let her go?"

"Yes, I confess my indiscretion. I was in haste to know the contents of the billet."

"And what is in it?" demanded Catherine.

"I thought it would be wanting in respect toward Your Majesty to read this precious billet first."

"Then, give it to me, prince."

And, with a respectful bow, Monsieur de Joinville handed the paper to the queen-mother.

They all crowded around Catherine, curiosity getting the better of deference.

"Mesdames," said Catherine, "perhaps this letter contains a family secret. Let me first read it alone, and I promise you that if it may be read aloud, it is a pleasure of which I will not deprive you."

They fell away from Catherine; by the act, a candelabrum was unmasked, and the queen was enabled to read the note.

Monsieur de Joinville anxiously watched the changes of Catherine's countenance, and, when she had finished, he said, —

"Mesdames, the queen is about to read."

"Really, prince, I think you very hasty. I do not know whether I ought thus to disclose the love secrets of my good friend, Madame l'Amirale."

"Then it is really a love-letter?" inquired the Duc de Guise.

"'Faith!" said the queen, "you shall judge for yourselves; because, for my part, I cannot think I have read aright."

"And for that reason you will read it again, will you not, madame?" said the impatient Prince de Joinville.

"Listen!" bade Catherine.

Perfect silence reigned, in which not a breath was heard, although fifteen persons were present.

The queen read: —

"Do not fail, dear love, to repair to-morrow an hour after midnight, to the Salles des Métamorphoses. The room in which we met last night is too near the apartments of the two queens; our confidante will see that the door is open."

There was a universal exclamation of astonishment.

It was a rendezvous, — a very explicit rendezvous; a rendezvous granted by the admiral's wife, since the note had fallen from her pocket.

Hence Madame l'Amirale's visit to the queen was but a pretext for visiting the Louvre, and, as Dandelot was on duty, the admiral's wife could undoubtedly count on her brother-in-law, and depart when she pleased.

But who could the man be?

They reckoned up all Madame l'Amirale's friends, one after the other; but Madame de Coligny led a life so strict that they knew not on whom to fix.

They went so far as to suspect Dandelot himself, so easy was it to be suspicious in that corrupt court.

"But," observed the Duc de Guise, "there is a very simple way of discovering the gallant."

"How?" was demanded on all sides.

"The rendezvous is evidently for to-night?"

"It is," answered Catherine.

"Well, we must serve the lovers as the Olympian gods served Mars and Venus."

"And visit them while they sleep!" cried Monsieur de Joinville.

The court dames looked at each other.

They were dying to welcome the proposition with unanimous applause; but they dared not confess to the desire. It was half an hour past midnight.

There was a half-hour to wait, but, in slandering a neighbor, a half-hour is quickly whiled away.

And they slandered the admiral's wife; in anticipation they pictured her confusion, and the half-hour passed.

But no one was more delighted than Catherine at this excellent idea of taking her dear friend, Madame l'Amirale, in the act.

One o'clock sounded.

All clapped their hands, so impatiently had they awaited the hour.

"Come," cried the Prince de Joinville; "forward, march!"

But the Maréchal de Saint André stopped him.

"O imprudent youth!" said he.

"Have you any suggestion to make?" demanded Monsieur de la Roche-sur-Yon.

"Yes," answered the maréchal.

"In that case, listen," rejoined Catherine, "and religiously, messieurs. Our friend, the maréchal, has had wide experience in all things, and particularly in affairs of this kind."

"Well," said the maréchal, "this is what I wish to say to curb the impatience of my son-in-law, Monsieur de Joinville: it sometimes happens that a rendezvous is not held at the precise hour, and that, were we to arrive prematurely, our plans would run the risk of defeat."

The prudent counsel of the Maréchal de Saint André was adopted, and all agreed with Queen Catherine that he was past master in matters of such nature.

It was agreed, therefore, to wait half an hour longer.

The half-hour rolled away.

But by that time the impatience had reached such a height that, whatever observations the Maréchal de Saint André might have made, they would not have been heeded.

He therefore hazarded none, perhaps because he knew it to be quite useless, perhaps because he thought the hour for attempting the expedition had indeed arrived.

Be that as it may, he promised the gay troop to accompany them as far as the door, and, once there, to await the result.

It was arranged that the queen-mother would retire to her bed-chamber, to which the Prince de Joinville should repair to give an account of all that might happen.

All formalities being thus regulated, every one took a candle in hand.

The young Duc de Montpensier and the Prince de la Roche-sur-Yon each carried two, and the cortége, with Monsieur de Guise at its head, moved solemnly in the direction of the Salle des Métamorphoses.

Arrived at the door, they came to a stand-still, and each applied his ear to the keyhole.

Not the slightest sound could be heard.

They remembered that, on this side, they were still separated from the Salle des Métamorphoses by an ante-chamber.

The Maréchal de Saint André gently pushed the door of the ante-chamber, but the door resisted.

"*Diable!*" he exclaimed, "we had not thought of this; the door is locked from within."

"Burst it open!" suggested the young princess.

"Softly, messieurs!" said Monsieur de Guise, "we are in the Louvre."

"That may be!" retorted the Prince de la Roche-sur-Yon; "but we are of the Louvre."

"Messieurs! messieurs!" insisted the duke, "we come to expose a scandal; let us not do so by creating another."

"True!" said Brantôme, "and the counsel is good. I once knew a beautiful and virtuous dame — "

"Monsieur de Brantôme," broke in the Prince de Joinville, laughing, "we are making a story at this present moment, not relating one. Find some means of entering, and there will be another chapter to add to your 'Dames Galantes.'"

"Ah! well," returned Monsieur de Brantôme, "do as they do at the king's apartment, — scratch gently on the panel, and perhaps it will be opened."

"Monsieur de Brantôme is right," said the Prince de Joinville. "Scratch, father-in-law, scratch!"

The Maréchal de Saint André scratched.

A valet who was on guard, or asleep, rather, in the ante-chamber, and who had heard nothing at all of the dialogue we have just reported, the dialogue having been conducted in whispers, awoke, and, supposing Lanoue had come to reconduct Mademoiselle de Saint André, as she was in the habit of doing, he set the door ajar and, rubbing his eyes, demanded, —

"Who is there?"

The Maréchal de Saint André drew back, and the valet found himself face to face with Monsieur de Guise.

At sight of all those candles, all those lords, all those ladies, all those laughing eyes, all those jibing mouths, the valet began to think it a trick, and he tried to close the door again.

But the Duc de Guise had already set one foot within the ante-chamber, true capturer of strongholds that he was, and the door, in closing, met the leather of his boot.

The valet continued to push with all his strength.

"Stop, knave!" said the duke; "open this door!"

"But, monseigneur," protested the poor devil, all in a tremble as he recognized the duke, "I have strict orders —"

"I know your orders; but I know, too, the secret of the matter going on within, and it is in the king's service, and with his consent, that we would enter here, these gentlemen and I."

He might have added, "these ladies," for five or six

inquisitive dames, laughing under their hooded cloaks, were of the troop.

The valet-de-chambre, who, like every one else, knew the power Monsieur de Guise exercised at court, imagined, in fact, that it was a question of some matter settled upon between the duke and the king. He first opened the door of the ante-chamber, then that of the Salle des Métamorphoses, rising on tip-toe to take in something of the scene about to be enacted.

It was not an entrance, it was an irruption. The wave dashed into the room like a surging tide, and —, —

XVIII.

IN WHICH MONSIEUR DE JOINVILLE IS FORCED TO RELATE HIS MISADVENTURE.

"I THINK, monseigneur," said Robert Stuart, the first to emerge from his retreat, "that you have no great reason to eulogize His Majesty, and that if His Majesty now fails to grant you Anne Dubourg's pardon, you will no longer have such pressing arguments against my project."

"You deceive yourself, monsieur," said the Prince de Condé emerging from the opposite side and regaining his feet; "had he far more seriously wronged me, the king is ever the king, and I could not avenge a personal injury upon the head of the nation."

"What has just happened, however, in no respect alters the promise you made me, does it, monseigneur?"

"I promised, monsieur, to ask a pardon for Councillor Anne Dubourg at the king's levee. This morning, at eight o'clock, I shall be at the Louvre to seek the pardon."

"Frankly, monseigneur," said Robert Stuart, "do you believe that it will be granted?"

"Monsieur," replied the Prince de Condé with great dignity, "rest assured that I would not take the trouble to ask this favor, if I were not almost sure of obtaining it."

"May it be so!" murmured Robert Stuart with a gesture indicating that he had not the same confidence; "in a few hours it will be daylight, and we shall see then —"

"Now, monsieur," said the prince looking on all sides, "the question is to find a way out of here promptly and understandingly. Thanks to your two letters and your very unusual manner of delivering them, the doors of the Louvre are guarded as if it were in a state of siege, and I suspect it would be difficult for you, especially in the uniform you are wearing, to get out of here before to-morrow morning. I beg you then to observe that, in taking you away with me, I am extricating you and your friend, the lender of the uniform, from a very bad predicament."

"Monseigneur, I never forget either benefit or injury."

"Pray believe that it was not my purpose to claim your gratitude, but to prove the fairness of my intentions, and in that way to set you an example; for you are aware that I should have only to abandon you here to be quit of my oath, without, however, having forfeited my word."

"I know the integrity of Monsieur le Prince de Condé," replied the young man with some emotion, "and I think he will have no cause to complain of mine. From this day I am your servant, body and soul. Obtain my father's pardon and you will have no retainer readier than I to die for you."

"I believe you, monsieur," returned the Prince de Condé, "and, although the occasion of our encounter and the manner in which we have met is very unusual, I will not conceal from you that in virtue of the motive which incited you to the act itself, however blameworthy it may be in the eyes of every honest man, I feel toward it a degree of indulgence amounting almost to sympathy. Only I would like you to explain one thing, — that is, how it happens that you bear a Scotch name and that the councillor Anne Dubourg is your father."

"It is very simple, monseigneur, as are all love stories. Twenty-two years ago, the councillor Anne Dubourg was twenty-eight years of age; he went to Scotland to visit his friend John Knox. While there he became intimate with a daughter of Lothian; she was my mother. Only on his return to Paris did he learn that the young girl was with child. He had never doubted her virtue, consequently he acknowledged as his son and commended to John Knox the child she brought into the world."

"Very well, monseiur," said the Prince de Condé, "I know what I desired to know. Now, let us busy ourselves about getting out of here."

The prince advanced first and half opened the door of the Salle des Métamorphoses. The corridor had again become dark and deserted; they entered it therefore with a certain degree of security. Arrived at the door of the Louvre, the prince cast his mantle around the Scotchman's shoulders and sent for Dandelot.

Dandelot came.

In few words, the prince acquainted him with what had taken place, but only with regard to the king, Mademoiselle de Saint André, and the unwelcome visitors who had come to rouse them from their slumbers. Of Robert Stuart, he said only these three words: —

"*Monsieur accompanies me!*"

Dandelot comprehended the necessity of Condé's getting away from the Louvre as fast as possible. He caused a private door to be opened, and the prince and his companion found themselves outside.

Both swiftly made their way to the river without the exchange of a single word, proving that both duly appreciated the danger they had just escaped.

Arrived at the embankment, the Prince de Condé asked the Scotchman which way he was going.

"To the right, monseigneur," he answered.

"And I to the left," returned the prince. "Now, this evening, at ten o'clock, let me find you in front of Saint-Germain-l'Auxerrois. I hope I shall have good news to tell you."

"Thanks, monseigneur!" said the young man bowing respectfully, "and allow me to repeat that, from this hour forth, I am at your service, body and soul."

And each went his way.

Three o'clock was striking.

At that very moment, the Prince de Joinville was being ushered into the bed-chamber of Catherine de Médicis.

Why was the young prince, in spite of himself, and at such an hour, entering the queen's chamber, and by what right was the nephew encroaching upon the uncle's privileges?

We are about to tell you.

The poor prince was not there of his own free will, or with a light heart.

Here, in fact, is what had happened.

It will be remembered that the queen-mother had remained in her room, announcing that she was about to go to bed, where she would expect Monsieur le Prince de Joinville, chief promoter of all the scandal, to come and tell her what happened.

We know what happened.

Now, the Prince de Joinville, quite abashed at his discovery, was less disposed than any one to constitute himself the historian of a catastrophe in which his conjugal honor, even before he was married, played such a sorry rôle.

And so without having forgotten his promise, the Prince de Joinville was in no hurry to fulfil it.

But Catherine did not share the same unconcern with regard to the unknown secret. She had been disrobed by her women, had retired to her bed, had sent away all in attendance save her confidante, and had waited.

Two o'clock in the morning struck. No time had been lost as yet.

Then a quarter past two, then half past two, then a quarter to three.

Finally, seeing neither uncle nor nephew appear, she had whistled for her femme-de-chambre, — the invention of bells dates back as far only as Madame de Maintenon, — and given orders that they must search for the Prince de Joinville and bring him to her, dead or alive.

The prince was discovered holding high conference with the Duc François de Guise and the Cardinal de Lorraine.

Of course the family council decided that a marriage between the Prince de Joinville and Mademoiselle de Saint André had become utterly impossible.

In face of the queen-mother's summons, there was no drawing back.

The Prince de Joinville had started with bowed head, and he arrived with his head bowed lower still.

As for the Duc de Montpensier and the Prince de la Roche-sur-Yon, they had slipped away.

Later, we shall discover with what intent.

Every moment increased Catherine's impatience. Although the lateness of the hour urged her to sleep, she was kept awake by the idea that she was about to hear of some escapade to the confusion of her dear friend, Madame l'Amirale.

"Is it he, at last?" she said to herself.

Then, the moment the young man appeared she cried rudely enough, —

"Come along, now, *Monsou* de Joinville. I have been waiting for you an hour!"

The prince approached the bed, stammering some excuse, out of which Catherine could make nothing but these words: —

"May Your Majesty pardon me — "

"I will not pardon you, *Monsou* de Joinville," said the queen-mother with her Florentine accent, "unless your story amuses me as much as your absence has annoyed me. Take a stool and sit here at my bedside. I see by your face that something extraordinary has happened."

"Yes," murmured the prince, "very extraordinary, in fact, something we were very far from expecting."

"So much the better! so much the better!" exclaimed the queen-mother, rubbing her hands; "tell it all and omit not a single detail. It is a long time since I have had such grounds for laughter. Ah! *Monsou*, there is no more laughing at court."

"That is true, madame," replied Monsieur de Joinville with a funereal air.

"Ah well, when the opportunity offers for one to divert one's self a little," resumed Catherine, "one must run to meet it, instead of allowing it to escape. Therefore, begin your story, *Monsou* de Joinville. I am listening and I promise you not to lose a word of it."

And, in fact, Catherine settled herself in her bed like a woman making herself thoroughly comfortable beforehand, so as to be in no way disturbed in the enjoyment of which she is about to partake.

Then she waited.

But the recital was difficult for *Monsou* de Joinville, as Catherine called him, to enter upon, so *Monsou* de Joinville sat mute.

The queen-mother at first thought the young man was collecting his ideas; but, as the silence continued, she craned her neck without otherwise deranging her body, and cast upon him an indescribable look of interrogation.

"Well?" she demanded.

"Well, madame," answered the prince, "I confess that my embarrassment is great."

"Your embarrassment! Why?"

"Why, in telling Your Majesty what I saw."

"Then what did you see, *Monsou* de Joinville? I confess that you drive me wild with curiosity. I have waited, it is true," continued Catherine, rubbing her beautiful hands together, "but it seems that I shall have lost nothing by waiting. Come, now. Ah! then this was really the evening, for you remember, do you not, dear *Monsou* de Joinville, that the billet you picked up said 'to-morrow,' it is true, but it bore no date?"

"This was the evening, indeed; yes, madame."

"So they were in the Salle des Métamorphoses, were they?"

"They were there."

"Together?"

"Together."

"Still Mars and Venus? *Ah ça!* tell me. I know who Venus was, — but Mars?"

"Mars, madame?"

"Yes, Mars. I do not know who was Mars."

"Really, madame, I am at a loss as to whether I ought to tell you."

"What, whether you ought to tell me? I think you ought indeed, — if you have any scruples, we will waive them. Come now, — Mars! — Young or old?"

"Young."

"Of good figure?"

"Of good figure, certainly."

"Of rank, doubtless?"

"Of the highest rank."

"Oh! oh! what are you saying, *Monsou* de Joinville?" exclaimed the queen-mother sitting bolt upright.

"The truth, madame."

"What, was it not some page, both blind and unsophisticated?"

"It was no page."

"And this bold young man," demanded Catherine, unable to resist her desire to indulge in sarcasm, "this bold young man holds a position at court?"

"Yes, Your Majesty, a very high position, even."

"Very high? Well, for God's sake, speak out, *Monsou* de Joinville! Your words are wrung from you as if a state secret were concerned."

"A state secret is concerned, in truth, madame," said the prince.

"Ah! then, *Monsou* de Joinville, I no longer request, I command you. Tell me the name of this person."

"Do you insist?"

"I insist."

"Well, madame," said the Prince de Joinville, lifting his head, "this person, as you call him, is no other than His Majesty, King François II."

"My son?" cried Catherine, bounding up in bed.

"Your son, yes, madame."

An arquebuse exploding unexpectedly in her room could not have produced greater consternation in the queen-mother's face, or more sudden discomfiture.

She passed her hand across her eyes as if the obscurity of the room, lighted by a single lamp, made it difficult for her to distinguish objects; then fixing a piercing gaze upon Monsieur de Joinville and leaning forward in such a way as almost to touch him, she said in a low voice, but with an accent which had changed from playful to terrible, —

"I am wide awake, am I not, *Monsou* de Joinville? I heard aright? You certainly told me just now that the hero of this adventure was my son?"

"Yes, madame."

"Do you repeat it?"

"I repeat it."

"Do you affirm it?"

"I swear it."

And the young man raised his hand.

"Very well, *Monsou* de Joinville!" continued Catherine, solemnly; "now I understand your hesitation, I ought even to have understood your silence. Oh! the blood surges into my face? Is it really possible! my son, possessing a young and charming wife and taking a mistress who is more than twice his age; my son going over to my enemies; my son, —*par le Christ!* it is impossible! — my son, the lover of Madame l'Amirale!"

"Madame," said the Prince de Joinville, "how the note came in Madame l'Amirale's pocket, I do not know. But I do know, unfortunately, that it was not Madame l'Amirale who was discovered in the room."

"What!" cried Catherine, "what are you saying now, — that it was not Madame l'Amirale?"

"No, madame, it was not she."

"But if not she, who was it then?"

"Madame —"

"*Monsou* de Joinville, the name of this person, her name instantly!"

"Will Your Majesty deign to excuse me —"

"Excuse you, and why?"

"Because I am the only one, in truth, from whom no one has the right to exact such a revelation."

"Not even I, *Monsou* de Joinville?"

"Not even you, madame. Besides, your curiosity is easily satisfied, for the first member of the court that you question in my place —"

"But, to question such a person, I must wait until to-morrow, *Monsou* de Joinville. I wish to know the person's name now, instantly even. What assurance have you that I may not resort to such measures as brook no delay?"

And Catherine's eyes blazed as they fastened themselves upon the young man.

"Madame," said he, "seek throughout the entire court for the only person whom I cannot name. Do you name her. But — for me, oh! for me, it is impossible!"

And the young prince raised both hands to his face, in part to hide his blush of shame, and in part his angry tears.

A thought flashed like lightning through Catherine's brain.

She uttered a cry, and, grasping and dashing away the young man's hands in one movement, she exclaimed, —

"Ah! Mademoiselle de Saint André!"

The prince did not answer; but to give no answer was a confession.

Moreover, he dropped down upon the tabouret placed beside the bed.

Catherine regarded him an instant, her pity being mingled with scorn.

Then, in tones which she forced herself to render most caressing, she said, —

"Poor child! I pity you with all my heart; for it

would appear that you love that perfidious girl. Approach, give me your hand, and pour out your sorrows into the heart of your dear mother, Catherine. I understand now why you were silent, and I am filled with remorse for having so insisted. Forgive me then, my son; and now that I know the wrong, let us seek a remedy. There are other maidens in our court besides Mademoiselle de Saint André, and if there are none noble enough and beautiful enough for you in our court of Paris, we will search for one in the court of Spain or of Italy. Therefore, compose yourself, my dear prince, and, if possible, let us talk seriously."

But Monsieur de Joinville, instead of replying to this discourse which evidently had a visible aim and a secret one, — to console him and to sound his affection, — Monsieur de Joinville fell upon his knees beside the queen-mother's bed, and, sobbing, buried his face in the cover.

"Pardon, Your Majesty!" he cried, "pardon, and thanks for your tender solicitude; but, at this moment, I have strength only to realize my shame and feel my sorrow. Therefore, I beg Your Majesty will permit me to withdraw."

The queen-mother rested a look of profound disdain upon this young man bowed down in his grief.

Then, her voice betraying none of the feeling portrayed in her face, she said, extending to the young prince her beautiful hand which he fervently kissed, —

"Go, my child! and come to-morrow morning and talk with me. Until then, good-night, and God keep you!"

Monsieur de Joinville instantly took advantage of the permission granted him, and left the room.

Silently Catherine followed him with her eyes until he had disappeared behind the curtain; then her look concentrated itself upon the tapestry until the motion which the prince's exit had communicated to the fabric had ceased.

Then she rested her elbow on the pillow, and, in hollow tones, her eyes glowing with a baleful light, she said, —

"From to-night I have a rival, and from to-morrow I have lost all power over my son's mind, — if I do not look to it."

Then, after a moment of silent meditation, a smile of triumph came to her lips.

"I will look to it!" she said.

XIX.

A TID-BIT.

Now, while Monsieur le Cardinal de Lorraine is being put to bed by his valet-de-chambre; while Robert Stuart is making his way back to his friend Patrick's; while Monsieur de Condé is regaining his hotel, cursing and laughing in a breath; while Madame l'Amirale keeps turning her pockets in search of the unlucky billet that has occasioned all this scandal; while the king is cross-questioning Lanoue in the effort to learn from her how a rumor of his rendezvous could have been noised abroad; while the Maréchal de Saint André is asking himself whether he ought to bless God or curse luck for what has happened; while Mademoiselle de Saint André is dreaming that her neck is encircled with the jewels of Madame d'Étampes and the Duchesse de Valentinois, and that Marie Stuart's crown rests upon her head, let us discover what is occupying the young Princes de Montpensier and De la Roche-sur-Yon, to whom we promised to return.

The two gay and handsome young men, witnesses of what they pronounced a capital spectacle, had been forced to contain themselves in presence of the three serious faces, — faces more serious than usual just then, — of Monsieur de Guise, Monsieur de Saint André, and the Cardinal de Lorraine. They did more: assuming an air of sympathy, they very decorously offered their condolences to Monsieur le Cardinal de Lorraine, to Monsieur le Maréchal de Saint André, and to Monsieur de Guise. Then, profiting by the first turn in the corridor that would aid them to escape, they remained silent and in the shadow until the last one had taken himself off and disappeared in whatever direction it suited him to take.

Once safely alone, the laughter that had been stifled in their bosoms with the utmost difficulty found vent in such explosions that the windows of the Louvre rattled as if a heavy chariot were rolling by.

Propped against the wall, facing each other, their hands on their sides, and their heads thrown back, they writhed in such contortions that they might have been taken for two epileptics, or, as they said in those days, for two persons possessed.

"Ah! my dear duc!" ejaculated the Prince de la Roche-sur-Yon, the first to recover breath.

"Ah! my dear prince!" gasped the other in return.

"And to think — to think that there are — are people who pretend that we never — never laugh any more in this poor Paris!"

"They are ill — ill-conditioned people."

"Ah! — *mon Dieu!* — how good it feels — and how it hurts — to laugh!"

"Did you see Monsieur de Joinville's face?"

"And the Maréchal de Saint André's?"

"I regret but one thing, duc," said the Prince de la Roche-sur-Yon, calming himself a little.

"And I regret two, prince," answered the other.

"It is, not having been in the king's place, had all Paris been looking on!"

"And I, that all Paris was not looking on, with me in the king's place."

"Oh! regret nothing, duc, — to-morrow, before noon, all Paris will know it."

"If you are of my mind, prince, all Paris shall know it this very night."

"And how?"

"Easily enough."

"But how —"

"*Parbleu!* by shouting it from the housetops."

"But Paris is asleep."

"Paris ought not to sleep when the king wakes."

"You are right! I can answer for it that His Majesty has not yet closed his eyes."

"Then, let us wake Paris."

"Oh! the madness of it!"

"Do you refuse?"

"By no means! Since I pronounce it madness, I consent to it naturally."

"All right, then."

"Come on! I am afraid the whole town already knows part of the story."

And the two young men, rushing headlong down the steps, descended the staircase of the Louvre like Hippomenes and Atalanta competing for the prize in the race.

Having reached the court, they made themselves known to Dandelot, to whom they took care to say nothing, deterred by the rôle his sister-in-law had played in the affair, and a fear that he might oppose their going out.

Dandelot identified them to the guard as in the case of the Prince de Condé, and caused the door to be opened for them.

Arm in arm, laughing in their sleeves, the two young people darted out of the Louvre, crossed the drawbridge, and found themselves near the river, where an icy wind began to cut their faces. Then, on a pretext of warming themselves, they gathered up some stones and threw them at the windows of the neighboring houses.

They had just broken a pane a-piece for two or three windows, and were promising themselves more of that engaging sport, when two men enveloped in cloaks, seeing the two youths on the run, barred their way and called out to them to stop.

Both halted. They were running, but not in flight.

"And what right have you to stop us?" cried the Duc de Montpensier, advancing upon one of the two men. "Go your own road and allow two gentlemen of rank to amuse themselves in their own fashion."

"Ah! pardon! monseigneur; I had not recognized you," said the one whom the Duc de Montpensier had addressed. "I am Monsieur de Chavigny, commander of the hundred archers of the guard, and I was returning to the Louvre in company with Monsieur de Carvoysin, first equerry to His Majesty."

"Good evening, Monsieur de Chavigny!" responded the Prince de la Roche-sur-Yon, walking up to the commander of the hundred archers and extending his hand, while the Duc de Montpensier responded courteously to the bow of the first equerry. "Did you say that you are returning to the Louvre, Monsieur de Chavigny?"

"Yes, prince."

"Well, we are coming from there, ourselves."

"At this hour?"

"Pray observe, Monsieur de Chavigny, that if the hour is suitable for entering, it ought to be equally so for leaving."

"Be assured, prince, where you are concerned, I am not so indiscreet as to question."

"And you are wrong, my dear monsieur; for we have very interesting news to tell you."

"Apropos of the king's service?" inquired Monsieur de Carvoysin.

"Precisely, the king's service. You have hit it, Monsieur le Grand Écuyer," cried the Prince de la Roche-sur-Yon, bursting into a laugh.

"Indeed?" inquired Monsieur de Chavigny.

"Upon honor."

"What is it about, messieurs?"

"The great honor with which His Majesty has just overwhelmed one of his most illustrious captains," returned the Prince de la Roche-sur-Yon.

"And my brother, De Joinville," said the Duc de Montpensier, "schoolboy as he is."

"Of what honor do you speak, prince?"

"Who is the illustrious captain, duc?"

"Messieurs, it is the Maréchal de Saint André."

"And what honors can His Majesty yet add to those he has already heaped upon Monsieur de Saint André: Maréchal of France, first gentleman of the Chamber, the grand-cordon of Saint Michel, Chevalier de la Jarretière? Some people are very fortunate!"

"That depends!"

"What! That depends —?"

"Doubtless; it is a bit of fortune that would not suit you, perhaps, Monsieur de Chavigny, who possess a pretty young wife, nor you, Monsieur de Carvoysin, who have a pretty young daughter."

"In truth?" cried Monsieur de Chavigny, who was beginning to comprehend.

"You have it, my dear fellow," said the Prince de la Roche-sur-Yon.

"But are you quite certain of what you say?" demanded Monsieur de Chavigny.

"*Parbleu!*"

"This is a very serious matter, prince!" replied Monsieur de Carvoysin.

"Do you think so? As for me, on the contrary, I find it excruciatingly funny."

"But who told you?"

"Who told us? No one. We saw it!"

"Where?"

"I saw it, as also did Monsieur de la Roche-sur-Yon, Monsieur de Saint André, my brother, De Joinville, who, by way of parenthesis, ought to have seen even more than the rest, for he held a candelabrum — with how many branches, prince?"

"With five branches!" declared the Prince de la Roche-sur-Yon, beginning to laugh louder than ever.

"The alliance of His Majesty with the maréchal is therefore no longer to be doubted," seriously began the Duc de Montpensier, "and, from now on, let the heretics look out for themselves. We are about to publish the news to the true Catholics of Paris."

"Is it possible?" cried Monsieur de Chavigny and Monsieur de Carvoysin simultaneously.

"It is exactly as I have the honor to inform you, messieurs," replied the prince. "Our news is quite fresh, not yet an hour old; so that in sharing it with you, we think we are giving you a real proof of friendship, — on condition, be it understood, that you cause it to circulate and communicate it to all whom you happen to meet."

"And as, at this hour, one runs across few friends, unless by some good chance like the one that has brought us together, we invite you to do as we are doing, cause closed doors to be opened, make your friends get up if they have gone to bed, and confiding the secret to them, as the barber of King Midas did to the reeds, tell them, — 'King François II. is the lover of Mademoiselle de Saint André.'"

"Ah! by my faith! messieurs," said the grand equerry, "I shall do as you say. I cannot endure the Maréchal de Saint André, and I know of a friend of mine near by to whom the news will give such pleasure that I should not hesitate, on leaving you, to go and wake him up if he were sound asleep."

"And you, my dear Monsieur de Chavigny," said the Prince de la Roche-sur-Yon, "knowing that you cherish no affection for Monsieur de Joinville, I am sure you will follow Monsieur de Carvoysin's example."

"'Faith, yes!" cried Monsieur de Chavigny; "instead of going to the Louvre, I shall return home and tell the affair to my wife. To-morrow morning, before nine o'clock, four of her friends will know it, and that I promise you is the same as if you were to send four trumpeters to the four cardinal points of the compass."

Upon this, the gentlemen saluted each other, the two young people followed the bank of the river toward the Rue de la Monnaie, while Messieurs de Chavigny and Carvoysin, instead of continuing their course to the Louvre, each conscientiously did his part to publish the news of the day, or, rather, of the night.

Having reached the Rue de la Monnaie, the Prince de la Roche-sur-Yon observed a lighted window over a sign that hung creaking in the wind.

"Hold," said the duc, "a wonder! there is a bourgeois' window alight at half-past three in the morning. It is either a bourgeois just married, or a poet making verses."

"There is some truth in what you say, my dear fellow, and I had forgotten that I was invited to the wedding. Faith, I should like to show you Master Balthazar's bride. You would find that, although the girl is not the daughter of a French maréchal, she is none the less a beautiful girl; but, for want of the bride, I am going to show you the husband."

"Ah! dear prince, it would not be charitable to bring the poor man to the window at such a time."

"Good!" said the prince; "he is the only man who has nothing to fear on that score."

"And why?"

"Because he always has a cold. I have known him for ten years; I have never yet been able to get from him a clear and distinct 'good day, prince.'"

"Let us see the man, then."

"And all the more, since besides being an inn-keeper, he is a bath-keeper, with houses on the Seine, and to-morrow morning, while rubbing down his patrons, he will repeat the story that we tell him."

"Bravo!"

Our two young people, like two schoolboys following the side of the river and filling their pockets with pebbles to skip on the water, had filled their own with small stones, which they meant to use as catapults against the houses to which they hoped to lay siege.

The prince took a pebble from his pocket, and, falling back two steps to gain an impetus, just as we have seen Robert Stuart do, but with a more sinister purpose, he shot the stone through a pane of the lighted window.

The window was opened so promptly that one might have thought the pebble had produced that effect.

A man in a nightcap appeared, candle in hand, and essayed to shout, —

"Robbers!"

"What is he saying?" demanded the duke.

"You see for yourself that one must be accustomed to him in order to understand him. He is calling us robbers."

Then, turning toward the window, the prince shouted,

"Don't get excited, Balthazar; it is I."

"You — Your Highness? — May Your Highness excuse me! — Your Highness certainly has a right to break my windows."

"Ah! *bon Dieu!*" cried the duke, laughing with all his might, "what language does your good man speak, prince?"

"People who know call it a jargon of Iroquois and Hottentot. Nevertheless, in his sort of growl, he has just made a very obliging remark."

"What is it?"

"That we have a right to break his windows."

"Ah! *pardieu!* that deserves thanks."

Then, addressing Balthazar, he said, —

"Friend, news reached the court that you were married this evening, and that your wife is pretty. Now, we have come from the Louvre expressly to congratulate you."

"And to tell you, my dear Balthazar, that the weather is cold and now is the proper time for the good things of earth."

"While, on the other hand, His Majesty's heart is warm, — which will profit the Maréchal de Saint André."

"I do not understand."

"Never mind! repeat what we have said, my dear Balthazar. Others will understand, and know all it implies. Our compliments to madame."

And the two young men went up the Rue de la Monnaie, shouting with laughter as they heard the grumbling and wheezing of the host of The Black Cow, who could very easily shut his window again but could not mend his window-pane.

XX

TIRE-LAINE AND TIRE-SOIE.

Laughing still, the two young men continued up the Rue de la Monnaie and came to the Rue de Béthisy.

On turning the corner, they seemed to hear, in the direction of the Hôtel de Coligny, a great clashing of swords and a formidable outcry of voices.

The scene which gave rise to the clashing of swords and the sound of voices was in the shadow twenty or thirty paces distant from them.

They stepped back out of sight under the porch of a house at the corner of the Rue de la Monnaie and the Rue de Béthisy.

"Aha!" said a firm voice in tones full of menace, "you are thieves it seems."

"*Parbleu!*" responded an impudent one, "you will do well if you meet honest men in the street at this hour of the night!"

"Robbers!" exclaimed a voice less assured than the first.

"Where is the thief that is not something of a robber, and where is the robber that is not something of a thief?" responded the second voice, which seemed to be that of a philosopher.

"Would you assassinate us, then?"

"By no means, your lordship!"

"Then, what do you want?"

"To relieve you of your purse, that is all."

"I swear," returned the first voice, "there is not much of anything in my purse, but, such as it is, you shall not look into it."

"You are wrong to be so obstinate, monsieur!"

"Monsieur, we give you notice that you are two against eleven; moreover, your companion seems to be only your lackey. All resistance would be folly."

"Stand aside!" cried the voice, becoming more and more threatening.

"You appear to be a stranger in this good city of Paris, monsieur," said the voice that appeared to belong to the leader of the band, "and perhaps it is not that you are so niggardly, but that you fear to be without lodging if left without money; but we are civilized thieves, monsieur, *tire-soie*, not *tire-laine*, and we know what is due in such a case. Deliver up your purse gracefully, monsieur, and we will give you back a crown, that you may not be left without money for your lodging, unless you would prefer the address of a respectable hotel where, with suitable references, you would be quickly admitted. A man like you cannot lack friends in Paris, and to-morrow, or rather to-day, — for I would not mislead you, it is almost four in the morning, — to-day, you can call on your friends, who will assuredly relieve your embarrassment."

"Stand aside!" repeated the same voice. "You can take my life, since you are eleven against two; but, as for my purse, you shall not have it."

"Your remark is illogical, monsieur," returned the one who seemed authorized to speak for the band; "for, if once we have your life, we are at liberty to take your purse."

"Back, scoundrels! and look out for yourselves, — we have between us two good swords and two good dirks."

"And, what is more, good law. But what does good law amount to when evil is the stronger?"

"Meanwhile," retorted the gentleman, who appeared to be the less tolerant of the two, "parry that."

And he made a frightful lunge at the chief of the band, who, fortunately for himself, being accustomed no doubt to this kind of sally, was on his guard, and sprang back so promptly and so cleverly that only his doublet was pierced.

Then began the clashing of swords and the cries heard by the Prince de la Roche-sur-Yon and the Duc de Montpensier.

While striking out, one of the men attacked shouted for help. But, as if the other must have understood that it was useless to call for help, or else that he scorned to make an outcry, he thrust in silence, and, from one or two blasphemies uttered by his adversaries, it could be divined that he did not thrust the air.

When we said the silent gentleman must have considered it useless to call for help, we hoped the reader would grasp our meaning.

It was of no use to seek aid from men whose business it was to dispense it in such an instance, that is, from the agents of Monsieur de Mouchy, *grand inquisiteur* of the law of France. These agents, called *mouchis*, or *mouchards*, went the rounds of the city day and night for the purpose of arresting, it is true, all of whom they were suspicious.

But Messieurs *les mouchis* or *mouchards*, whichever one prefers to call them, did not appear to suspect the hordes of evil-doers infesting Paris, and more than once even, when the occasion had seemed opportune, and the spoil promised to be rich, Monsieur de Mouchy's agents had assisted the suspicious characters, whether they belonged to the class of *tire-soie*, or gentleman thieves, who never molested any but people of quality, or to the class of *tire-laine*, poor devils, thieves of the lowest degree, who were content to strip the bourgeois.

Outside of the two great categories which we have just mentioned, there was besides, a gang of *mauvais garçons*, a band of ruffians organized and divided into sections, who hired out as assassins to any that would honor them, we will say, with their confidence. And, let us add in passing, during that era of the fulness of love and hate, the number of those desiring to be rid of another being great, there was no lack of work.

None of these were regarded as suspicious characters by Monsieur de Mouchy's agents. It was known that in general they were employed by rich and noble lords, even by princes, indeed, and good care was taken not to disturb them in the performance of their duties.

Still there remained the *guilleris*, *plumets*, and *grisons*, who corresponded to our cutpurses, pickpockets, and panders. But these fellows were such low rascals that, had Monsieur de Mouchy's agents considered them suspicious characters, Monsieur de Mouchy's agents would not have deigned to be seen in their company.

It was, therefore, very rare for gentlemen to venture into the streets of Paris at night otherwise than well armed and accompanied by a certain number of attendants. Hence it was very imprudent for our young men to be out at such an hour, unattended, and nothing less than a matter of such importance as the one that had brought them out could induce us to overlook such rashness on their part.

This explains how the chief of the *tire-soie* recognized, on attacking the man with the threatening voice, that the latter must be a gentleman from the provinces.

After what we have said of the customs of Monsieur de Mouchy's agents, no astonishment will be felt that none of them appeared at the valet's cries. But his shouts had evidently been heard by a young man who was leaving the Hôtel de Coligny. Comprehending the difficulty, he had wrapped his mantle around his left arm, had drawn his sword in his right hand, and rushed forward shouting, —

"Stand fast, monsieur! If you want help, here it is!"

"I did not call for help," angrily replied the gentleman, as he wielded his long sword; "it was this squalling La Briche, who thinks he is justified in disturbing a gentleman and waking up the quarter on account of five or six miserable assassins."

"We are not assassins, monsieur," replied the leader of the band, "as you can see from the courtesy with which you are treated. We are *tire-soie,* as we have already told you, freebooters of good family, all having lands of our own; and we rob only gentlemen. Instead of calling to your aid a third person, who will add fuel to the fire, you would do much better to yield with a good grace and not force us to resort to violence, which we dislike beyond expression."

"Not a pistole!" returned the gentleman assailed.

"Ah! thieves! — ah! dogs! — ah! wretches!" shouted the gentleman from the admiral's, as he flung himself into the midst of the fray.

One of the *tire-soie* gave a groan which testified that the new-comer had joined word and deed.

"Come!" said the leader of the band, "since you are obstinate, I see indeed that we must fight it out."

And, in the shadow, the shapeless group became more animated, shrieks issued from the throats of the wounded, fast and faster flew the sparks from dirk and dagger.

La Briche, while striking out his best, continued to shout for help. It was his system, and he could maintain that it was a good one, since it had already succeeded.

His screams could have but one result, — a theatre once provided.

"We cannot let those three men be slaughtered in cold blood," exclaimed the Prince de la Roche-sur-Yon, drawing his sword.

"True, prince," said the Duc de Montpensier, "and, really, I am ashamed to have delayed so long."

And the two young men, responding to the call of La Briche, as the gentleman emerging from the Hôtel Coligny had done just a moment before, rushed upon the field of action, crying in turn, —

"Stand fast, messieurs! here we come! to the death! to the death!"

The *tire-soie*, compelled to face the three men, having already lost two of theirs, and seeing this new reenforcement preparing to charge their rear, resolved to make a last stand, although they were now but nine to five.

The leader, with five of his men, confronted the three they had first assailed, while four of the bandits faced about to receive Messieurs de Montpensier and de la Roche-sur-Yon.

"To the death, then, gentlemen, since you will have it so!" cried the chief.

"To the death!" repeated the band.

"With all my heart! have at them, comrades! To the death!" cried the gentleman from the Hôtel Coligny. "By all means! — to the death! There — !"

And, with a lunge as great as his slight stature permitted, he passed his sword through the body of one of the assailants.

The wounded man gave a groan, took three steps backward, and fell stone dead on the pavement.

"A pretty stroke, monsieur!" exclaimed the gentleman first assaulted. "But I think I can match it for you. There!"

And, with a lunge in turn, he buried his sword to its basket-hilt in a bandit's body.

At almost the same moment, the Duc de Montpensier's poniard disappeared to the guard in the throat of one of his adversaries.

The bandits were now but six to five, as much as to say that they were becoming the weaker party, when suddenly the door of the Hôtel Coligny opened wide, and the admiral, followed by two torch-bearers and four armed lackeys, appeared under the lighted archway, sword in hand, and wearing a dressing-gown.

"Ho, there, clowns!" he called out, "what are you about? Clear the street, and quickly, too, or I will nail every man of you like crows to the great door of my hôtel."

Then, turning to his lackeys, he said, —

"Come, my lads, upon the rascals!"

And setting the example, he started for the field of battle.

This time, there was no chance to make a stand.

"Every man for himself!" cried the chief, parrying, but a little too late, a sword thrust which had yet force enough to pierce his arm. "Every man for himself! it is the Prince de Condé!"

And darting swiftly to the left, he took to his heels.

Unfortunately, five of his comrades were unable to profit by this charitable warning. Four were stretched on the ground, and the fifth was forced to lean against the wall to save himself from falling.

This last stroke was the work of the Prince de la Roche-sur-Yon, so that each had done his duty.

As for the gentlemen, they had received but scratches or slight wounds.

The gentleman first assailed, learning to his great astonishment that the one who had first come to his rescue was no other than the Prince de Condé, turned and bowed with deference, saying, —

"Monseigneur, I have double reason to thank Providence: first, for my safety; and in the second place, for having sent as the instrument of my salvation, — with no reflection upon these noble lords, — the bravest gentleman in France."

"By my faith! monsieur," said the prince, "I am happy that chance brought me at this hour of the night to my cousin, the admiral's, and at the same time placed me in the way of being of service to you. Now, as you have thanked me in such pleasant terms for the little I have done, I should esteeem it a favor if you would tell me your name."

"My name, monseigneur, is Godefroi de Barri."

"Ah!" interposed Condé, "Baron de Périgord, Seigneur de la Renaudie?"

"And a good friend of mine," said the admiral, extending one hand to La Renaudie and the other to the Prince de Condé. "Now, if I mistake not," continued the admiral, "it is a long time since the king's pavement has seen such a gallant gathering, — Monsieur le Duc de Montpensier and Monsieur le Prince de la Roche-sur-Yon."

"In person, Monsieur l'Amiral!" said the Prince de la Roche-sur-Yon, while La Renaudie turned toward him and his companion, saluting them both; "and, if it can please these poor devils to know that those who have given them their passes to hell are not exactly peasants, they can rest in peace, well satisfied!"

"Messieurs," said the admiral, "the door of the Hôtel de Coligny is open. That is to say, if you will do me the honor to enter and have some refreshment, you shall be welcome."

"Thanks, dear cousin," said Monsieur de Condé. "But you know that I left you ten minutes ago with the intention of returning home. I did not suspect that I should have the pleasure of meeting at your door a gentleman whose acquaintance you had promised me."

And he courteously saluted La Renaudie.

"A brave gentleman whom I have seen at work, cousin, and who, I give you my word, acquits himself marvellously well," continued the prince. "Have you been long in Paris, Monsieur de Barri?"

"I have just arrived, monseigneur," replied La Renaudie in accents of profound melancholy, and casting a final glance at the wretch whom his last sword-thrust had stretched dead on the pavement; "and I did not expect," he added, "to be the cause of a man's death, and to owe my own life to a great prince before a half-hour had rolled away after I had passed the gates."

"Monsieur le Baron," said the Prince de Condé, holding out his hand to the young man with his accustomed graciousness and urbanity, "pray believe that I shall be greatly pleased to see you again. The friends of Monsieur l'Amiral are the friends of the Prince de Condé."

"Well said, my dear prince!" remarked Coligny, with an inflection that signified,—"That is no idle speech you are making, and we shall recur to it later."

Then, turning to the young men, he asked,—

"And you, messieurs, will you not do me the honor

to enter? Before I became your father's enemy, Monsieur de Montpensier, or, rather, before he became mine, we were hearty comrades. I hope," he added with a sigh, "that it is the times that are changed, and not our hearts!"

"Thanks, Monsieur l'Amiral," returned the Duc de Montpensier, answering for himself and the Prince de la Roche-sur-Yon, as Coligny's words had been addressed to him especially, "we should be most happy to accept your hospitality, were it only for a moment; but the Hôtel de Condé is at some distance from here, bridges must be crossed, bad quarters traversed, and we are about to ask the prince the favor of escorting him."

"Go, messieurs, and may God keep you! For that matter, I should not advise all the *tire-soie* and the *tire-laine* of Paris banded together to attack three men so valiant as you."

This entire conversation had taken place on the very scene of the fight, the victors standing with their feet in blood, and none of them, excepting La Renaudie, a man seemingly of another epoch, glanced at the five wretches, of whom three were already corpses, but two of whom were still in the throes of death.

The Prince de Condé, the Prince de la Roche-sur-Yon, and the Duc de Montpensier saluted the admiral and La Renaudie, and turned in the direction of the Pont-aux-Moulins, an edict forbidding the ferry-men to ply their boats after nine o'clock at night.

Left alone with La Renaudie, the admiral extended his hand.

"You were on your way to my house, were you not, my friend?" said he.

"Yes; I come from Geneva, and have most important news to give you."

"Come in! My house is yours at any hour, day or night."

And he pointed to the door of the hôtel, open and waiting for the guest who must have come in the Lord's care, since the Lord had so miraculously saved him.

Meanwhile, the two young men who, it is readily seen, had not accompanied the prince merely for the sake of providing him an escort, but rather for the purpose of relating the adventure of the king and Mademoiselle de Saint André, narrated, without omitting a detail, the occurrence which he himself, with details quite as exact in other respects, had just related to the admiral.

The news had been quite fresh for Monsieur de Coligny. Madame l'Amirale had returned and shut herself in her room without saying a word, not only of this occurrence, which she could not have foreseen, but also of the loss of the billet, chief cause of all this tumult; so that, however well-informed Monsieur de Condé might be as to all the rest, he was still ignorant — so true it is that there is always something for us to learn — as to how and on what information all the court, headed by Monsieur de Saint André and Monsieur de Joinville, had burst into the Salle des Métamorphoses.

That was a secret which could be divulged by the two young princes.

They told him then, speaking by turn like the shepherds of Virgil, how the admiral's wife had laughed until she cried; how, crying still more than she laughed, she had drawn her handkerchief from her pocket to wipe her eyes; how, in drawing her handkerchief from her pocket, she had at the same time drawn with it a billet which had fallen on the floor; how Monsieur de Joinville had picked up the billet; how, after Madame l'Amirale's departure, the young prince had exhibited the note to the queen-mother; how the queen-mother, thinking that the said billet concerned her good friend, the admiral's wife, had suggested the surprise; how the surprise-party, decided upon by a unanimous vote, had set out; and how, in the end, the surprise had reacted on those who had intended to surprise.

The end of the story brought them to the door of the Hôtel de Condé. The prince in turn gave the young men the invitation extended by the admiral to all, but they declined it; however, they confessed to the prince the true cause of their refusal. They had lost some precious time in that unexpected affair of Monsieur de la Renaudie's, and they had still many friends to whom they wished to communicate the story which they had just told Monsieur de Condé.

"What pleases me most in this affair," said the Prince de la Roche-sur-Yon, shaking hands a last time with Monsieur de Condé, "is the face that Mademoiselle de Saint André's adorer must draw upon learning this news."

"What! her adorer?" said the Prince de Condé, retaining Monsieur de la Roche-sur-Yon's hand which he was on the point of releasing.

"What! don't you know about that?" inquired the young man.

"I know nothing, messieurs," replied the prince laughing. "Speak! speak!"

"Ah! bravo!" cried the Duc de Montpensier; "for that is the prettiest part of the story."

"Were you not aware," continued the Prince de la Roche-sur-Yon, "that besides a fiancé and a lover, Mademoiselle de Saint André has still another devotee?"

"And who is this devotee?" demanded the prince.

"Ah! in faith, you ask too much, this time; I do not know his name."

"Is he young? is he old?" asked the prince.

"We cannot see his face."

"Really?"

"No. He is always enveloped in a great mantle which conceals all the lower portion of his face."

"He is some Spaniard from the court of King Philip II.," added the Duc de Montpensier.

"And where does this wooer appear, or rather this shadow?"

"If you were less seldom at the Louvre, my dear prince, you would not have put such a question."

"Why?"

"Because for the last six months, now, he has walked after nightfall under his lady-love's windows."

"Nonsense!"

"It is truth."

"And you do not know the man's name?"

"No."

"You have never seen his face?"

"Never."

"You have not recognized his figure?"

"He is always wrapped in an immense cloak."

"And you have no suspicions as to who he is, prince?"

"None."

"Not the slightest suspicion, duc?"

"Not the slightest."

"Yet some conjecture has certainly been made!"

"One among others," said the Prince de la Roche-sur-Yon.

"What is it?"

"It has been said that it was you," continued the Duc de Montpensier.

"I have so many enemies at the Louvre!"

"But there is nothing in it, of course?"

"Pardon, messieurs, it was I!"

And, with a bow and a cavalier wave of the hand to the two young men, the prince entered his hôtel, and shut the door behind him, leaving Monsieur de Montpensier and Monsieur de la Roche-sur-Yon standing there, stupefied with amazement in the middle of the street.

XXI.

LIKE MOTHER, LIKE SON.

The queen-mother had not closed her eyes during the whole night.

Thus far, her son, a puny, sickly child, scarcely matured, married to a coquettish young queen, interested in nothing but love, hunting, and poetry, had left to her — to her and the Guises — the entire management of affairs, what kings call the burden of state, and yet are so jealous of maintaining.

To Catherine, reared in the midst of the intrigues of Italian politics, — paltry, petty politics, fit for a small duchy like Tuscany, but unworthy of a great kingdom such as France was beginning to be, — power was life.

Now, what did she see dawning on the horizon opposed to her own?

A rival — not in her son's love; for her son's love she could have been consoled. Who does not love has no right to exact love; she loved neither François II. nor Charles IX.

She was dismayed, therefore, this farseeing Florentine, at discovering in her son a sentiment which was unknown to her, which was not inspired by herself, which had been developed without her, and which had suddenly burst upon the court, surprising them, surprising her at the same time, and, consequently, still more than it surprised others.

And she was especially terrified, knowing the one to whom her son had turned; for out of the young girl's sixteen years, she had seen in lightning flashes the ambition of the woman.

When day dawned, she sent her son a message saying that she was suffering, and that she begged him to come to her room.

In her own room, Catherine, like a clever actor in his own theatre, was free to select her position and command the stage. She established herself in the shadow, where she remained but dimly visible; she placed those who approached her in the light where she could see all. This is why, instead of going to seek her son, she pretended to be ailing and summoned him to visit her.

The messenger returned saying that the king was still asleep.

Catherine impatiently waited an hour, and sent again.

The same answer.

She waited with increasing impatience for another hour. The king was still asleep.

"Oh! oh!" murmured Catherine, "the sons of France are not in the habit of sleeping so late. This slumber is too pertinacious to be natural."

And she left her bed, where she had waited in the hope of being able to play out the scene that she had meditated, half-hidden by the curtains, and gave the order for herself to be dressed.

The theatre was changed. Everything that would have been of service to Catherine in her own apartment was wanting in her son's. But she considered herself a sufficiently clever comedian for this change of scene to have no effect on the result.

Her toilet was hurried, and when it had been achieved, she directed herself in all haste to the apartment of François II.

Without ceremony she entered the king's room as any mother enters her son's. None of the valets or officers stationed in the ante-chambers dreamed of stopping her.

She therefore proceeded through the first hall leading to the king's apartment, and raising the portière of the bed-chamber, she saw him, not lying down, not asleep in his bed, but sitting before a table, facing the embrasure of a window.

With his elbow resting on the table, and his back turned to the door, he was regarding some object so attentively that he did not hear the portière rise in front of his mother and fall behind her. Catherine stood still at the door. Her eye, which had at first sought the bed, became fixed upon François II.

Her glance flashed with a light in which there was certainly more of hate than of love.

Then she slowly advanced, and with no more noise than if it had been her shadow instead of herself, she leaned on the back of the arm-chair, and looked over her son's shoulder.

The king had not heard her approach. He was sitting in an ecstasy before a portrait of Mademoiselle de Saint André.

The expression of Catherine's face hardened and, with a quick muscular contraction, turned into the most accentuated hatred.

Then, by a powerful self-control, the muscles of her face relaxed, the smile returned to her lips, and she bent her head until it almost touched the king's.

François shivered with terror as he felt a warm breath fan his hair.

He turned sharply and recognized his mother.

By a movement as quick as thought, he overturned

the portrait on the table with the face down and placed his hand upon it.

Then, instead of rising and embracing his mother, as was his wont, he rolled his chair and moved away from Catherine.

Then he nodded to her coldly.

"Well, my son," demanded the Florentine, without appearing to notice the frigidity of his greeting, "what has happened?"

"Do you ask me what has happened?"

"Yes."

"Why, nothing at all that I am aware of, mother!"

"I beg your pardon, my son. Something extraordinary must have happened."

"And why?"

"Because it is not your custom to remain in bed until this hour. It is true, I may have been deceived, or the messenger has misunderstood."

François remained silent, regarding his mother almost as steadily as she regarded him.

"Four times have I sent to you this morning," continued Catherine. "I was told that you were asleep."

She paused; but the king continued to maintain silence, looking at her as if to say, "Well, what then?"

"So that," Catherine continued, "being alarmed at such persistent sleeping, I feared you were ill and came to see you."

"I thank you, madame," vouchsafed the young prince, inclining his head.

"You should never alarm me thus, François," insisted the Florentine. "You know how much I love you, how precious your health is to me! Do not, therefore, trifle longer with the anxiety of your mother.

Enough annoyances assail me from others, without my children's adding still more to them by their indifference toward me."

The young man appeared to have formed a resolution. A wan smile played on his lips, and, extending his right hand to his mother, while the left still rested on the portrait, he said, —

"Thanks, dear mother; with all the exaggeration there is some truth in what has been told you. I have been ailing; I have spent a restless night, and I arose two hours later than usual."

"Oh!" exclaimed Catherine, very dolefully.

"But," continued François II., "I am quite myself now, and ready to work with you, if such is your good pleasure."

"And why, my dear child," said Catherine, retaining François' hand in one of her own, holding it against her heart, and passing her other through his hair, "why have you spent such a restless night? Do I not take on myself all weighty affairs, leaving you only the pleasures of royalty? How does it happen that any one has permitted himself to impose upon you fatigue which should have been mine? For I presume that they were affairs of state that troubled you, were they not?"

"Yes, madame," answered François II. with such precipitation that Catherine would have guessed the lie, had she not known beforehand the true cause of that night's restlessness.

But she guarded well against expressing the least doubt, and, on the contrary, feigned to have implicit confidence in her son's words.

"Some important question is to be decided, is there not?" continued Catherine, visibly determined to force her son to the wall; "a question of engaging an enemy, of repairing an injustice, of lessening a heavy tax, of confirming a death-sentence?"

At these words, François remembered indeed that he had been asked the day before to fix the execution of Councillor Dubourg for that same evening.

He eagerly seized upon the cue that was given him.

"It is just that, mother," he answered. "It is the question of passing a sentence of death upon one man by another, although that other is a king. A death-sentence is always such a solemn matter, — and that is the real cause of the trouble in which I have been since yesterday."

"You fear to sign the death-warrant of an innocent man, do you not?"

"Of Monsieur Dubourg, yes, mother."

"That comes from a good French heart, and you are the worthy son of your mother. But, in this case, fortunately, there is no mistake to be made. Councillor Dubourg has been found guilty of heresy by three different jurisdictions, and the signature for which you are asked, that the execution may take place this evening, is a simple formality."

"That is what seems so terrible, mother," said François, — "that a simple formality should suffice to take a man's life."

"What a heart of gold you have, my son!" exclaimed Catherine, "and how proud I am of you! However, be reassured. The safety of the State is to be considered before the life of a man, and in this instance, you need hesitate the less, since the councillor must die, first because it is right, next because it is necessary."

"You are not unaware, my dear mother," said the young man after a moment's hesitation, and turning pale, "that I have received two threatening letters."

"Liar and coward!" muttered Catherine between her teeth. Then aloud and with a smile she said, —

"My son, it is just because you have received these two threatening letters with regard to Monsieur Dubourg, that Monsieur Dubourg must be condemned; otherwise, it would be thought you had yielded to threats and that your clemency arose from fear."

"Ah!" said François, "do you think so?"

"Yes, I think so, my son," replied Catherine; "while, on the contrary, if you proclaim these two letters by sound of trumpet and, immediately after them, the arrest, it will reflect great glory on you and great shame on Monsieur Dubourg. All who now are neither for nor against him will be against him."

François appeared to be reflecting.

"From the nature of these two letters," continued Catherine, "I should not even be surprised if a friend had written them instead of an enemy."

"A friend, madame?"

"Yes," insisted Catherine, "a friend, careful at once of the welfare of the king and of the glory of the kingdom."

The young man lowered his dull gaze under his mother's keen one.

Then, raising his head after a moment's silence, he said, —

"You had those two letters written to me, did you not, madame?"

"Oh!" said Catherine, in a tone that belied her words, "I do not say that, my son."

Catherine had a double motive for allowing her son to think the two letters had emanated from her: first, to make him blush for his cowardice, next, to remove the fear with which the two letters had inspired him.

The youth, whom those letters had cruelly tormented, and who preserved a doubt in the depths of his mind, cast at his mother a quick glance of anger and hate.

Catherine smiled.

"If he could strangle me," she said to herself, "he would certainly do it at this moment. But, fortunately, he cannot do it."

Thus, Catherine's affectation of maternal tenderness, her protestations of devotion, her cat-like wheedling had in no respect been able to touch the heart of François. The queen-mother likewise saw that her fears were about to be realized, and that, unless she remedied the matter with all possible haste, she was on the point of losing her influence over him. She completely and instantly changed her plan of attack.

She heaved a sigh, shook her head, and assumed a look of the deepest dejection.

"Ah! my son," cried she, "I must needs be convinced of what I have hesitated to believe, but which I am no longer permitted to doubt."

"What, madame?" demanded François.

"My son, my son," said Catherine, essaying to call a tear to her aid, "you no longer have confidence in your mother."

"What do you mean?" returned the young man with an air of gloomy impatience. "I do not understand."

"I mean, François, that you are suddenly forgetting the fifteen years of mortal anxiety, fifteen years of watching at your pillow; I mean that you are forgetting the terrors that I underwent during your infancy, the constant care with which my solicitude has surrounded you from the cradle."

"I understand you still less, madame, but I have been schooled to patience; I am waiting and listening."

And the young man's nervous hand gave the lie to his boast of patience, by clutching at the portrait of Mademoiselle de Saint André with an almost convulsive movement.

"Well," replied Catherine, "you shall understand me. I say that, thanks to the care I have taken of you, François, I know you as well as you know yourself. Now this night has been full of trouble for you, I know; but not because you have considered the welfare of the State, not because you have hesitated between severity and clemency, but because your secret amours with Mademoiselle de Saint André are revealed."

"Mother!" cried the young man into whose countenance surged all the shame and anger he had endured on the preceding night.

Ordinarily pale, with an unwholesome, deadly pallor, François became as red as if a wave of blood had passed over his face.

He rose, but stood with his hand clutching the back of his chair.

"Ah! do you know that, mother?"

"What a child you are, François!" said Catherine, with that good nature which she knew so well how to affect. "Do not mothers know everything?"

François stood silent, his teeth set, his cheeks quivering. Catherine continued in her softest tones, —

"Tell me, my son, why you have refused to confide this love to me? Doubtless, I should have reproved you; doubtless, I should have reminded you of your duties as a husband; doubtless, I should have endeavored to turn your eyes to the grace, the beauty, the intelligence of the young queen."

François shook his head with a gloomy smile.

"It would have availed nothing?" resumed Catherine. "Well, discovering the disease to be incurable, I should not have tried to cure it; I should have counselled you. Is a mother not her child's visible Providence, and, seeing you so devoted to Mademoiselle de Saint André, — for you love Mademoiselle de Saint André very much, as it seems?"

"Very much, yes, madame!"

"Well then, I should have shut my eyes. It would have been easier for me to shut them as a mother than to shut them as a wife. Did I not, for fifteen years, see Madame de Valentinois share your father's heart with me, at times even take it from me altogether? Now, do you think that what a woman has done for her husband, a mother cannot do for her son? Are you not my pride, my joy, my happiness? How does it happen, then, that you have loved in secret without telling me?"

"Mother," replied François, with a self-possession that would have done credit to her own powers of dissimulation in the eyes of Catherine herself, if she could have known what was to follow, "mother, you are really so kind to me that I blush for having deceived you so long. Well, yes, I confess, I love Mademoiselle de Saint André!"

"Ah!" exclaimed Catherine, "you see, indeed —"

"Observe, mother," added the young man, "it is the first time that you have spoken of the matter; and if you had spoken of it sooner, — having no reason for concealment from you, since this affection is not only firmly rooted in my heart, but, what is more, in my will, — if you had spoken of it sooner, I should have avowed it sooner."

"In your will, François!" cried the astonished Catherine.

"Yes. You are surprised, are you not, mother, that I have a will? But there is one thing at which I, too, am surprised," continued the young man, regarding her steadily; "it is that you have this morning just played this farce of the tender mother, when it was you who, last night, gave up my secret to the ridicule of the court, when you are the sole cause of what has happened."

"François!" cried the queen-mother, more and more amazed.

"No," pursued the young man, "no, madame, I was not asleep this morning when you sent for me. I was gathering information from all sources on the prime cause of this scandal, and all the information I have collected has resulted in convincing me that you are the one who laid the snare in which I was caught."

"My son! my son! be careful as to what you say!" replied Catherine with set teeth, and casting upon her son a look as glittering and as piercing as the blade of a poniard.

"First, madame, let us understand one thing: there is no longer any question of mother and son between us."

A gesture escaped Catherine in which were blended threat and terror.

"There is a king who, thank God, is of age; there is a queen regent who has nothing more to do, if it is this king's pleasure, with affairs of state. The king reigns at fourteen in France, madame, and I am sixteen. Well, I am weary of the rôle of infant which you continue to thrust upon me when I am past the age for it. I am tired of the sensation of leading-strings around me, as if I were still in swaddling clothes. In short, and to sum all, madame, henceforth, if you please, we will each assume our real position. I am your king, madame, and you are only my subject."

A thunderbolt falling into the room could not have produced a more terrible effect than this fulminating apostrophe bursting in the midst of Catherine's projects. Thus, then, what she had supposed she was saying in hypocritical jest was true. For sixteen years she had reared, cared for, led, instructed, directed this rickety child; like the keepers of the tawny brutes in our days, she had impoverished, exhausted, enervated this lion's cub, and behold, suddenly the young lion awoke, growled, showed his teeth, turned upon her his glowing eyes, and rushed at her the whole length of his chain. Who could answer whether he would not devour her if the chain were to break?

She recoiled in terror.

For a woman like Catherine de Médicis, there was something to shudder at in what she had just seen, in what she had just heard.

And what terrified her most, perhaps, was not the climax of the end, but the dissimulation of the beginning.

In her judgment, to know how to dissimulate was everything; the strength of the crafty policy brought by her from Florence was dissimulation. And it was a woman, a young girl, a child almost, who had produced this change, regenerated this sickly creature, endowed this sorry mortal with the hardihood to speak these strange words: "Henceforth, I am your king, and you are only my subject."

"Against the woman who has wrought this strange metamorphosis," thought Catherine, "the woman who has made of this child a man, of this slave a king, of this dwarf a giant, against that woman I must enter the lists."

Then, under her breath, as if regaining her faculties, the queen-mother murmured, —

"*Vrai Dieu!* I was worn out with having to deal with only a phantom. And so," she added aloud to François, quite prepared to support the attack, however unexpected it might have been, "and so it is I whom you accuse of being the author of last night's scandal?"

"Yes," dryly returned the king.

"You accuse your mother without certainty of her guilt. That is a good son!"

"Will you say, madame, that the affair did not emanate from your apartment?"

"I do not say that it might not have emanated from my apartment; I say that it did not emanate from me."

"Then who betrayed the secret of my rendezvous with Mademoiselle de Saint André?"

"A note."

"A note?"

"A note that fell from the pocket of Madame l'Amirale."

"A note fallen from the pocket of Madame l'Amirale? You are jesting!"

"God forbid my jesting on what gives you pain, my son!"

"But by whom was this note signed?"

"It bore no signature."

"By whom was it written?"

"The writing was unknown to me."

"But, in short, what became of this note?"

"There it is!" said the queen-mother, who had preserved it. And she handed the note to the king.

"Lanoue's writing!" cried the king.

Then, after a second, he said with growing amazement, —

"My own note."

"Yes; but admit that you alone would recognize it."

"And do you say this note fell from Madame l'Amirale's pocket?"

"It so surely fell from Madame l'Amirale's pocket, that everyone supposed it to implicate her, that it was she whom they were preparing to surprise; otherwise," added Catherine, shrugging her shoulders and smiling disdainfully, "otherwise, do you suppose that the two persons whom you must have seen on opening your eyes would have been the Maréchal de Saint André and Monsieur de Joinville?"

"And the secret of all this intrigue directed against myself and the woman I love?"

"Madame l'Amirale alone can give it to you."

François raised a small gold whistle to his lips and blew a shrill note.

An officer lifted the portière.

"Let some one go to the admiral's hôtel, Rue de Béthisy, and inform Madame l'Amirale that the king desires to speak with her immediately."

On turning back, François encountered his mother's fixed and gloomy stare riveted upon his face.

He felt himself blush.

"I ask your pardon, mother," said he, ashamed enough that his accusation had proved to be false, "I ask your pardon for having suspected you."

"You have done more than suspect me, François; you have gravely and harshly accused me. But I am not your mother for nothing, and I am prepared to bear with many more accusations."

"Mother!"

"Allow me to continue," said Catherine, frowning; for, seeing her adversary give way, she understood that then was the time to press him.

"I am listening, mother," said François.

"You have made a mistake in this, then, in the first instance, and, in the second, you made a still graver mistake when you called me your subject. I am no more your subject — do you hear? — than you are or ever will be my king. I repeat that you are my son, nothing more, nothing less."

The young man ground his teeth and paled almost to lividness.

"It is you, mother," warned he, with an energy which Catherine had not suspected in him, "it is you who strangely mistake: I am your son, it is true; but it is because I am your eldest son that I am at the same time the king, and I will prove it, mother!"

"You?" exclaimed Catherine, looking at him like a viper ready to strike; "you — king? and you will prove it, say you?"

She burst into a harsh, disdainful laugh.

"You will prove it — and how? Do you think yourself a match in the political arena for Elizabeth of England and Philip II. of Spain? You will prove it! How? By establishing peace between the Guises and the Bourbons, between the Huguenots and the Catholics? You will prove it! Will you do it by placing yourself at the head of the armies, like your grandfather, François I., or your father, Henri II.? Poor child! you — king? Why, are you not aware, then, that I hold your destiny and your very existence between my hands? I have but to say a word, and the crown slips from your head. I have but to give the signal, and the soul takes flight from your body. Look and listen, if you have eyes and ears, and you will see, monsieur, my son, how the people treat their king. You — king? Wretch that you are! The strongest is king — and look at you and look at me!"

As she uttered these last words, Catherine was terrible to behold.

Threateningly she advanced, like a spectre, on the young king, who recoiled three steps and leaned for support against the back of his arm-chair, as if ready to faint.

"Ah!" said the Florentine, "you see indeed that I am still the queen, and that you, you are only a weak and slender reed, which the slightest breath bends to the earth; and you think to rule! Why, look around you at the powerful ones in France who would be kings, were I not here to drive them back every time that they have endeavored to set foot on even the lowest step of your throne. Look at Monsieur de Guise, for example, that winner of battles, that taker of towns: why, his arms reach a hundred times as far as yours, monsieur, my son; and your head, even with its crown, is not worth his heel."

"Well, mother, I will bite Monsieur de Guise's heel. Death seized Achilles by the heel, as I have been taught, and I will reign in spite of him and in spite of you."

"Yes, quite so; and, when you have bitten Monsieur de Guise's heel, when your Achilles is dead, not from the bite, but from poison, who will fight the Huguenots? Do not deceive yourself; you are neither so handsome as Paris, nor so brave as Hector. Are you aware that, after Monsieur de Guise, you have only one great captain in France? For I trust indeed that you do not count as such your idiot of a Constable de Montmorency, who has been beaten in every battle where he has commanded, nor your courtier, the Maréchal de Saint André, whose conquests have been made in antechambers only? No! you have but one great captain, and that is Monsieur de Coligny. Well, that great captain, with his brother Dandelot, almost as great as he, will to-morrow, if he is not to-day, be at the head of the most formidable faction that ever threatened a state. Look at them and look at you; compare yourself with them, and you will see that they are oaks powerfully rooted in the earth, and that you are but a miserable reed bending under the breath of every faction."

"But, after all, what do you desire, what do you exact from me? Am I, then, but an instrument in your hands, and must I resign myself to being the bauble of your ambition?"

Catherine repressed the smile of joy ready to play on her lips and betray her. She was beginning to recover her power. With the tip of her finger she touched the string of the puppet which for an instant had made a feint of acting independently, and she was again about to move it to her liking. But she by no means desired to let her triumph be seen, and, enchanted with this beginning of his defeat, she resolved to complete her victory.

"What I desire, what I exact of you, my son," returned she in her hypocritical voice, more to be feared perhaps than when it was cajoling or threatening, "is no more than this: that you allow me to establish your power, to insure your happiness; nothing more, nothing less. What signifies the rest to me? Am I thinking of myself, in speaking as I do and acting as I speak? Is not my every effort put forth to make you happy? Eh! *mon Dieu!* do you think, then, that the burden of a government is so pleasant and so light a mattter that

I find pleasure in carrying it? You talk of my ambition! Yes, I have one, — to fight until I have overthrown your enemies, or at least until they are worn out one after the other. No, François," said she, with apparent self-abnegation, "on the day when I see you the man I desire you to be, the king that I hope for, I will joyfully, believe me indeed, place the crown on your head and the sceptre in your hand. But were I to do it to-day, I should be giving you a reed instead of a sceptre, a crown of thorns instead of a crown of gold. Grow, my son, strengthen, mature under your mother's eyes as a tree under the sun's rays, and then, then, tall, strong, and mature, be a king!"

"But what must be done, mother, to accomplish that?" cried François, in tones that were almost despairing.

"I will tell you, my son. You must, first of all, renounce the woman who is the chief cause of this scandal."

"Renounce Mademoiselle de Saint André!" cried François, expecting anything but this condition; "renounce Mademoiselle de Saint André!" he repeated, with concentrated rage. "Ah! then that is what you are aiming at?"

"Yes, my son," said Catherine, coldly, "renounce Mademoiselle de Saint André."

"Never, mother!" returned François with a resolute air, and with the energy of which he had already given proof two or three times since the beginning of the conversation.

"Pardon me, François," said the Florentine with the same gentle but resolute tone; "she must be given up. It is the price I place on our reconciliation; if not — there can be none!"

"But do you not know, then, how desperately I love her, mother?"

Catherine smiled at the naïveté of her son.

"Then wherein would be the merit of renouncing her, if you did not love her?" said she.

"But, *mon Dieu!* why should I renounce her?"

"In the interests of the State."

"What has Mademoiselle de Saint André to do with the interest of the State?" demanded François II.

"Do you wish me to tell you?" asked Catherine.

But the king, interrupting her as if having beforehand no doubt of her logic, said, —

"Listen, mother. I know the supreme genius with which God has gifted you; I know the weakness and inertness that he has placed in me; in short, I recognize your authority, present and future, and I trust blindly to you in the decision of public matters and in all concerning the interests of the kingdom which you govern so wisely. But, in return, mother, in return for yielding up to you all these rights, which would be so precious to another, I beg you to allow me free control of my private affairs."

"In every other instance, yes! and I thought even that you had nothing with which to reproach me on this subject. But to-day, no!"

"But why not to-day? Why this severity with regard to the only woman I have ever truly loved?"

"Because this woman, more than any other, my son, can create civil strife in your dominions, because she is the daughter of the Maréchal de Saint André, one of your most devoted servants."

"I will send Monsieur de Saint André to govern some great province, and Monsieur de Saint André will shut his eyes. Besides, Monsieur de Saint André is entirely devoted just now to his love for his young wife, and his young wife will be very glad to be rid of a step-daughter, her rival in wit and beauty."

"It is possible that it may be so in the case of Monsieur de Saint André, whose jealousy has become proverbial, and who keeps his wife shut up quite as if he were a Spaniard of the days of the Cid. But will Monsieur de Joinville, — Monsieur de Joinville, who passionately loves Mademoiselle de Saint André, and who was to have married her, — will he, too, shut his eyes? And if he consents to close them out of reverence for the king, will he shut them before his uncle, the Cardinal de Lorraine, and his father, the Duc de Guise? Really, François, permit me to tell you that you are a poor diplomat, and that, if your mother were not watchful, in less than eight days the foremost despoiler of royalty would snatch your crown from your head, as the first *tire-laine* he meets strips the cloak from the bourgeois' shoulders. A last time, my son, I insist that you renounce this woman, and at this price, do you hear, I repeat that we shall be fully reconciled, and I will arrange the matter with the Messieurs de Guise. Do you understand me, and will you obey me?"

"Yes, mother, I understand you," said François II.; "but I will not obey you."

"You will not obey me!" cried Catherine, coming into collision for the first time with an obstinacy which, like the giant Antæus, arose with renewed strength when supposed to be vanquished.

"No," continued François II., "no, I will not, and I cannot, obey you. I love, I tell you; I am in the first hours of a first love, and nothing can prevail on me to renounce it. I know that I have entered on a thorny path; perhaps it leads to a fatal end; but, I tell you, I love, and I will not look beyond that word."

"You are firmly resolved, my son?"

In those two words, "my son," usually so sweet from a mother's lips, there was an indescribably threatening accent.

"Firmly resolved, madame," answered François II.

"Do you accept the consequences of your foolish obstinacy, whatever they may be?"

"Whatever they may be, I accept them; yes!"

"Then, adieu, monsieur! I know what remains for me to do."

"Adieu, madame!"

Catherine took a few steps toward the door and stopped.

"You will take the blame on yourself?" said she, attempting a last menace.

"I will take the blame on myself."

"Remember that I am in no way responsible for this foolish resolution of yours to strive against your real interests; that, whether misfortune comes upon you or me, all the responsibility will fall on you alone —"

"So be it, mother. I accept the responsibility."

"Then, adieu, François!" said the Florentine with a laugh and a terrible glance.

"Adieu, mother!" answered the young man, with a laugh no less evil, with a look no less threatening.

And mother and son parted, each filled with profound hatred for the other.

XXII.

IN WHICH MONSIEUR DE CONDÉ PREACHES REVOLT TO THE KING.

WE must bear in mind the promise made by the Prince de Condé to Robert Stuart on the preceding evening, and the rendezvous that he had appointed with the young man for the following night on the Place Saint-Germain-l'Auxerrois.

The Prince de Condé entered the Louvre just as the queen was leaving her son's apartment.

He came to fulfil his promise of asking the king to pardon Anne Dubourg.

He was announced to the king.

"Let him enter!" returned the king in a feeble voice.

The prince entered and saw the young monarch lying rather than sitting in his arm-chair, and wiping with his handkerchief the perspiration that covered his forehead.

His eyes were set, his mouth was open, his face livid.

He might have been taken for a statue of Fear.

"Ah! ah!" murmured the prince, "the child is in trouble."

Let it not be forgotten that the prince had been present to the end of the interview between the king and Mademoiselle de Saint André, and had heard the promises made by the former to his mistress.

At sight of the prince the king's face suddenly brightened. The sun in person entering the gloomy chamber could not more suddenly have illumined it. One would have said that the young king had just made a great discovery. An inspiration lighted up his face with hope. He rose and went to meet the prince. One would have thought him about to cast himself on the other's bosom in an embrace.

It was the attraction of strength for weakness, as powerful as that of the magnet for iron.

The prince, who seemed but moderately desirous of an embrace, bowed at the first step he saw the king make to advance toward him.

Restraining his first impulse, François paused and extended a hand to the prince.

The latter, being unable to dispense with kissing the hand extended to him, bravely performed his part.

Only, in pressing it to his lips, he asked himself, —

"How the devil can I be of use to him, that he gives me such a welcome to-day?"

"Oh! how glad I am to see you, cousin!" said the king tenderly.

"And I, sire, am at once glad and honored."

"You could not have come more opportunely, prince."

"Am I so fortunate?"

"Yes; I have been horribly vexed."

"Indeed," said the prince, "just as I entered, Your Majesty was looking profoundly annoyed."

"Profoundly, that is the word. Yes, my dear prince, I am frightfully plagued."

"Royally, in short," said the prince, with a smile and a bow.

"And the sadness of it is, cousin," continued François II., with an air of profound melancholy, "that I have no friend to whom I can confide my troubles."

"Has the king troubles?" asked Condé.

"Yes; and serious ones, real ones, my dear cousin."

"And who, then, is audacious enough to cause Your Majesty trouble?"

"A person who, unfortunately, has the right, cousin."

"I know of no one, sire, that has the right to annoy the king."

"No one?"

"No one, sire."

"Not even the queen-mother?"

"Ah! ah!" thought the prince to himself, "the queen-mother, it seems, has been whipping her baby."

Then, aloud, the prince repeated, —

"Not even the queen-mother, sire."

"Is that your opinion, cousin?"

"It is not only my opinion, sire, but it is also, I presume, that of all Your Majesty's faithful subjects."

"Do you know that you are saying a very serious thing, Monsieur cousin?"

"Serious in what respect, sire?"

"You are preaching revolt to a son against his mother."

And as he spoke he looked on every side, like a man afraid of being overheard, although apparently alone.

In fact, François knew that for any one in possession of their secret, the walls of the Louvre transmitted sounds as readily as water infiltrates through sand.

Not daring then to express all his thought, he contented himself with saying, —

"Ah! in your opinion the queen-mother has no right to interfere with me. What would you do then, cousin, if you were king of France and the queen-mother crossed you? In short, and to be brief, what would you do if you were in my place?"

The prince understood the king's fear; but as he was, under all circumstances, in the habit of saying what he thought, he returned, —

"What would I do in your place, sire?"

"Yes!"

"In your place, I should revolt."

"You would revolt?" repeated François, joyfully.

"Yes," returned the prince briefly.

"But how can I revolt, my dear Louis?" demanded François, drawing near the prince.

"Why, as any one revolts, sire, — by revolting. Consult those who are accustomed to such acts. The ways are not numerous, — by refusing to obey, for instance, or, at least, by doing all that one can to exempt one's self from an unjust authority, an implacable tyranny."

"But, cousin," said François, thoughtfully, and evidently meditating upon the prince's words, "a serf can revolt in that way against a lord; but a son can no more revolt against his mother, it seems to me, in the absolute sense of the word, than a subject against his king."

"And," said the prince, "what are these thousands of Huguenots who seem to be suddenly springing up from the depths of your farthest provinces, in the Netherlands, and in Germany, doing at this moment, if they are not engaged in a great revolt against the pope? And he is a king, if ever was one!"

"Yes, prince," answered François, from pensive becoming gloomy, "yes, you are right, and I am grateful to you for speaking to me thus. I see you too rarely, cousin. You are a member of my family, the man in whom I have the most confidence, the courtier for whom I entertain the most friendship. From my infancy, dear prince, I have had a sympathetic affection for you, which your courageous frankness has fully justified. No one else would have spoken to me as you have just done. I especially thank you; and, as a proof of my gratitude, I am going to bestow on you a confidence which I have intrusted to no one, and which the queen-mother has just now wrested from me."

"Do so, sire."

The king threw his arm around Condé's neck.

"The more, my dear prince," he continued, "as I shall perhaps need not only the advice that I have just asked of you, but your support also."

"I am in every way at Your Majesty's service."

"Well, my dear cousin, I am desperately in love."

"With Queen Marie? — I know that, sire," said Condé, "and it really creates a scandal in the court."

"No, not with Queen Marie, but with one of her maids of honor."

"Ah!" cried the prince, assuming an air of deepest amazement. "And of course Your Majesty is paid in kind?"

"I am loved beyond all expression, cousin."

"And has Your Majesty received proofs of this love?"

"Yes."

"I should have been surprised, sire, were it otherwise."

"You do not ask me who she is, Louis."

"I would not permit myself to question the king; but I am waiting until he is pleased to complete his confidence."

"Louis, she is the daughter of one of the greatest lords of the French court."

"Ah, indeed!"

"She is the daughter of the Maréchal de Saint André, Louis."

"Accept my sincere congratulations, sire. Mademoiselle de Saint André is one of the most beautiful persons in the kingdom."

"Is she not? That is your opinion, is it not, Louis?" cried the king, overwhelmed with joy.

"For a long time I have entertained of Mademoiselle de Saint André exactly the same opinion as Your Majesty."

"It is another congenial sentiment between us, my dear cousin."

"I should not dare to boast of it, sire."

"And so you think I am right, do you?"

"A hundred times right! When king or peasant meets a girl, he always does right to fall in love with her, and especially to make her fall in love with him."

"So that is your opinion, is it?"

"And it will be every one's, excepting Monsieur de Joinville's. Fortunately, the king, I presume, will not seek his advice; and as it is probable that he will always be ignorant of the honor the king has done his fiancée — "

"There you mistake, Louis," said the king; "he does know it."

"Does Your Majesty mean that he suspects something?"

"I tell you that he knows all."

"Oh! it is impossible — "

"But since I say it is so!"

"Incredible, sire!"

"And yet it must be believed. However," continued the king, knitting his brow, "I should not attach any great importance to this fact, if it had not been followed by an extraordinarily grave occurrence which led to the violent scene between my mother and me, something of which I have told you."

"But what so serious can have happened, sire? I wait Your Majesty's pleasure to reveal the depths of this mystery," ingenuously continued the Prince de Condé, who, however, knew the whole affair better than any one.

Thereupon, the king began to relate in rueful accents, which from time to time assumed a certain fierce energy, the violent scene that had just taken place between himself and his mother.

The prince listened with profound attention.

Then, when François had ended, he said, —

"Well, now, sire, it seems to me that you have come off well enough, and you are this time your own master."

The king regarded the prince and, drawing the arm of the latter within his own, he said, —

"Yes, cousin, yes, I came off very well; as long as she was present, at least, something resembling the joy of the slave that breaks his fetters gave me strength. I permitted the queen to leave me with the belief that my revolt was serious. But when the door had closed behind her, and I was left alone, — come, I must be frank with you, — every muscle in my body, every fibre of my brain relaxed, and if you had not come, cousin, I believe that I should, as at other times, have gone to find her, to throw myself at her feet and entreat her forgiveness."

"Oh! beware of that, sire!" cried Condé; "you would be lost!"

"I know that very well," said the king, clinging to Condé's arm as a shipwrecked mariner clings to the floating spar by which he hopes to save his life.

"But to inspire such terror, the queen-mother must

have threatened you with some dire misfortune, some imminent peril."

"She threatened me with civil war."

"Ah! And where does Her Majesty look for civil war?"

"Why, where you yourself saw it but a moment ago, cousin. The Huguenot party is powerful; but Monsieur de Guise, its enemy, is also powerful. Well, my mother, who sees only with the eyes of the Guises, who governs the kingdom only under the direction of the Guises, who has married me to a woman that is related to the Messieurs de Guise, threatens me with the wrath and, what is more, the desertion of the Messieurs de Guise."

"And in that case, sire?"

"The heretics are masters of the realm."

"And you answered, sire?"

"Nothing, Louis. What could I say?"

"Oh! many things, sire."

The king shrugged his shoulders.

"One among others," continued the prince.

"But what?"

"That there was one means of preventing the heretics from becoming the masters of the realm."

"And this means?"

"Is to place yourself at the head of the heretics, sire."

The young king remained thoughtful, for a moment, with knitted brows.

"Yes," said he, "that is a very wise conception, my dear cousin; one of those games of see-saw, at which my mother is an adept. But the Protestants hate me."

"And why do they hate you, sire? They know that, thus far, you have been but an instrument in your mother's hands."

"Instrument! instrument!" repeated François.

"Said you not so yourself just now, sire? The Huguenot party has not sided against the king; it hates the queen-mother, that is all."

"Indeed, I hate her myself," muttered the young king under his breath.

The prince overheard the words, low as they had been spoken.

"Well, sire?" he demanded.

The king looked at his cousin.

"If the plan seems good to you," continued the prince, "why not adopt it?"

"They would not trust me, Louis; they must have some pledge, and — what pledge have I to give them?"

"You are right, sire; but the season is propitious. It is in your power to give them a pledge at this moment, a truly royal pledge, a man's life."

"I do not understand," said the king.

"You can pardon Councillor Dubourg."

"My dear cousin," said the king, turning pale, "here, in this very room, my mother said to me just now, speaking of him, — 'He must die!'"

"And you yourself, sire, then said that he must live?"

"What! pardon Councillor Dubourg!" whispered the young king looking about him, as if frightened at the bare thought that he could grant a pardon.

"Why, yes, sire, pardon Councillor Dubourg. What, then, is so astonishing in that?"

"Nothing, certainly, cousin."

"Is it not your right?"

"It is the king's right, I know."

"Well, are you not the king?"

"I have not yet been so, at least."

"Well, sire, it would be a noble approach to royalty, a lofty step to the throne."

"But — the councillor, Anne Dubourg?"

"Is one of the most upright men in your kingdom. Ask Monsieur de l'Hospital, who knows."

"I know, indeed, that he is an honest man."

"Ah! sire, it is already much for you to have said that."

"Much?"

"Yes. A king does not condemn to death a man whom he has declared to be an honest man."

"He is dangerous."

"An honest man is never dangerous."

"But the Messieurs de Guise detest him."

"Ah!"

"And the queen-mother detests him."

"The more reason, sire, for beginning your rebellion against the Messieurs de Guise and against the queen-mother by pardoning Councillor Dubourg."

"My dear cousin!"

"*Dame!* I hope that Your Majesty is not giving himself the trouble to revolt against the queen-mother merely for amusement."

"True, Louis; but Monsieur Dubourg's death is decided upon. The question has been settled by the Messieurs de Guise, my mother, and myself; there is no escaping that."

The Prince de Condé could not refrain from casting a look of disdain upon this king, who regarded the death of one of the most upright magistrates of the realm as a settled thing, and one from which there was no escape, while this magistrate was still alive, and the king had but to say one word in order to prevent his death.

"As the question is 'settled,' sire," he repeated, with an accent of profound contempt, "let us say no more about it."

And he was about to salute the king and retire, but the king arrested him.

"Yes, that is it," said he, "let us say no more about the councillor; let us talk of something else."

"And of what, sire?" demanded the prince, who had come for that alone.

"Why, in short, my dear prince, is there but one way out of the embarrassing situation? You are an inventive genius; find me a second means."

"Sire, it was God who found you the first. Man will invent nothing to equal it."

"In truth, my dear cousin," said the young king, "I myself feel compunction at the thought of causing an innocent man to die."

"Then, sire," continued the prince with real solemnity, "listen to the voice of your conscience. Good deeds are fruitful, causing love for his king to flourish in the heart of the subject. Pardon Monsieur Dubourg, sire, and from the day on which you grant the pardon, thus asserting your royal prerogative, all will know that you reign as the sovereign, the true king!"

"Do you wish it, Louis?"

"Sire, I ask it as a favor, and that I swear in the interest of Your Majesty!"

"But what will the queen say?"

"Which queen, Sire?"

"The queen-mother, *pardieu!*"

"Sire, there should be no queen in the Louvre other than the virtuous spouse of Your Majesty. Madame Catherine is queen because she is feared. Make yourself loved, sire, and you will be king!"

The king appeared by an effort to arrive at a final resolution.

"Well, I will repeat the word that you so sharply caught up. It is 'settled,' my dear Louis," said he. "Thank you for your wise counsel, thank you for prompting me to do an act of justice, thank you for arousing my remorse! Give me pen and parchment."

The Prince de Condé drew the king's chair up to the table.

The king sat down.

The Prince de Condé presented the parchment for which he had asked. The king took the pen which the prince handed him, and wrote the essential clause: —

"François, by the grace of God, king of France, to all to whom these presents shall come, greeting: — "

He had written thus far when the officer whom he had sent to the Hôtel Coligny entered and announced Madame l'Amirale.

The king broke off at that point, rose abruptly, and from the gentle look his face had been wearing, it took on an indefinable expression of ferocity.

"What is the matter, sire?" inquired the Prince de Condé, struck with amazement at sight of this brusque change of countenance.

"You shall see, cousin."

Then, turning to the officer, he said, —

"Show in Madame l'Amirale."

"Madame l'Amirale is undoubtedly admitted to an audience with Your Majesty on some personal matter, sire?" said the prince. "I will retire, if Your Majesty will permit."

"No! On the contrary, I desire you to remain, my dear cousin, to be present at our conversation, to lose not a word of it. You already know how I pardon," said he, pointing to the parchment. "I will show you how I punish."

The Prince de Condé felt something like a shudder pass over him. He felt that the audience of the admiral's wife with the king, where she never came except when constrained by force, had some connection with the cause that had brought himself there, and he had a vague presentiment that he was about to witness a terrible scene.

A few moments after the tapestry had fallen it was raised again, and the wife of the admiral appeared.

XXIII.

IN WHICH THE KING CHANGES HIS MIND WITH REGARD TO MONSIEUR DE CONDÉ AND COUNCILLOR ANNE DUBOURG.

BEFORE perceiving the king, Madame l'Amirale had first caught sight of the Prince de Condé upon whom she was prepared to cast a very smiling and affectionate glance, when that glance unexpectedly encountered the king's face.

The angry expression imprinted upon his countenance made the admiral's wife lower her head, and approach with trembling.

Arrived before the king, she courtesied.

"I have sent for you, Madame l'Amirale," said the king, his lips blanched and his teeth set, "to demand the answer to an enigma over which I have puzzled in vain since this morning."

"I am always at Your Majesty's command," stammered the admiral's wife.

"Even to the solution of enigmas?" continued François. "So much the better. I am delighted to know it, and we will forthwith set to work."

Madame l'Amirale bowed.

"Will you, therefore, explain to our dear cousin De Condé and to us," resumed the king, "how it happens that a note written by our order to a member of the court was lost by you last evening in the apartment of the queen-mother?"

The time had come for the Prince de Condé to understand the portent of the shudder he had felt when Madame l'Amirale was announced.

The whole truth rose before his eyes as if it had sprung from the earth, with the king's terrible words humming in his ears: "I will show you how I can punish!"

He glanced at the admiral's wife.

The latter's eyes were fixed upon him, as if she were inquiring, "What must I answer the king?"

The king did not observe the pantomime of the two accomplices, and continued, —

"Well, Madame l'Amirale, there is the enigma stated; we ask you for the key to it."

Madame l'Amirale was silent.

The king went on, —

"But perhaps you have not quite understood my question: I will repeat it. How does it happen that a note which was not addressed to you came into your hands, and by what carelessness or by what perfidy was this note dropped from your pocket on the carpet of the queen-mother's apartment to find its way into the hands of Monsieur de Joinville?"

The admiral's wife had had time to collect her thoughts.

"Very simply, sire," said she, recovering her self-possession. "I found the note in the corridor of the Louvre leading to the Salle des Métamorphoses. I picked it up, I read it, and, not knowing the writing, I carried it with me to the queen-mother's room purposing to ask if she were wiser than I. There was with Her Majesty a large assemblage of writers and poets, and among them Monsieur de Brantôme, who told such ridiculous stories that all laughed till they cried, I with the rest, sire, and so heartily that while laughing I drew out my handkerchief, and my handkerchief of itself caused that unfortunate note which I had forgotten, to slip out and fall to the floor. When I tried to find it, it was no longer there, neither in my pocket nor beside me, and I presume that Monsieur de Joinville had already picked it up."

"The thing has a semblance of truth," said the king with a derisive smile; "but I do not accept it for the truth, however much it may resemble it."

"What may Your Majesty mean?" demanded the admiral's wife with misgiving.

"You found this note?"

"Yes, sire."

"Well, then, nothing is easier than for you to tell me in what it was wrapped."

"Why," stammered the admiral's wife, "it was not wrapped in anything, sire — "

"It was not wrapped in anything?"

"No," said the admiral's wife turning pale; "it was simply folded in four."

A light flashed through the brain of Monsieur le Prince de Condé.

Evidently Mademoiselle de Saint André had explained to the king the loss of her note by the loss of her handkerchief. Unfortunately, what became clear to Monsieur de Condé remained obscure to Madame l'Amirale.

She hung her head then under the king's scrutinizing eye, more and more disconcerted, confessing by her silence that she had merited the anger which she felt resting upon her.

"Madame l'Amirale," said François, "you must confess that, for a devout person like yourself, this is one of the boldest of lies."

"Sire!" stammered the admiral's wife.

"Are these the fruits of the new religion, madame?" continued the king. "Here was our cousin Condé, although a Catholic prince, just now preaching the reformation to us in truly touching terms. Answer Madame l'Amirale yourself, dear cousin, and tell her in our behalf that, to whatever religion one belongs, it is never safe to deceive one's king."

"Pardon, sire," stammered the admiral's wife, as she saw the king's wrath mounting with the swiftness of the tide.

"And with regard to what are you asking pardon, Madame l'Amirale?" said François. "I would have staked my life but an hour ago, whatever might have been said of you, that you were the strictest person in my kingdom."

"Sire!" cried the admiral's wife, proudly lifting her head, "your anger, if you will, but not your derision. It is true I did not find the note."

"Ah! you confess it?" cried the king triumphantly.

"Yes, sire," replied the admiral's wife simply.

"Then some one gave it to you."

"Yes, sire."

The prince was following the conversation with the manifest intention of engaging in it when he should deem the moment opportune.

"And who gave it to you, Madame l'Amirale?" demanded the king.

"I cannot name the person, sire," said Madame de Coligny, firmly.

"But why not, cousin," said the Prince de Condé, interrupting her.

"Yes, why not?" rejoined the king, enchanted that re-enforcement was at hand.

The admiral's wife looked at the prince as if to ask an explanation of his words.

"Of course," continued the prince, in response to the mute interrogation of the admiral's wife, "I have no reason for concealing the truth from the king."

"Ah!" exclaimed the king, turning toward the Prince de Condé, "you know the rights of this story, do you?"

"Perfectly, sire."

"And how does that happen?"

"Why, sire, because I played a leading rôle in it."

"You, monsieur?"

"I myself, sire."

"And how does it happen that you have not said a word to me about it until now?"

"Because, sire," replied the prince without discomfiture, "because you have not done me the honor to question me, and because I could not permit myself to relate an anecdote, whatever it might be, to my gracious sovereign, without being authorized by him."

"I like your deference, cousin Louis. However, respect has its limits, and one can anticipate the questions of his sovereign when one thinks to be of use or, at least, agreeable to him. Do me the favor then, monsieur, to disclose all you know of the matter, and the rôle you have played in this story."

"I played the part of accident. It was I who found the note."

"Ah! it was you!" said the king, frowning and regarding the prince with severity. "Then I am no longer surprised that you awaited my questions. Ah! it was you who found the note?"

"It was I, yes, sire."

"And where?"

"In the lobby leading to the Salle des Métamorphoses, as Madame l'Amirale just now had the honor to tell you."

The king's glance shot from the prince to the admiral's wife, as if endeavoring to fathom whatever of connivance might exist between them.

"Then, my dear cousin," said he, "since you found it, you must know in what it was confined."

"It was not confined, sire."

"What!" cried the king with blanched face, "dare you tell me that the note was not confined?"

"Yes, sire, I have the boldness to tell the truth, and I have the honor to repeat to Your Majesty that the billet was not confined, but daintily enveloped."

"Enveloped or confined, monsieur," said the king, "is it not the same thing?"

"Ah! sire," said the prince, "there is an extraordinary difference between the two words. A prisoner is confined, but a letter is enveloped."

"I did not know you were so skilled in linguistics, cousin."

"The leisure that peace affords permits me to study letters, sire!"

"Finally, monsieur, to make an end of this, tell me in what the note was enveloped or confined."

"In a delicate handkerchief embroidered in the four corners, sire, and it was in one of these corners that the billet was knotted."

"Where is the handkerchief?"

The prince drew the handkerchief from his pocket.

"Here it is, sire!"

The king violently snatched the handkerchief from the Prince de Condé's hands.

"Good! But now, how does it happen that the note

found by you should be in Madame l'Amirale's hands?"

"Nothing could be simpler, sire. In descending the stairs of the Louvre, I met Madame l'Amirale and said to her, 'Cousin, here is a note lost by some gentleman or lady of the Louvre. Be so kind as to learn who has lost a note, an easy matter for you, through Dandelot, who is in charge, and return the note, I beg, to its owner!'"

"That was very natural, certainly, cousin," said the king, who did not believe a word of the whole story.

"Then, sire," said the Prince de Condé, moving as if to retire, "since I have had the honor to satisfy Your Majesty entirely — "

But the king stopped him by a gesture.

"One word more, cousin, if you please," said he.

"Willingly, sire!"

"Madame l'Amirale," said the king, turning to Madame de Coligny, "I know that you are a loyal subject; for in the position in which you were placed before Monsieur le Prince de Condé you said all you could say. I ask your pardon for having put you to inconvenience. You are free and continue in our good graces. The remainder of the explanation rests with Monsieur de Condé."

The admiral's wife saluted and withdrew.

Monsieur de Condé would gladly have done as much; but he was detained by the king's order.

The admiral's wife having departed, the king approached the prince with his teeth set, his lips purple.

"Monsieur," said he, "you had no need to resort to Madame l'Amirale to find out to whom the note was addressed."

"Why not, sire?"

"Because here in one corner of the handkerchief are the initials, and in another the arms, of Mademoiselle de Saint André."

It was Monsieur de Condé's turn to hang his head.

"You knew the note belonged to Mademoiselle de Saint André, and knowing that you allowed it to fall into the hands of the queen-mother."

"Your Majesty will at least do me the justice to admit that I was ignorant of its having been written by his order, and that its being known could compromise him."

"Monsieur, you who so well know the force of the words of the French language, ought to know that nothing can compromise my majesty. I do what I please, and no one sees anything or says anything about it, and the proof — "

He went to the table and lifted the parchment already crossed by a line and a half of his writing.

"And the proof, here — "

He was about to tear the parchment.

"Ah! sire, let your anger fall upon me, and not on an innocent man!"

"From the moment that my enemy protects him, he is no longer innocent in my eyes, monsieur."

"Your enemy, sire!" cried the prince; "does the king consider me his enemy?"

"Why not, since from this moment I am yours?"

And he rent the parchment.

"Sire, sire, in the name of heaven!" cried the prince.

"Monsieur, here is my answer to the threats you just now made in the name of the Huguenot party. I defy it, monsieur, and you along with it, if perchance you should see fit to assume its command. This day, Councillor Anne Dubourg shall be executed."

"Sire, the blood of an innocent man, a just man, will flow."

"Well," said the king, "let it flow, and let it fall drop by drop on the head of him who spilled it."

"And that, sire?"

"Is you, Monsieur de Condé!"

And, pointing to the door, he said to the prince, —

"Go, monsieur!"

"But, sire —" insisted the prince.

"Go, I say!" repeated the king between his set teeth and with a stamp of his foot. "It is not safe for you to remain ten minutes longer in the Louvre!"

The prince bowed and retired.

Overcome, the king fell back into his chair, his elbows on the table, his head in his hands.

XXIV.

A DECLARATION OF WAR.

One can easily understand that, if the king was furious, the Prince de Condé was preyed upon by a rage no less great, and his rage was the more intense because he could blame no one but himself for what had happened, since it was he who had gone to Mademoiselle de Saint André's, it was he who had discovered the note in the handkerchief, it was he, in short, who had delivered the note to Madame de Coligny.

And so, like all people who find themselves involved in embarrassments by their own fault, he resolved to brave it through to the end, and to burn the very last ship by which he might make a retreat.

Besides, after suffering all he had suffered at the hands of Mademoiselle de Saint André, an act of deeper despair, for it would have resembled shame and impotence, would have been to retire without shooting as he went the Parthian dart of revenge, which so often returns to pierce the heart of the lover that aims it.

Now, his revenge on the king was already shaped; but revenge on Mademoiselle de Saint André, — he hesitated.

For an instant, he asked himself whether it was not rather cowardly for him, a man, to avenge himself on a woman; but even as he questioned, he told himself that here was no weak enemy, — this young girl with her crafty, vindictive nature, who would be, that very day, undoubtedly, the declared mistress of the king.

Yes, certainly, it would be risking less danger to challenge the bravest and most skilful gentleman of the court than to engage in a merciless quarrel with Mademoiselle de Saint André.

He well knew that once embroiled with her it was war to the death, without truce or respite, that he would need to stand firm, and that this war, teeming with dangers, with snares, with attacks open and underhanded, would last as long as the king's love endured.

And, considering the splendid beauty of his enemy, her multiple character, her temperament, full of lascivious intoxication, he understood that this love, like that of Henri II. for the Duchesse de Valentinois, would endure as long as life.

Therefore, although he was not facing the danger of the brave man who goes to beard the lion, he was courting the peril, as serious in another way although apparently less grave, of the imprudent traveller who, armed with a simple stick, amuses himself by teasing the beautiful cobra whose least bite is deadly.

This danger was in reality so great, that the prince asked himself an instant whether it was necessary, indeed, to add this fresh bolt to the thunder and lightning already rumbling above his head.

But, as he had hesitated when, before this reflection, he had feared to stoop to a cowardly act, so he felt himself irresistibly impelled when he saw that his action, cowardly in appearance, was in reality rash to very folly.

Had he been obliged to descend the stairs, cross the court, ascend again into the main building, to give himself, in short, time for more serious reflection between leaving the king's apartment and entering Mademoiselle de Saint André's, perhaps reason would have come to his aid, and, like Minerva of old leading Ulysses from the fray, the frigid goddess might have led him away from the Louvre. But unfortunately, the prince had but to follow the corridor in which he then was to find at his left, after two or three turns, Mademoiselle de Saint André's door.

Every step that he took he felt to be bringing him nearer to it, and at every step the pulsations of his heart increased in rapidity and violence.

At last he arrived abreast of the door.

He could turn his head, pass by, and continue on his way. Such, doubtless, was the advice given him by his good angel, but he listened only to his bad one. He stood as if his feet were taking root in the floor, and Daphne changed into a laurel-tree was not, seemingly, more immovably fixed in the earth.

After a moment, not of hesitation, but of reflection, he exclaimed, like Cæsar hurling his javelin from the other side of the Rubicon, —

"*Alea jacta est!*"

And he knocked.

The door was opened.

There might yet remain to the prince the chance that Mademoiselle de Saint André was out, or that she would not receive him.

Destiny was written, however, and Mademoiselle de Saint André was at home, and the two words, "Admit him," reached the prince's ears.

In the interval occurring during his passage from the antechamber where he awaited the answer, to the boudoir where this answer had been uttered in tones sufficiently loud for him to hear, Louis de Condé saw like a vision before his eyes and his heart the whole great panorama of the six months that had just rolled away, from the day on which, in a frightful rain-storm, he had met the young girl in that shabby inn near Saint Denis, down to the hour when he had seen her enter the Salle des Métamorphoses with a branch of myrtle entwined in her hair, and when his indiscreet gaze had not lost sight of her an instant, until the moment when, of all her adornings worn on entering the Salle, she had preserved but that branch of myrtle.

And, as this panorama unrolled before his sight, he saw repeated, rapidly though it was, that scene of the night at Saint Cloud between the young girl and the page; then he saw her again at the edge of the great basin in the half light which the trembling shadow of plane-trees and willows shed upon her; then he saw himself standing motionless under her windows, longing for a blind to be opened and a flower or a note to fall at his feet; finally, he saw himself again beneath the bed where on the first night he had waited in vain when one had not come, and where, on the second, he had seen not only those come whom he was expecting, but others still whom he was not expecting; and all these various sensations, the vision of the inn, the jalousie with its concealed witness, the contemplation of the girl admiring herself in the pond, the impatient waiting beneath her window, the anguish of the lover in the Salle des Métamorphoses, — all these sensations mounting to his brain, causing his temples to throb, rending his heart, torturing his vitals, seized and assailed him at once in the space of a few seconds.

Thus it was, trembling and pale with anger, love, shame, and hate, that he discovered himself in the presence of Mademoiselle de Saint André.

Mademoiselle de Saint André was alone.

When she perceived the prince hiding all the opposing sentiments which were struggling within him under a tolerably impertinent air, when she saw the smile of derision perched on his lips like the American mocking-bird upon its branch, the young girl knitted her brows, but imperceptibly. Hers, in the matter of dissimulation, was a soul quite as hardened in one sense as that of the Prince de Condé.

The prince bowed with an easy air.

Mademoiselle de Saint André did not mistake the significance of that bow; she understood that an enemy was in her presence.

But she permitted not a gleam of penetration to be apparent, and, to the prince's graceful bow and mocking smile, she replied with a low and gracious courtesy.

Then, smiling at him with the gentlest of eyes and addressing him in the most winning of tones, she asked, —

"To what saint, prince, do I owe thanks for this visit, as early as it is unexpected?"

"To Saint Aspasia, mademoiselle," returned the prince, bowing with feigned respect.

"Monseigneur," replied the girl, "I doubt whether I shall find her name on the calendar in this year of grace, 1559, however minutely I may search."

"Then, mademoiselle, if you absolutely must thank some saint for the slender favor of my presence, wait until Mademoiselle de Valentinois is dead and has been canonized, — which cannot fail to happen, if you recommend it to the king."

"As I doubt whether my influence extends so far, monseigneur, I will limit myself to thanking you yourself, at the same time asking very humbly what procures me the pleasure of seeing you."

"What! Can you not guess?"

"No."

"I have come to tender my very sincere congratulations on the recent favor with which His Majesty has honored you."

The young woman flushed scarlet; then, by a sudden reaction, her cheeks were overspread by a deadly pallor.

And yet she was very far from suspecting the truth. She thought merely that the night's adventure had already been noised abroad, and that the echo had reached the ears of the prince.

She contented herself therefore by turning on the prince a look which preserved a medium between inquiry and defiance.

The prince appeared to observe nothing of the look.

"Well," asked he smilingly, "what is the matter now, mademoiselle, and how can the congratulations I have had the honor of addressing to you have been able instantaneously to lend your cheeks the color of your lips, — it is true they did not retain it long, — and then that of the handkerchief that you did me the honor to present me the other night?"

The prince dwelt on these last words so significantly that there was no longer any doubt as to the expression on Mademoiselle de Saint André's face.

It turned wholly to defiance.

"Beware, monseigneur!" said she in a voice the more terrible for affecting perfect calmness. "I believe you have come here with the intention of insulting me."

"Do you think me capable of such audacity, mademoiselle?"

"Or of such cowardice, monseigneur. Which of the two words would be the more appropriate in this case?"

"It is what I asked myself at the door, mademoiselle. My response was, 'Audacity!' — and I entered."

"Then you confess that such was your intention?"

"Perhaps. But, upon reflection, I have preferred to present myself in quite a different character."

"And what is that?"

"As an old adorer of your charms, transformed into a courtier of your fortune."

"And, doubtless, in this capacity, you come to seek a favor."

"A great favor, mademoiselle."

"What is it?"

"That you will consent to pardon me for having been the cause of last night's untimely visit."

Mademoiselle de Saint André stared at the prince with an air of doubt, for she could not believe that a man would so imprudently and deliberately walk into an abyss. From pale, she became livid.

"Prince," said she, "is it really as you say?"

"It is."

"In that case, let me tell you that you must simply have lost your mind."

"I simply think, on the contrary, that I had lost it up to that moment, and that at that moment only did I find it again."

"But do you think, too, that such an insult will remain unpunished, monsieur, prince though you are, or do you hope that I will not inform the king?"

"Oh! that is unnecessary."

"It is unnecessary?"

"*Mon Dieu*, yes, because I have just informed him myself."

"And did you tell him also that on leaving him you intended coming here?"

"No, by my faith! for I had not thought of it; the idea occurred to me on the way. Your door lay in my path, and you know the proverb: 'Opportunity makes the thief.' I said to myself that it would be truly curious if by good luck I were the first to congratulate you. Am I the first?"

"Yes, monsieur, and I accept the compliment," said Mademoiselle de Saint André, haughtily.

"Ah! since you take it so well, let me pay you another."

"On what?"

"On the taste of your toilet upon so momentous an occasion."

Mademoiselle de Saint André bit her lips. The prince was enticing her on ground where it was difficult to defend herself to advantage.

"You are a man of imagination, monseigneur," said she, "and have you not surely, thanks to your imagination, accredited me with a toilet very superior to the one that I wore in reality?"

"No, I swear; it was simple, on the contrary. There was especially a spray of myrtle entwined in those beautiful tresses."

"A spray of myrtle!" cried the girl. "How did you know that I wore a spray of myrtle in my hair?"

"I saw it."

"You saw it?"

Mademoiselle de Saint André began to be thoroughly mystified, and felt her self-possession deserting her.

"Come, prince," said she, "continue; I enjoy fables."

"Then you must remember that of Narcissus — Narcissus enamored of himself and gazing at his reflection in a stream."

"What, then?"

"Well, on the night before last, I saw something similar, or rather, quite as admirable in a different way: it was a young girl enamored of herself and regarding her image in a mirror with no less pleasure than Narcissus felt when gazing into the brook."

Mademoiselle de Saint André uttered a cry. It was impossible for the prince to have invented that, or that it should have been told him. She was alone, or rather she thought she was alone in the Salle de Métamorphoses when the scene to which he referred had taken place. The blush gained the upper hand, — she became purple.

"You lie!" she exclaimed.

Mademoiselle de Saint André's voice was a snarl between her teeth; however, she endeavored to dissemble the snarl under a burst of laughter.

"Oh!" she continued, "what a fine story you have composed."

"Yes, you are right, the story is fine; but what is it in comparison with the reality? Unfortunately, the reality was as transitory as a dream. The beautiful nymph awaited a god, and after all the god could not come, the goddess, his wife, having fallen from her horse like a simple mortal and sustained an injury."

"Have you yet other tales of that sort to relate, monsieur?" said Mademoiselle de Saint André between her teeth, quite ready, in spite of her strength, to allow her wrath to gain the mastery.

"No, I have only a word more: the rendezvous was postponed until the next night. This is all I came to tell you; and, with this, in the hope of the future, permit me to conclude as if I were the king, the present visit having no further purpose, — with this, I pray God to have you in his high and holy keeping!"

And, with this, in fact, the Prince de Condé retired with the insolence that, two centuries later, made the reputations of Lauzun and Richelieu.

At the head of the stairs he paused and cast a glance behind.

"Good!" said he, "here am I embroiled with the queen-mother, with the king, with Mademoiselle de Saint André, — and all at one blow. A fine morning, in faith! for a younger son of Navarre. Bah!" added he philosophically, "it is true that younger sons get off where their elders could not."

And he slowly descended the stairs, cavalierly crossed the court, and saluted the sentinel, who presented arms.

XXV.

THE SON OF THE CONDEMNED.

WE have said that the prince had made an appointment to meet Robert Stuart between the hours of seven and eight o'clock in the square in front of the church of Saint-Germain-l'Auxerrois.

To repair to the rendezvous he could easily cross the bridge of Notre-Dame and the Pont aux Moulins; but a magnet drew him toward the Louvre. He crossed the river with the ferry-man, and went ashore in front of the Tour de Bois.

His way lay to the right, he kept to the left.

He went toward danger as the imprudent moth flies to the light.

He knew this road well; during four or five months he had hopefully followed it every evening.

Now that he hoped no longer, why did he still choose it?

He pursued then the old course; and, passing under the windows of Mademoiselle de Saint André, he stopped as he had been in the habit of stopping.

He knew those windows well!

The first three were those of Charlotte's bedroom and boudoir; the other four were the maréchal's.

Then, beyond the maréchal's four windows came still another window, to which he had never paid any attention.

That window was always dark, perhaps because the room on which it opened was never lighted, perhaps because thick curtains carefully drawn kept the light from filtering through.

This time, as at others, he would have paid no attention to that window, had he not heard a creaking of its hinges. Then he thought he saw a hand reach through the half-opened shutters, and from the hand flit like a night-moth a little paper which, borne on the evening breeze, seemed to be making every effort to reach its destination.

The hand disappeared, and the window was shut before the paper had yet touched the ground.

The prince caught it on the wing, without, indeed, accounting for his action, or knowing whether it was intended for him.

Then, as the hour of half-past seven sounded from the clock of Saint-Germain-l'Auxerrois, he remembered his appointment and turned in the direction whither the vibrating bronze seemed to be calling him.

Meanwhile, he turned over and over the note in his hands; but the darkness of the night prevented his learning the import of his frail conquest.

At the corner of the Rue Chilpéric was a small inn, in the wall of which a niche had been contrived. In the niche was a little Madonna of gilded wood, and before the Madonna burned a resin candle, a sort of beacon directing the course of zealous Catholics to a Christian inn and a devout inn-keeper, but which to the belated traveller cried aloud, "You can get a night's lodging here."

The Prince de Condé approached the house, mounted the stone bench placed beside the door, and, standing under the beacon's flickering light, he read with amazement the following lines: —

"The king is momentarily reconciled with the queen-mother; this evening they will be present at the execution of Anne Dubourg. I dare not say, fly! but I do say, enter the Louvre under no pretext whatever; your life is at stake."

The amazement with which the prince read the first lines changed to stupefaction with the last sentence. Whence came this warning? From a friend certainly. But of what sex was this friend? Was it a man or a woman? No, it was a woman; a man would not have written thus.

Besides, there were no men in the palace of the Louvre. There were only courtiers, and a courtier would have thought twice before risking the disgrace that his charity would earn.

So it was not a man.

But if it was a woman, who was she?

What woman could have taken a lively enough interest in him to get embroiled at a stroke, supposing the charitable warning which she had given the prince were known, — to get embroiled at a stroke, we repeat, with the king, the queen-mother, and Mademoiselle de Saint André?

But perhaps it was Mademoiselle de Saint André herself!

Oh! as to that, after a moment's reflection, the prince knew well that it was impossible. He had too cruelly wounded the lioness, and the lioness must still be nursing the wound he had inflicted.

He had, indeed, in the Louvre two or three former mistresses, but he had quarrelled with them, and when women no longer love, they hate.

Only one had still perhaps some remaining tenderness for him, pretty Mademoiselle de Limeuil, — but he knew of old the pothooks of the charming child; it was not her writing, and no one would take the chances of employing a secretary to write such a note. After all, was it a woman's handwriting?

The prince stood on tiptoe to get as near as possible to the light.

Yes, it was certainly a woman's writing, and in spite of the masterly turn of those characters which we can compare only to a fine English hand of our time, an expert would not have been deceived, and the prince, from the great number of their letters received, had become an expert with regard to women's handwriting. While the down-strokes were strong, the up-strokes were delicate, graceful, and effeminate.

Then the little billet was so neat altogether, the paper so fine, so velvety, so silky, and betrayed so sweet a perfume of feminine bedroom or boudoir, that most decidedly it was from a woman.

Then again arose the question which had received no answer, — who was she?

The Prince de Condé, who had completely forgotten his rendezvous, being wholly preoccupied with his letter, would have spent the night in seeking this woman's name, and, in all probability he would have sought in vain, if, fortunately for him, Robert Stuart, who saw him in the distance perched on his bench, and whose heart was agitated by a preoccupation quite as profound, had not suddenly appeared, as if he had sprung from the earth in the circle of light thrown out by the candle.

He bowed low before the prince.

The prince blushed at being surprised in reading the note, and the way in which he blushed confirmed his own certainty that it had come from a woman.

"It is I, prince," said the young man.

"You see, monsieur, that I keep my word," said the prince, leaping down from the stone bench.

"And I," said Robert Stuart, "am waiting for an opportunity to show you that I will keep mine."

"I have sad news to give you, monsieur," said the prince with emotion.

The young man smiled bitterly.

"Speak, prince," said he. "I am prepared for anything."

"Monsieur," said the prince with a degree of impressiveness that might have been regarded as surprising in a man who was generally considered to be one of the most frivolous of his day, "we are living in a period when notions of good and ill are confused, changing, undecided. For some time the world has seemed to be in a sort of childbirth, and the throes of its travail have cast sinister enlightenment into the souls of some, while those of others have been plunged into profoundest darkness. What will be the result of the encounter of the passions conflicting at this moment, I do not know — "

"Why do you not say at once, prince, — 'Young man, your father is condemned. I promised you your father's pardon, and the pardon has been denied me. I told you that your father should not die, and your father is to die this night.' "

"Monsieur," said the prince, almost ashamed of the subterfuge by whose aid he was attempting to deceive the young man, "monsieur, matters are not so bad as you say."

"Do you tell me to hope, prince?" demanded Robert Stuart.

Condé dared not answer; there was in the young man's look an expression which checked the words on his lips.

"Yesterday, the sentence of death was not yet approved, not yet signed by the king. To-day, in spite of my efforts, it is signed, it has been served; in an hour perhaps he will be executed."

"An hour!" muttered the young man between his teeth. "Many things can be done in an hour!"

He darted away and went nearly twenty steps; then,

returning to the prince and grasping his hand which he covered with kisses and bathed with tears, he said, —

"From to-day, from this moment, prince, you have not a more faithful, more devoted servant than I. I am yours, body, soul, brain, arms, heart, and I surrender you my life even to the last drop of my blood!"

And this time he moved away at a slow pace and, after giving the prince a final inclination of the head, he disappeared at the turn of the quay.

XXVI.

HIS OWN MASTER.

THE young man was already abreast of the point of La Cité, and the prince had not yet emerged from the reverie into which he had fallen.

It is true that his reverie had perhaps, by one of the frequent whims of memory, reverted from Robert Stuart to the note dropped from a window of the Louvre, and which the prince had just read half an hour before in the glimmering light of the Madonna's lamp.

Whatever might have been the tendency of his brown study, he was drawn from it by a new and unexpected incident.

A youth, bareheaded and without his doublet, dashed out of the Louvre and with panting breath crossed the square at a run, as if he had been pursued by a mad dog.

The prince recognized him as the page of the Maréchal de Saint André, whom he had seen first at the inn near Saint Denis, and again in the park at Saint Cloud.

"Hey!" cried the prince when he was ten paces away, "where are you running so fast, my young master?"

The youth stopped as suddenly as if an insurmountable barrier had presented itself in his path.

"Is it you, monseigneur?" cried he in turn recognizing the prince, in spite of the dark cloak enveloping him and the broad-brimmed hat that covered his eyes.

"*Parbleu!* yes, it is I; and it is you also, if I mistake not? You are Mézières, Monsieur de Saint André's young page, are you not?"

"Yes, monseigneur."

"And, what is more, if I am to trust appearances, enamored of Mademoiselle Charlotte?" added the prince.

"Oh! I was, yes, monseigneur, but I am not so any longer."

"Good!"

"I swear it!"

"You are very fortunate, young man," said the prince half gayly, half sadly, "to be able thus to discard your loves; but I do not believe it."

"Why, monseigneur?"

"If you were not in love like a madman, or as mad as a lover, nothing would explain this disheveled race in the darkness and at this hour of the night."

"Monseigneur," said the page, "I have just suffered the most deadly outrage that a man ever endured."

"A man!" laughed the prince. "Of whom are you speaking? Not of yourself?"

"Why should it not be of myself?"

"Because you are but a child."

"I tell you, monseigneur," continued the youth, "I tell you that I have been most dreadfully maltreated. Man or child, as I have the right to wear a sword at my side, I will be revenged."

"If you have the right to wear a sword at your side, you should have made use of it."

"I was caught by the valets, overcome, bound down, and —"

The young man broke off with a gesture of unspeakable wrath, and his blue eyes, like the eyes of night-prowling beasts, flashed twin streams of light into the darkness.

By that token, the prince recognized the man of hate and of bloodshed.

"And — " repeated the prince.

"And whipped, monseigneur!" added the youth, with a cry of rage.

"Then," said the prince lightly, "you must see that you were not treated as a man but as a child."

"Monseigneur, monseigneur," cried Mézières, "children quickly become men, when they are seventeen years old and have such an insult to avenge!"

"That is right!" said the prince again becoming serious. "I like to hear you speak thus, young man. But how did you incur such an affront?"

"I was, as you have just said, monseigneur, madly in love with Mademoiselle de Saint André. Pardon this confession made to you, monseigneur — "

"And why should I have anything to pardon?"

"You loved her almost as much as I."

"Ah! ah!" said the prince, "you were aware of that, young man?"

"Prince, you will never repay me in good the hundredth part of the heartache that you have made me suffer."

"Who knows? Proceed."

"I would have given my life for her," continued the page, "and, however great the barrier raised between us by her birth, I felt destined, if not to live, at least to die for her."

"I understand that," said the prince, smiling and making a sign of the hand, as if he would ward off a disagreeable thought. "Proceed."

"I loved her so much, monseigneur, that I should have been willing to see her the wife of another, providing the other would have loved and respected her as I should have loved and respected her myself. Yes, to know her loved, happy, and honored would have sufficed.

That shows you, monseigneur, the height of my ambitious views and loving desires."

"Well," said the prince, "what happened?"

"Well, monseigneur, when I learned that she was the king's mistress, when I learned that she was deceiving not only me, who was more than her adorer, her slave! not me alone, I say, but you who worshipped her, Monsieur de Joinville who was to wed her, and the entire court who, in the midst of that squad of shameless and abandoned maids, believed her to be a chaste, pure, open-hearted child; when I experienced this revelation, monseigneur, when I learned that she was another man's mistress —"

"Not another man's, monsieur," interrupted Condé with an untranslatable accent, — "a king's."

"Very well! a king's; but it is none the less true that I thought of killing this man, king though he is."

"*Diable!* my fine page," said he, "you go at it tooth and nail. To kill the king for a love affair! If you were merely whipped for that idea, it seems to me that you do wrong to complain."

"Oh! I was not whipped on account of that," said Mézières.

"Why then? Do you know that your story begins to interest me? Only, do you mind telling it as we walk? First, because my feet are literally frozen, and again because I have business in the direction of the Grève."

"Little does it matter to me where I go, monseigneur," said the young man, "provided I go away from the Louvre."

"Well, that suits marvellously well," said the prince, stamping his feet on the pavement. "Come with me, I am listening."

Then regarding him with a smile, he continued, —

"You see however what a common misfortune will do. Yesterday, you thought I was loved and it was I whom you wished to kill. To-day, as it is the king who is loved, misfortune draws us together and here I am your confidant, and a confidant in whose loyalty you have such faith that you have just confessed your great desire to kill the king. However, you have not killed him, have you?"

"No; but I spent an hour in my room a prey to a burning fever."

"Good!" murmured the prince, "that is like me."

"Having reached no resolution at the end of two hours, I knocked at Mademoiselle de Saint André's door to upbraid her for her infamous conduct."

"Still like me," murmured the prince.

"Mademoiselle de Saint André was not at home."

"Ah!" thought the prince, "here the likeness disappears. I was more fortunate, myself!"

"It was the maréchal who received me. The maréchal was very fond of me; so he said, at least. He was alarmed at seeing me so pale.

"'What is the matter, Mézières?' asked he. 'Are you ill?'

"'No, monseigneur,' I answered.

"'What then is troubling you to such a degree?'

"'Oh! monseigneur, my heart is bursting with bitterness and hate.'

"'With hate, Mézières, at your age? Hatred is unbecoming at the age of love.'

"'Monseigneur, I hate, I wish to be revenged. I came to ask advice of Mademoiselle de Saint André.'

"'Of my daughter?'

"'Yes; and, as she is not here—'

"'As you see.'

" 'I will seek your advice.'

" 'Speak, my child.'

" 'Monseigneur,' I continued, 'I was ardently in love with a young —'

" 'Good, Mézières!' said the maréchal laughing, 'tell me of your love affairs. The language of love comes as naturally to the lips at your age as the flowers of the garden come in the spring; and is your love requited by the one whom you love so ardently?'

" 'Monseigneur, I did not even aspire to that. She was so much above me in birth and fortune that I worshipped her from the bottom of my heart as some divinity, the hem of whose robe I dared scarcely dream to kiss.'

" 'It is a court lady, then?'

" 'Yes, monseigneur,' I stammered.

" 'And do I know her, too?'

" 'Oh! yes.'

" 'Well, what is the difficulty, Mézières? Is your divinity about to be married, to become the wife of another, and is that what troubles you?'

" 'No, monseigneur,' I answered, emboldened by the anger awakened within me by these words; 'no, the woman I love is not about to be married!'

" 'And why not?' demanded the maréchal, looking at me apprehensively.

" 'Because the woman I love is publicly the mistress of another.'

"At these words, the maréchal became disconcerted in his turn.

"He became as pale as death, and took a step forward while he regarded me sternly and steadily.

" 'Of whom are you speaking?' he demanded in broken tones.

"'Ah! you know well, monseigneur,' I answered; 'and the reason I speak to you of my vengeance is because I presume that you are at this hour seeking some one to aid yours.'

"Just then the captain of the guard entered.

"'Silence!' said the maréchal to me. 'On your life, silence!'

"Then, as if he judged it more prudent still to dismiss me entirely, he said, —

"'Go!'

"I understood, or rather, I thought that I understood. If ill befell the king, and the harm came through me, the maréchal would be compromised if seen talking with me by the captain of the guard.

"'Yes, monseigneur,' I replied, 'yes, I am going.'

"And I rushed out by one of the inner private doors so as not to encounter the captain of the guard, either in the corridor or in the antechamber.

"However, once outside of the room, once out of sight, I stopped; then I returned on tiptoe, then I applied my ear to the portière, the only obstacle that prevented my seeing what was about to take place, but which did not interfere with my hearing.

"Judge of my astonishment, of my indignation, monseigneur!

"Letters patent for the governorship of Lyons were brought to Monsieur de Saint André.

"The maréchal received title and favors with the humility of a grateful subject, and the officer was charged to convey the father's thanks to the daughter's lover!

"Scarcely had he gone, when I made but one bound from my hiding-place into the maréchal's presence.

"I do not know what I said to him, I do not know with what insult I branded the father who was selling his daughter; but what I do know is that, after a desperate struggle in which I sought and begged for death, I found myself bound, tied down, in the hands of lackeys, given over to the whip, to the rod, to infamy!

"Through my tears, or rather through the blood streaming from my eyes, I saw the maréchal looking on from a window of his apartment. At the sight I swore a solemn oath that the man that had caused to be whipped the one who had offered to avenge him, should die only by my hand.

"I do not know whether it was from pain or rage, but I fainted away.

"On returning to myself I found that I was free again, and I rushed out of the Louvre, renewing the solemn oath that I had taken. Monseigneur! Monseigneur!" continued the page with increasing excitement, "it may be true that I am but a child; yet from my love, from my hatred, I think differently! But you are yourself a man! you are a prince! Well, I tell you now as I told you before, — the maréchal shall die only by my hand!"

"Young man!"

"And still less for the insult that he has inflicted upon me than for the one that he has accepted."

"Young man," said the prince, "do you know that such an oath is blasphemous?"

"Monseigneur," said the page, wholly absorbed in the thought that was mastering him, and as if he had not heard the prince's words, "monseigneur, it is a miracle of Providence that on coming out of the Louvre you should be the first person I should meet. Monseigneur, I tender you my services; our love was the same, if our hatred is not. Monseigneur, in the name of our common love, I beseech you to take me among your servants. My head, my heart, my hand shall be yours, and at the first opportunity I will prove that I cannot be accused of ingratitude. Do you accept, monseigneur?"

The prince remained thoughtful for a moment.

"Well, monseigneur," repeated the young man impatiently, "do you accept the offer of my life?"

"Yes," returned the prince, taking the youth's two hands within his own, "but upon one condition."

"Name it, monseigneur."

"That you renounce your project of assassinating the maréchal."

"Oh! anything else that you will, monseigneur, but not that!"

"So much the worse, then! for that is the first condition that I should impose upon you in entering my service."

"Oh! monseigneur, I beg you on my knees, do not exact that of me!"

"If you do not promise what I ask, leave me at once, monsieur; I do not know you, — I do not wish to know you."

"Monseigneur! monseigneur!"

"I command soldiers, not desperadoes."

"Oh! monseigneur, can one man possibly deny another the right to avenge a mortal insult?"

"In the manner you speak of, yes."

"But is there any other way in this world?"

"Perhaps."

"Oh!" said the young man shaking his head, "never would the maréchal consent to cross swords with one who had been of his household."

"Naturally," replied the prince, "in a regular duel, no; but such an occasion may present itself when the maréchal cannot refuse you that honor."

"How?"

"Suppose that you were to meet him on the battlefield."

"The battlefield?"

"Well, on that day, Mézières, I pledge myself to yield up my place to you, if I instead of you should meet him face to face."

"But, monseigneur, will that day ever come?"

"Sooner than you think, perhaps," answered the prince.

"Oh! if I were sure of that!" cried Mézières.

"Who the deuce is sure of anything in this world?" said the prince; "there is a probability of it, that is all."

The young man in turn remained thoughtful for a moment.

"Stay, monseigneur," he said at last, "I know not whence there comes to me a presentiment, indeed, of something strange and threatening in the air; besides, it has been predicted that I — I accept, monseigneur."

"And do you take the oath?"

"Not to assassinate the maréchal treacherously, yes; but if I meet him on the field of battle —"

"Oh! in that case, I deliver him over to you, he is yours; yet beware!"

"Of what?"

"The maréchal is a tough soldier."

"Oh! as for that, monseigneur, I will take my chances. May my good or my bad angel conduct me to him, — that is all I ask."

"Then, it is settled, and on this condition you enter my service."

"Oh! monseigneur!"

The youth seized the prince's hand and kissed it.

They were abreast of the Pont aux Moulins; the quay

was beginning to be thronged with people who were hurrying toward the Place de Grève. The prince deemed it prudent to rid himself of Mézières as he had disembarrassed himself of Robert Stuart.

"Do you know the Hôtel de Condé?" the prince asked the lad.

"Yes, monseigneur," replied the latter.

"Very well, present yourself there, say that from to-day you are one of my household, and ask for a room in the quarters set apart for my equerries."

Then the prince added, with that charming smile which, when he desired, made friends of his enemies and zealots of his friends, —

"You see that I treat you as a man, since I am making you your own master."

"Thanks, monseigneur," respectfully answered Mézières; "from this moment, dispose of me as of a thing wholly your own."

XXVII.

WHAT THE PRINCE DE CONDÉ'S HEAD IS WORTH.

Now, let us tell something of what was passing at the Louvre while the events which we have related in the preceding chapters were taking place; that is to say, during the two conversations of the Prince de Condé with Robert Stuart and Mézières.

We have seen how Monsieur de Condé took leave of the king, and how Mademoiselle de Saint André took leave of Monsieur de Condé.

Monsieur de Condé having gone, the girl had been left overwhelmed with mortification. Like a wounded lioness that, at first fallen under a blow, gradually recovers herself, tosses her head and shakes it, spreads her claws and examines them, and gains the neighboring stream to gaze in it at her leisure and see if she is, indeed, still herself, Mademoiselle de Saint André had sought her mirror to learn whether, in the terrible conflict, she had lost anything of her marvellous beauty; and, finding herself as alluring as ever under the redoubtable smile beneath which she had concealed her spite, she no longer doubted the might of her charms, and she took her way to the king's apartment.

Everybody already knew the event of the night before, so that all doors were open to Mademoiselle de Saint André; and, upon her signifying that she did not desire to be announced, officers and ushers ranged themselves against the walls, and were content to indicate by a sign the door of the bed-chamber.

The king was sitting in his great chair, lost in thought and meditation.

Scarcely had he resolved to be king, and already the burden of royalty was falling upon his shoulders with crushing weight.

And so, close upon his discussion with the Prince de Condé, he had sent a message to the queen-mother that she might command his presence in her apartment, or that she might do him the favor to come to his.

He then waited, not daring to look in the direction of the door, lest he should encounter the austere countenance of the queen-mother.

Instead of that austere countenance, however, the gracious face of a young girl emerged from the uplifted tapestry.

But François II. did not see her; he had turned his head away from the door, thinking that it would be time enough to turn around when he heard his mother's firm and rather heavy step creaking the parquetry beneath the carpet.

Mademoiselle de Saint André's footstep was not of a sort to creak the floor. Like the undines, the girl could have run along the tops of the rushes without causing them to bend; like the salamanders, she might have been lifted up to heaven on the crest of a column of smoke.

Therefore, she entered the room without being heard. She approached the young king, and when beside his chair, she slipped her arms affectionately around his neck, and, just as he was raising his head, pressed her glowing lips upon his forehead.

It was not Catherine de Médicis. The queen-mother had no such ardent caresses to bestow on her children; or, if she had, she reserved them for the favorite of her maternal affections, — for Henri III. But for François II., the child that was conceived during a period of illness and suffering, and in accordance with a physician's prescription, born into the world a sorry, sickly creature, she scarcely had the affection that a hireling sometimes feels for her nursling.

It was, therefore, not the queen-mother.

Still less was it the little Queen Marie.

The little Queen Marie, somewhat neglected by her spouse, having been injured by the fall from her horse, propped up in a reclining-chair, by order of her physicians who feared a miscarriage as the result of the fall, — the little queen, as she was called, was in no condition to come to her husband, and had small reason to lavish upon him her caresses, which were, for that matter, so fatal to all who received them.

It was, then, Mademoiselle de Saint André.

So the king had no need to see the smiling face above his own to occasion the cry, —

"Charlotte!"

"Yes, my beloved king!" responded the girl, "Charlotte; you can even say 'my' Charlotte, unless you permit me no longer to say 'my' François."

"Oh, always! always!" returned the young king, who recalled at what price he had just purchased the right in the terrible discussion in which he had engaged with his mother.

"Well, your Charlotte has come to ask a question."

"What is it?"

"What is the man's head worth," continued the girl, with a charming smile, "what is the man's head worth who has mortally insulted her?"

A quick blush suffused the wan face of François II., and he seemed for the moment to be alive.

"Has any man mortally insulted you, my darling?" he asked.

"Mortally."

"Ah! ah! this is a day of insults," said the king, "for a man has also mortally insulted me; unfortunately, I cannot avenge myself. So much the worse then for your insulter, my beautiful one!" said François with the smile of a child as it chokes a bird; "he shall pay for two."

"Thanks, my dear king! I doubt not that the more the one who has sacrificed everything for you were disparaged, the more you would be disposed to defend her honor."

"What punishment do you demand for the guilty man?"

"Have I not said that the insult was a mortal one?"

"Well?"

"Well, for a mortal insult, the death penalty."

"Oh! oh!" exclaimed the king; "it is not a day of mercy, at all events. Every one is demanding some one's death. And whose head do you demand, my cruel beauty?"

"I have told you, sire, — the head of the man that has insulted me."

"Yet, to give you the man's head," said François, laughing, "I must know his name."

"I believe the king's scales have but two pans, — one of life and one of death, that of the innocent and that of the guilty."

"Nevertheless, guilt is more or less heavy, innocence more or less light. Well, let us hear, — who is the guilty man? Is it another councillor of parliament like that unfortunate Dubourg who is to be burned tomorrow? If so, that would go of itself. My mother is full of heart-burning toward them just now; two of them would burn instead of one, and no notice would be taken of the second."

"No, it is not a man of the gown, it is a man of the sword."

"Provided that he is not associated with the Messieurs de Guise, nor with Monsieur de Montmorency, nor with your father, we shall still be able to encompass it."

"He not only is not associated with any of the three, but, what is more, he is their deadly enemy."

"Good!" declared the king. "Now all depends upon his rank."

"His rank?"

"Yes."

"I thought there was no rank for the king, and that all his inferiors belonged to him."

"Oh, my fair Nemesis, you go on at a great rate! Do you suppose, for instance, that my mother is my inferior?"

"I am not speaking of your mother."

"That the Messieurs de Guise are my inferiors?"

"I am not speaking of the Messieurs de Guise."

"That Monsieur de Montmorency is my inferior?"

"The constable is not in question."

An idea flashed into the mind of the king.

"Ah!" he exclaimed, "and a man, you pretend, has insulted you."

"I do not pretend, I affirm it."

"When did it happen?"

"But just now."

"Where?"

"In my own room, to which he came after leaving you."

"Ah!" returned the king, "I comprehend. My cousin, Monsieur de Condé, is the man."

"Exactly, sire."

"And you have come to demand the head of Monsieur de Condé?"

"Why not?"

"*Peste!* at what a pace you go, my darling! a prince royal!"

"A fine prince!"

"The brother of a king!"

"A fine king!"

"My cousin!"

"He is the more guilty; being of your family, sire, he owes you the greater respect."

"My angel, my angel, you are asking too much," replied the king.

"Oh! but you do not know what he has done."

"Yes, I know."

"You know?"

"Yes."

"Tell me, then."

"Well, in the corridor of the Salle des Métamorphoses, he found the handkerchief you had lost there."

"What next?"

"In the handkerchief was the note Lanoue had written."

"What next?"

"He gave the note to Madame l'Amirale."

"What next?"

"Mechanically or maliciously, Madame l'Amirale dropped it at the queen-mother's reception."

"What next?"

"Monsieur de Joinville found it, and, suspecting any one to be concerned rather than you, he showed it to the queen-mother."

"What next?"

"Then came the wicked prank, where, under the eyes of your father and of your fiancé — "

"And what next?"

"What! next?"

"Yes."

"Is not that all?"

"Where was Monsieur de Condé during that time?"

"I do not know, — at his hôtel, or hunting after adventures."

"He was not at his hôtel; he was not hunting after adventures."

"At any rate, he was not among those who surrounded us."

"No, but he was in the room."

"In our room?"

"In our room."

"Where, then? I did not see him."

"But he saw us, he saw me."

"Did he tell you that?"

"And many other things besides, as, for example, that he was in love with me."

"That he was in love with you!" exclaimed the king, excitedly.

"Oh! as for that matter, I knew it; he had said it to me, or written it, twenty times."

François turned as pale as death.

"And for the last six months," continued Mademoiselle de Saint André, "every night, from ten o'clock to midnight, he has been walking under my windows."

"Ah!" said the king in a hollow voice, and wiping away the perspiration that beaded his forehead, "that is another thing."

"Well, sire, is not Monsieur le Prince de Condé's head less secure than it was?"

"It is so insecure that, did I not restrain myself, the fire of my wrath would take it from his shoulders."

"And why restrain yourself, sire?"

"Charlotte, this is a serious matter, and I cannot determine it alone."

"Yes, you must ask your mother's permission, poor nursling infant, poor king in swaddling-clothes!"

François darted a threatening look at the girl who had just flung at him this double taunt; but he met her eye, itself so full of menace, that he turned away his own.

As happens in a fencing-match, steel turned steel.

The stronger disarmed the weaker.

And everybody was stronger than poor François II.

"Well," replied François, "if I must have her permission, I will ask it, that is all."

"And if the queen-mother refuses you?"

"If she refuses!" repeated the king, as he regarded his mistress with an expression of fierceness of which one would have thought his eye incapable.

"Yes, — if she refuses you?"

"I will dispense with it."

"Truly, Your Majesty?"

"As truly as it is true that I wish death to Monsieur de Condé."

"And for how many minutes do you ask me for the execution of this grand scheme of vengeance?"

"Ah! such schemes do not mature in minutes, Charlotte."

"How many hours?"

"The hours go quickly, and nothing is gained by haste."

"How many days?"

François paused in reflection.

"I ask a month," said he.

"A month?"

"Yes."

"That is to say, thirty days?"

"Thirty days."

"Thirty days and, consequently, thirty nights?"

François II. was about to respond, but the portière was lifted and the officer in waiting announced, —

"Her Majesty, the queen-mother!"

The king indicated to his mistress the little door of the alcove which opened into a room that had itself an outlet upon the corridor.

The mistress was no more disposed than was the lover to brave the presence of the queen-mother. She fled in the direction indicated; but, before disappearing, she still had time to cast these last words back to the king, —

"Keep your promise, sire!"

. . . . . .

A quarter of an hour after the execution of Anne Dubourg, the square of Saint-Jean-en-Grève, dark and deserted, lighted only by the last gleams of the burning fagots that blazed up from time to time, presented the appearance of a vast cemetery, and the vaulting sparks added to the likeness by representing the fire-flies flashing among the tombs during the long winter nights.

And this illusion was still heightened by the aspect of two men, who moved so slowly and so silently through the square that they impersonated ghosts.

They had waited, without doubt, to begin their evening promenade after the crowd had dispersed.

"Well, prince," demanded one of the two men as they halted a short distance from the funeral pile, "what do you think of all this?"

"I do not know how to answer you, dear cousin," responded the man addressed by the title of prince, "but I do know that I have seen many human creatures die; I have been present at death scenes of all sorts; twenty times have I listened to the death-rattle of dying men. Ah! well, never, Monsieur l'Amiral, has the death of a brave enemy, the death of a woman, the death of a child, produced in me such emotions as I felt when this soul was quitting earth."

"As for me," returned the admiral, whose courage was not to be questioned, "I felt myself seized with inexplicable terror; and had I been in the place of the condemned, my blood could not have curdled more horribly in my veins. In a word, my dear cousin," added the admiral, clutching the prince by the wrist, "I was afraid."

"Afraid, Monsieur l'Amiral!" said the prince, staring at Coligny in amazement. "Did you say that you were afraid, or did I misunderstand?"

"I did indeed say it; and you heard aright. Yes, I was afraid; yes, I cannot describe the icy chill that froze my veins, the dark presentiment of my own approaching end that thrilled my heart. Cousin, I am certain that I, I too, shall die a violent death."

"Then give me your hand, Monsieur l'Amiral, for I have been forewarned that I myself shall be assassinated."

There was a moment's silence.

Both stood, erect and motionless, in the ruddy light reflected from the dying flames of the fagots.

The Prince de Condé seemed plunged in a melancholy reverie.

The Admiral de Coligny was lost in meditation.

Suddenly, a man, tall of stature and enveloped in a great mantle, rose up before them, without their having heard even the sound of his footsteps, so profound had been their preoccupation.

"Who goes there?" challenged the two men with an apprehensive start, and mechanically laying hold of their swords.

"A man," replied the new-comer, "whom you last night honored with your conversation, and who would probably have been murdered on leaving your house, had he not been rescued by monseigneur."

And with these words, having removed his broad-brimmed felt hat and saluted the admiral, the new-comer turned to the Prince de Condé and bowed to him still more profoundly than to the admiral.

The prince and the admiral both recognized him.

"The Baron de la Renaudie!" they simultaneously exclaimed.

La Renaudie freed his arm from his cloak and quickly extended his hand to the admiral.

But, swift as had been his movement, a third hand was ahead of his.

It was the Prince de Condé's.

"You mistake, father," said he to the admiral; "there are three of us."

"Is it indeed true, my son?" cried the admiral.

By the lingering light of the funeral embers, they saw a body of men pouring into the farther side of the square.

"Ah!" said the admiral, "there is Monsieur de Mouchy and his men. Let us withdraw, my friends, and let us never forget what we have just witnessed, — let us never forget our compact."

Just as, by the light of the flames, the three conspirators had seen Monsieur de Mouchy, Monsieur de Mouchy had espied them, but without recognizing them, wrapped as they were in their mantles.

He ordered his men to advance upon the suspicious group.

But, as if awaiting only this order to go out, the last tongue of flame expired and the square was again in profoundest darkness.

And into this darkness vanished the three future leaders of the Protestant Reformation, who were to fall, one after the other, victims of the oath they had just taken.

THE END.

www.ingramcontent.com/pod-product-compliance
Lightning Source LLC
LaVergne TN
LVHW030908080826
845145LV00010B/2813

9781410100894